The Son Thief

SEAN MUNGER

Contents

Chapter 1: Tondoro

A blue and white SUV with dusty windows and mud-splattered sides rolls down a lonely highway through arid country spotted here and there with trees and other vivid patches of green. The woman driving the SUV is an American and this Namibian landscape might be compared to somewhere in the American desert southwest. But Sarah Brinson is very far from Albuquerque or El Paso. Not long ago she stopped for petrol in a long line of similarly dusty vehicles, at a town called Rundu, on the south bank of the Okovango River that separates Angola from Namibia. The gas stop took an hour, during which she checked and re-checked the map of her route. Her destination cannot be far now, but Tondoro is one of those places you can't see until you're there.

Suddenly, she is there: a ramshackle little town with tan and brown stucco buildings, houses spaced far apart, and a few of those same scrubby trees. Lots of orange-tan dust swirls in clouds and piles up against cinder block walls and barriers of rusty corrugated metal that separate the little farm plots. Two old women watch with hollow eyes as the SUV prowls slowly down Tondoro's main street. A block or so later Sarah must swerve, slowly, to avoid a boy of about eight leading a goat, its ribs visible through its skin, down the middle of the street. From a yard somewhere nearby, a radio plays bright-sounding music with a reggae beat. The town dead-ends just past the driveway of a two-story stucco-faced house, as tan as the sand, with a carefully-trimmed garden of flowers and hedges and a Range Rover parked in front.

Having come to the end of Tondoro, Sarah pulls into the house's driveway, backs out, and prowls again. She passes the boy with the goat, who eyes her suspiciously through the windshield.

Her destination is not hard to see. The large church steeple towers above everything else in town except the water tower, whose tank is square and made of wood. Near the church are several buildings, most looking brand new. Flower boxes overflow with red and yellow blossoms. It is February; the year is 2002. It's deep summer in the southern hemisphere. Visible beyond the church complex, the Okovango River shines blue and gold in the afternoon summer sunlight.

A painted sign in front of the church—the posts holding it up are surrounded by flowers—reads, *ST. AM-BROSE PARISH, TONDORO, NAMIBIA* and below that, *AD-MINISTERED BY THE MISSIONARY OBLATES OF THE MARY IMMACULATE.*

The SUV crackles to a stop in the paved driveway of the church complex. Music is drifting here too: the raised harmonious voices of children, singing some ancient Catholic hymn. Through the broad tall windows of the church the parishioners are visible, swaying and clapping. It is not Sunday, but the scene makes clear that this place is Tondoro's center of gravity, spiritually if not geographically.

The SUV's door opens and its driver steps out. Sarah Brinson is a short, stocky woman. Her auburn hair is cropped close to her head. She wears cargo shorts, hiking boots and an olive drab T-shirt. Tondoro reflects in her mirrored sunglasses as she pauses to take a long drink from an almost-drained bottle of water, which she tosses through the open door of the car before closing it. She begins walking up to the church. The hymn has just stopped, but not on her account.

A few moments later the front doors of the church open up and the parishioners stream out. Many are children. Some of the girls wear matching white shirts and skirts, the boys little blue caps and patent leather shoes. A few of the ordinary townspeople glance at this new white stranger.

A fortyish man in a white shirt and blue slacks approaches her. "Hello, may I help you?" He speaks English crisply, with an inflection that marks him as a native to this region, the Kavango.

"Yes, hello. My name is Sarah Brinson. I'm a private investigator. Is there someone I can speak to who's in charge here? Is there like a bishop or something?"

"An investigator?"

"Yes. I'm looking for someone who may have come through this town. An American."

The man in the white polo—his name is Joe Kimbeta —smiles, revealing a silver-capped tooth. "Someone who would come here from America would have a very long journey."

"Yeah, I've been on planes and in cars for most of the past 48 hours."

"You should speak to Father Ubate. This way, please."

Father Ubate is in his mid-80s, wizened, with a crescent of curly snow-white hair surrounding an otherwise bald brown pate. His office is in the rear of the complex, which is an L-shaped bank of new-looking buildings behind the church. The only decorations on his office wall are a crucifix with an agonized wooden Christ dripping painted blood, and a faded framed photo of John Paul II likely taken in the year he ascended to the papacy, nearly a quarter century past. Ubate's black cassock looks almost like velvet.

"You drove up here from Windhoek today, Ms. Brinson?"

"Yes. Long drive, but very beautiful."

"The Kavango is beautiful country. But you should have told us you were coming. We could have made arrangements for you."

"There are reasons why I didn't call first. I'm sorry for the inconvenience."

"We do have a small guest room in the complex where you may stay. I don't think you want to drive the eight hours back to Windhoek tonight."

"Thank you, most appreciated. I'll pay whatever you think is fair."

The elderly priest waves away her words with his wrinkled hand. "We don't run a boarding house for profit. We're a Catholic charity."

"Well, I do appreciate it."

"Unfortunately, I'm afraid you'll go back empty-handed." Ubate hands back to her the photograph she gave him a few minutes ago. "I can say with assurance that no such man has been in this town."

"He might have been in disguise. Are you absolutely sure?"

"We get very few visitors here. Driving to Tondoro from Windhoek, you yourself have seen how remote a place this is. I've been here forty years. I can count on one hand the number of Americans who have been here in that time, Father Tyler being one of them. I'm sorry. This person hasn't been here."

"Well, I appreciate your time." She puts the photo in a small leather folio that closes with a zipper. "Who's Father Tyler? He's American?"

"Yes, he is our Director of Outreach and Charities. I'll introduce you to him."

"Thank you. Would you mind if I also talked to others in the parish, just to be sure? Maybe they saw or heard something you weren't privy to."

"I know everything that goes on St. Ambrose Parish, Ms. Brinson."

"I'm sure you do. But I've come a very long way and my client will have to be absolutely satisfied that I've covered everything."

The priest spreads his hands. "Of course. We have no secrets here. Talk to anyone you like."

"Thanks."

The old priest brings her back to the church, now empty of parishioners. A young man is working his way through the aisles, setting Bibles and hymnals back neatly in their slots on the wooden backs of the pews. He must have heard them enter the church, but doesn't acknowledge them until Ubate speaks.

"Father Tyler? I'd like you to meet someone. A guest, and a countryman—*woman*—of yours."

The young priest looks up and smiles. "Oh, really? We don't see many Americans here."

"Less than six since 1962, counting you, if what Father Ubate has told me is right." The investigator extends her hand. "I'm Sarah Brinson."

"Evan Tyler. Very pleased to meet you."

He's an attractive young man in his early thirties. His hair is blond, shaved to military-length stubble. His piercing eyes are blue but appear more gray. He's of average build, not muscular, but clearly the kind of hardy type likely to thrive in the developing world. His handshake is firm and friendly, but he lets go quickly and snatches up a Bible and holds it in both hands at his waist, as if giving his hands something to do.

"If Americans are so rare here, Father Tyler, do you mind if I ask how *you* got here?"

"I was assigned by OMI about three years ago."

"OMI, that would be—?"

"Oblates of the Mary Immaculate. I volunteered to be a missionary in the developing world. They were originally going to send me to Thailand, but my assignment got changed to Namibia at the last minute." He chuckles. "Now you know everything."

"What exactly does the Director of Outreach and Charities do?"

Ubate speaks up. "Father Tyler is absolutely key to our parish. He holds most of the services, he teaches school, he handles the money. All the things I'm too old to do, or do well anymore."

"Not true at all," Tyler replies, "but I'll accept the compliment."

"I'm sure Ms. Brinson has questions for you. Father, when you're finished with her, bring her back to me and we'll get her situated in her room."

The old man hobbles away. Brinson and Tyler sit down in the front pew. The young priest still doesn't release the Bible he is holding.

"So, what would you like to ask me, Ms. Brinson?"

"Call me Sarah, please." She's already unzipped her folio and is reaching for the photo. "I'm a private investigator from Washington, D.C. I'm looking for someone who may have passed through this area a few months ago, in October, maybe. An American. Name is Michael Kimmissee."

Tyler takes the photo from her and studies it. "Hm. He doesn't look familiar. What was the name again?"

"Kimmissee, Michael Kimmissee. Now, that's funny that you ask that."

"Excuse me?"

"Father Ubate said there have been no Americans that have come through here in years. Even if you didn't remember what I said his name was a moment ago, how many Americans could there have been that you would need to distinguish them by name?"

Tyler's expression goes just a shade less cheerful. "You *are* a detective, aren't you?" He hands the photo back, "Well, it's an easy case for me, at least. There haven't been any Americans in months. A tourist couple came through here about six months ago. July and August—winter—is when the eco-tourists arrive. They come to see the Okovango."

"Why do they come in winter?"

"Well, this region, Okovango, is usually pretty arid. In the rainy season the run-off comes from central Africa, from the monsoons, and irrigates the river, but it takes a couple of months to get here. There are a lot of wildlife migrations that happen then—flamingos, lions, wildebeests, all that Animal Planet type of stuff."

"Do you remember their names, these tourists?"

Tyler shrugs. "No, I don't. I only met them briefly. But they were a lot older, the man at least was a lot older than the guy you're looking for. I'm sorry I can't be of more help."

On the walk through the florescent compound back toward Ubate's office Tyler's friendly smile returns. "You're from Washington, you say?"

"Not Washington itself, but Arlington."

"Did you grow up there?"

"There, and other places. My father was military, Navy. He was at the Pentagon for a long time. What about you, where'd you grow up?"

"Grand Rapids, Michigan."

"Oh, small world. I've been to Grand Rapids. My grandparents lived there for a while when my brother and I were kids. I have fond memories of the zoo there, Potter Park Zoo."

Tyler smiles. "I knew it well. Yes, it is a small world." They've reached the door of the complex wing near Ubate's office. The young priest tucks the Bible he's still carrying under his arm. "Pleased to meet you, Sarah. If there's anything you need during your stay with us, let me know."

"Thanks so much."

The room in which they've billeted her is small and austere, almost like a monk's cell in a monastery. There's a bed, a chair, a window, a wooden crucifix on the wall and little else. After dinner with Tyler, Ubate, and the other Namibian priest who works at the parish—a white man called Hague—Sarah Brinson returns to her room, sits on the small bed and removes something else from her leather folio: a small packet of photographs, snapshots and prints, a few of them color Xeroxes.

All of them show a young man at various ages, though pictures of him in his twenties predominate. One, evidently taken upon graduation from a seminary, shows him in clerical collar. The young man is blond and has bright blue eyes and an infectious smile. He's handsome. Another photo shows him with a slightly younger sister. Given the hairstyles and fashions it seems about a decade in the past. Indeed, the blue ball-point writing on the back of this photo reads, *Evan & Zoë Tyler, Memorial Day, 1992.*

That picture is ten years old, but even if it were the only one it would still be clear that the man here in Tondoro is not this person. The blond young man in the photo is built slightly differently. His nose is bigger, wider. His lips are fleshier.

Brinson studies the pictures carefully. Having apparently reached a conclusion, she zips them back in her folio and proceeds to get ready for bed.

There are two other things you must know. Michael Kimmissee has not been seen in Tondoro because he does not exist. The photo Sarah Brinson showed Frs. Ubate and Tyler is of a man named Ron Staley, an employee of Brinson's investigation firm.

Also, the Potter Park Zoo is in Lansing, not Grand Rapids, Michigan. Grand Rapids's zoo is called the John Ball Zoological Garden. Anyone who—like Sarah Brinson herself—actually *is* from Grand Rapids would know this, but the man passing himself off as Evan Tyler evidently does not.

Chapter 2: Grand Rapids

A few weeks earlier, in the conference room of an office converted from an old factory warehouse on the edge of downtown Grand Rapids, Sarah Brinson sat across a conference table from a man and two women who had brought with them a large three-ring binder full of photos, letters and documents. A single word, *EVAN*, was written on the binder's spine in black Sharpie ink. The man, Neil Tyler, was in his late sixties with whitening hair and a careworn face. Barbara, his wife, seemed 15 years younger; her hair was chemically blonde, but the wrinkles on her neck disclosed her true age. The younger woman, Zoë Tyler-Petrick, was heavy-set, well-dressed and spoke with a quietly intense quality. It was early January and bitterly cold. Outside the conference room windows, the vista of the city was almost uniformly white.

"Everyone I tell this story to says we're crazy." The man's voice was thin and gravelly. He did not look Sarah in the eye as he spoke, as if he were ashamed. "I mean, it *does* sound pretty strange—that our son has been re-placed with some sort of impostor. But there's just too many red flags. We've given the situation the benefit of the doubt as long as we possibly can."

Brinson, who said little during the long interview, had been taking copious notes on a yellow legal pad. She turned over to her third page, momentarily put down her pen and flexed her fingers.

"I want to make sure I understand this absolutely correctly. You suspect that someone has stolen your son's identity and is impersonating him, living as a priest at a parish in Namibia?"

The younger woman stared down at the table. "You don't believe us either. Dad, I told you it was hopeless."

Brinson held up a hand. "Now, just a minute. I didn't say that at all. I'm just trying to understand."

The older woman spoke. "Yes, the way you put it, that's the problem we have."

"And you haven't actually seen Evan in person in three and a half years?"

"That's right. Not since he left for Rome, before he got assigned to this mission in Africa. He spent several weeks with us that summer, and then he left. That was the last time we saw him in person."

"That was the last time you *saw* him. When was the last *contact* with him, of any kind?"

Neil, the father: "He talked to us on the phone at Christmas. The last three years, the only times he's ever called us is on Christmas. He didn't sound like himself. But then again it's harder than you think to remember exactly what a person's voice sounds like."

"You didn't record the conversation, did you?"

"No, we didn't. Maybe we should have."

"When did you first have suspicions that someone was impersonating Evan?"

The family members exchanged nervous, almost ashamed glances. It was Barbara who spoke up: "At least two years ago."

Her husband cut in, shaking his head. "No. Longer than that. I could tell something was off the very first time he called us from that place, Tondoro. And the letter we got from him, which is there in that binder—it just didn't sound like him. First of all, we never got letters from him before. When he was in Chicago, at seminary, before he left for Africa, he always just called. When he went there his whole mood, his whole personality changed. I couldn't put my finger on it until much later, of course, in part because we heard from him so seldom."

"That's another thing," said Zoë. "Before he left the country Evan was sick at the thought of being so far away from us. We thought he'd be calling and coming home to visit every chance he got. He never did."

The mother added: "Before he went, he told us he thought he'd be in Africa 18 months at the most. It's been more than three years now, and he has no interest in coming home. He keeps requesting that the OMI renew his assignment. I found that out from calling the Vatican myself, a few months ago."

Brinson was again writing copiously on her pad. She did not stop writing as she spoke. "The big question: if you're right, who is doing this? What would someone have to gain from impersonating your son?"

"We have no idea." Neil's voice sounded even thinner. "This is what we need help figuring out."

"If you don't mind me asking, Mr. Tyler, what's your net worth?"

"About two and a half million dollars."

"Does Evan have money of his own? A trust fund, an inheritance, something like that?"

"No, we spent most of what we saved for him to put him through college and seminary."

"Is he involved in businesses on the side?"

"Not that we know of."

Barbara Tyler: "You have to understand that God and the Catholic Church are Evan's whole life. There was nothing in the world he wanted more than to become ordained and go do missionary work."

"Does he have any enemies?"

"Again," said the father, "not that we know of."

In barely more than a whisper Barbara cut in: "Well, there was that time..." Her voice trailed off.

"What time? What?"

"That was almost 20 years ago." Neil said this more to his wife than to the investigator. "It can't have anything to do with this."

"What happened, please? I need to know everything."

The father gave a little defeated sigh.

"When he was 12, my son was kidnapped. It was a mistake. His best friend at the time was Brent Van Cordt. The kidnappers evidently mistook Evan for him. They were going to hold him for ransom, but they realized they kidnapped the wrong boy and let him go. They threw him out of a van on the side of the highway. Evan was in the hospital for a while. Eventually the police found the two men who did it. Petty crooks just looking for quick cash. Evan recovered just fine. We don't talk about the incident, but it did happen."

Brinson kept scrawling on her pad. "When was this? What year?"

"It was 1984, I think."

"Where are these kidnappers now, do you know?"

"One is in prison for another crime. The other died a couple of years ago."

"Do you have a relationship with the Van Cordt family, other than Evan's friendship with that other boy?"

"I practice at the law firm of Novak Porter & Tyler. We've represented various members of the Van Cordt family for many years. I've been Roger Van Cordt's principal tax lawyer for over 20 years."

After another half a minute or so, Brinson finished writing, put down the pen and flexed her hand again. Then she turned to the binder. It was well-organized: in its plastic sleeves were photographs of Evan Tyler from infancy to adulthood, brief notes written by him (and showing his signature), a Xerox copy of his travel itinerary to Rome dated August 1998, copies of the Tylers' long-distance phone bills, with a few select entries, the numbers beginning with +264—the country code for Namibia—highlighted in yellow. There was also a printout of a web page with a brief directory article on St. Ambrose Parish in Tondoro, Namibia. It included very small thumbnail photographs of the various officials of the parish: Fathers Olo Ubate, Mattias Hague and Evan Tyler. The picture of Tyler, being low-resolution, was blurry but appeared to show a young man with close-cropped blond hair.

Sarah tapped the photo on the page. "What do you think of this picture? Is it him?"

Zoë answered: "It's too blurry to tell. It *could* be him, but we can't be sure. Something looks off to me."

The mother said: "So far as we know, that's the only picture of him taken since he arrived in Namibia."

"Does he have any other distinguishing characteristics? Birth marks, tattoos?"

The father: "He does have a tattoo. He got it while he was at seminary. A sacred heart of Jesus on his arm, the top part of his arm."

Sarah wrote this down and circled it. "Which arm, right or left?"

"I honestly don't remember."

The last entry in the binder was a sheet of typing paper, folded in thirds, with computer printed text and a signature—*EVAN*—in blue ball-point ink. It was dated December 9, 2001, barely a month ago. Its text was vapid and empty. *"Dear Mom & Dad: Well, it will be Christmas again soon. Everything is going well here in Tondoro. The children are putting on a Nativity play..."*

"If I were to take your case," said Sarah Brinson, in a no-nonsense, almost steely tone, "I would want to be sure, from the outset, that my expectations—and yours—are absolutely clear. There are a couple of related issues here. If I took the case, the first thing would be for me to determine for certain whether the man at this parish in Africa is or is not your son. That job would have two, potentially two steps. First, all the research and background I can do from here. Second, if that's not conclusive, and from what you've told me I can obviously tell you think it won't be, it would require somebody, probably me, to travel to Namibia and see this man face-to-face."

"Are you saying that you *will* take the case?"

"No, I'm not saying that. I *might* take the case. I'm just setting out, if I do, what will be involved."

"Well, yes. It seems like someone will have to go to Namibia and meet him."

"You *do* realize, Mr. Tyler, how expensive that would be? I've never in my career traveled that far on a case. *If* I take the case, I'd be willing to go all the way to Africa, but we're talking about a lot of expenses, a lot more than would be usual on a normal identity tracing matter."

Tyler nodded. "I'm prepared for that. This is not a normal matter. What then?"

"Well, it depends on what I find out in Namibia. If that *is* Evan in Tondoro, and I verify that, is my work done? We don't have to decide that now, but you will eventually. Let's say I prove you right, that that isn't Evan in Tondoro. What then? Are you going to want me to find out what happened to the real Evan Tyler? I know you can't make a decision until we know what the circumstances are, but I'm just trying to give you a road map of what we might be facing."

"I think we all realize," said Barbara Tyler, "this could be a long haul."

"It might be. But then again it might not be."

"What do you mean?"

Brinson sighed. "I have to tell you frankly, Mrs. Tyler, that the resolution you hope for might not be realistic. Having your son back here in the States and in contact with you and the same relationship he had with you before he went to Namibia, that may not happen, may never happen. Despite what you've told me—and obviously you did a lot of soul-searching before you came to see me—honestly, I think your suspicions are probably not founded. Let me explain why I say that. It's not because I think the suspicions you've raised aren't good ones or that you don't have valid reasons for your concerns. Clearly you do. You aren't making this stuff up. But it's a simple fact that, in the real world, the scenario you're describing is *extremely* unlikely, more so because there's no obvious reason why some stranger would want to switch places with your son. If there's no obvious gain in it, why would anyone do it? This kind of thing just doesn't happen very often. For that reason alone, I think the man down there at St. Who's-its Parish *is* probably your son. What you would be effectively hiring me to do is to rule out a vanishingly small possibility of an extremely unlikely situation. You understand that, right?"

For the first time, one of the family reacted with what seemed like emotion. "That may be how you see it," said Zoë tersely. "I want to know if that really *is* my brother down there. If it is, fine. If it is him, and he wants to stay there and wants us, his family, to butt out of his life, that's fine. But I want *him* to tell us that, face-to face, and with no doubt whatsoever that it's him."

"I understand that, but I'm telling you that you may not get that resolution. I'm confident that I can verify his identity. But I can't make him—whether he's Evan or not, I can't make him talk to you or prove himself to you if he doesn't want to. If I call you from Namibia and say, 'Yes, it's him, and he refuses to speak to you,' there's nothing more I can do beyond that. Understood?"

There was silence in the conference room for a while. The father said: "What if we were to start with just the basic question—*is* that Evan down there or not? Whatever we decide to do after that, can you commit to finding that out for us?"

Brinson paused, and pursed her lips slightly.

"Let me think about it for 48 hours. If I feel, for any reason, that I can't make you a reasonable guarantee that I'll be able to determine if this man is or is not Evan, I won't take the case and you won't owe me anything."

The lawyer glanced at his wife and his daughter, and nodded. "That's fair."

"May I keep the binder until I make my decision?"

She was looking at the binder again, several hours later, while sitting at the dining table of the house on Juneberry Avenue that Sarah Brinson shared with her partner, Gwen Carrigan. A glass of wine was on the table in front of her. From the kitchen the aromas of home-cooked Thai food—Gwen was an enthusiastic amateur chef—poured from the kitchen in sizzling waves. The couple's fawn-colored French bulldog, Cracker, prowled the kitchen floor for dropped morsels. Not far away, Vincent, Gwen's 15-year-old son, sprawled on the living room sofa, bundled in a comforter, engrossed in watching *The Matrix*. The DVD was a present to him from Sarah and Gwen for Christmas, only two weeks past.

Over the sizzle of her pan Gwen spoke to her partner: "Where the hell is Namibia?"

"It's in southern Africa. Just above South Africa, on the western coast. It's mostly desert, I think. It used to be a German colony."

"How long do you think you'd be gone?"

"I can't imagine it'd be more than, I don't know, a week, maybe two. But it's premature to talk about that. I haven't taken the case."

"You will, though." Gwen scraped freshly-cut chili peppers from a plastic cutting board into her pan. "You're too intrigued by it, I can tell."

"It's definitely unusual." Sarah reached for her wine glass. "Better than asset tracing, at least."

Sarah turned one of the plastic-sleeved pages in the binder. A snapshot of Evan Tyler, age 20, with his arm around a much-younger Zoë, taken Memorial Day 1992, stared back at her.

"Well, then, what's your hesitation?"

"I'm a little wary of the possible Van Cordt connection. The client is Roger Van Cordt's tax lawyer. This guy who's now in Africa was Roger's son's best friend as a kid. It could be a coincidence, but I can't assume it is. The Van Cordts don't much like me. If this does involve them somehow, I might be opening a can of worms I'd be better off leaving alone."

"You can't run any kind of business in this town without rubbing shoulders with the Van Cordts in one way or another. Are you suspicious of this guy, the client? Because of that?"

"No. I think he's an honest guy at the end of his rope, and his story is crazy enough that no one else will pay attention."

"Then what's your problem?"

Sarah shrugged. "I guess there isn't one. Other than just a vague bad feeling." She reached for her wine glass and took a sip.

Chapter 3: Identity

Sarah Brinson arrived on Thursday. After a restful night in the guest room, on Friday morning she asks Father Ubate for access to the parish business office to use the phone. When she emerges she tells Father Ubate, "I've made my arrangements to return to the States, but I can't fly out from Windhoek until Sunday. I don't want to impose on you any more, but would it be possible for me to stay another day? Then I'll drive back tomorrow, stay in Windhoek tomorrow night and start fresh on my way back home on Sunday." Ubate readily agrees.

"Maybe I could look around a bit in the meantime?" she says. "I'm intrigued by what you guys are doing here. Is it OK if I take some pictures?" She does not mention the imaginary Michael Kimmissee.

If the elderly priest suspects she has an ulterior motive, he gives no indication of it. "Of course. We're very proud of what we've accomplished here in Tondoro. We want the whole world to know."

Tondoro is a small village, but it's part of a network of small settlements and farms across the region. Sarah walks the town from end to end several times. There are small houses made of cinder blocks; chickens are pecking in the dusty street. Young boys fish along the banks of the Okovango River. A small store sells basic staples. The place has a run-down, vaguely desperate look that contrasts with the natural beauty surrounding it. Standing on the banks of the river, Sarah takes many photos with her digital camera.

The buildings of St. Ambrose Parish stand in contrast to the rest of the village. A few are old, and the pinkish stucco-walled structure that used to be the church is obvious, but the rest of the compound looks new. The buildings—church, office wing, schoolroom, medical clinic, cafeteria—are well-constructed, sturdy, clean and attractive. Brinson takes her time examining the clinic, the newest building. It is built from modular steel prefabricated structures. Its windows still have the little stencils in their corners noting the company name and date of manufacture of the glass panels: April 2001.

Sarah slips into a corner of a classroom where Father Tyler is teaching. His assistant is a tall raw-boned youth, about 17, called Moses Mbwele, also a student but one of the older ones. Tyler seems to rely on him as sort of a junior teacher. Mbwele keeps younger children in line and occasionally translates some of Tyler's instructions into a tribal language, perhaps more than one. "We left off last time on page 23 in our English books. Okay. In English, for many words, we have what are called contractions. They're short versions of phrases. *Do not* is often shortened to *don't*. They mean the same thing. You see?" The English textbooks, paperback, though dog-eared, are not very old. Tyler marches through the English lesson methodically, cheerfully. Sarah takes several more pictures.

She walks with Tyler to lunch in the cafeteria. "You're a gifted teacher. It's obvious those kids love you."

"Well, I love doing it."

"Is this what you wanted to do with your life? Missionary work?"

"Before I came here, I didn't know what I wanted to do. But after spending some time here, yes, it's very fulfilling. All I ever wanted to do was serve God."

She smiles. "You're making me rethink my opinion of missionaries."

The man pretending to be Evan Tyler laughs. "We aren't all colonialists, you know."

Classes resume after lunch. But something is different this time: the schoolroom, whose door and windows have sat open all the previous day, is now closed up, and the blinds are drawn over the windows. Sarah approaches, but Moses Mbwele blocks her way. "I'm sorry, ma'am. You are not to come in."

"I can't sit in on the lesson?"

"Not this one." The look in Mbwele's eyes is icy. "Bible study is private. Only certain students allowed."

Tyler, who is the last to come to the classroom, slips past Mbwele and Sarah, and steps inside the school module. Mbwele follows him in, and closes the door.

The schoolroom is not really built for secrecy, however. Twenty minutes later, she's crouching beneath one of the windows on the rear of the structure. There's a small chink between the edge of the window and the blinds inside. Sarah surreptitiously brings the lens of her small digital camera to the crack and takes a few pictures, but mostly she listens.

The pictures aren't that interesting. Father Tyler stands at the front of the classroom, lecturing to twenty or so students, all Black, from ages roughly ten to about sixteen. Some sit on the floor at his feet. Others sit at desks. Mbwele and a few of the other boys have taken off their shirts and tied them around their heads, Arab burnoose style.

"So, you remember what we were talking about last time, Christ's secret nature. Does anyone remember from the last class the name of the star Christ came from, the Christmas star? Yes, Joseph." (The child's answer is inaudible). "Correct. Sirius. Sirius is known as the dog star. It's about eight light-years away. What was the name of Christ's race, his people? Who remembers? Kenny." (Again inaudible, followed by laughter). "No, not the dog people. Anyone remember this word?" (Silence; he's apparently writing on the black board). "*Annunaki*. Say it with me. Ann-u-nak-i. This is a highly intelligent race of alien beings. They're also known as the 'Seeders' or sometimes the 'Preservers.' They go around from planet to planet, scooping up people who are in danger of extinction and transporting them to other planets where they won't be in danger. This is how human beings came to Earth originally, millions of years ago. The human race came in flying saucers, UFOs. You remember what a UFO is? Yes, Elizabeth."

Sarah's remains, brow furrowed, frozen in a crouch beneath the window, listening in puzzlement and anticipation.

"Now, when Christ returns to Earth, which is foretold in Revelations—what's that called, the word for that? Emmanuel? Right, the Rapture. He will come, but

He won't be alone. He'll come with the Annunaki. This is going to happen on April 5, 2011. We Christians call this the Rapture, but others, not necessarily Christians, some will call this First Contact. They'll think it's the first time humans come into contact with aliens, but it really isn't, because of course Christ was an alien. Okay, here's what you need to know about this event..."

Eventually she withdraws, creeping along the back wall to the corner of the schoolroom, where she can retreat behind a tree and emerge back into the compound unobserved. Brinson pockets her camera and walks back toward the complex.

Next, she visits the clinic. It is staffed mostly by volunteers from the village. Many are parents of the students now attending school. It's a light day; an elderly woman has suffered a minor burn accident and a volunteer—it happens to be Moses Mbwele's mother—is bandaging it. While Sarah is there, Father Ubate pays a visit. She asks him, "How long has the clinic been operating? You're very well-equipped. You must have had some wealthy donors help you out."

"Father Tyler is very good at soliciting donations."

"He seems to be good at a lot of things. He teaches a lot of classes too. What does he teach?"

"A little bit of everything. He's our primary schoolteacher here. There is another school in the town, a public school, but most of Tondoro's children come here."

"He's doing Bible study right now. Do you, ah, sit in on those classes?"

Ubate smiles. "Fortunately, I no longer have to teach any classes. I'm an old man and teaching is a hard job.

Father Tyler assuming that duty was just one of the many wonderful things he's done."

"So you *don't* know what he's teaching in there?"

"He's teaching our children to love Jesus. That's the most important thing."

She does not push the issue.

Communication with the outside world from Tondoro—at least a form of communication that doesn't depend on the cooperation of officials of St. Ambrose Parish—is difficult. The nearest internet café is in Rundu, an hour or so away. It may be that Sarah Brinson considers driving there; we can't know for sure, but the rental car remains, for the time being, where it's parked. Perhaps she figures the timing of her report to her clients in Grand Rapids isn't necessarily urgent. She will be back in Windhoek tomorrow night in any event, on the first leg of her journey home.

But she does, in a small notebook kept in her zipper-closed folio, record a short page of notes about what she's seen in Tondoro. Sitting on her bed in the small monastery cell room, she writes:

Tondoro, Namib. — 2/15/02 — St. Ambrose Parish — Observation subject is clearly not Evan Tyler - physical & facial differences - laid several seed questions (zoo, etc.) & clear this is diff. person. Have not observed tattoo - not nec. conclusive (though if he has matching tat, proves considerable deliberate plan to impersonate)

Obs. subj. American — white M 28-35 – slight E. coast inflection (NY?) – seems unquestioned by parish officials (real E. Tyler prob. never here, substitution probably 1998 (?) Obs. subj. probably upper middle class – teaching children strange lesson (UFOs, apocalypse) – Star Trek fan! Officials seem unaware of content of his lessons – ppl at parish treat him w/cult-like reverence

Impersonating Catholic priest, reasons not clear — check finances of St.A. Par. (if client wishes to move fwd.) — Suspect financial scam - Parish has many new bldgs. — Sr. Fr. (Ubate) remarked obs. subj. "handles the money" and made reference to donations solicited by subj.

MUST CONSULT W/CLIENT BEFORE LVNG COUNTRY.

After she's been writing a while there comes a knock on the door. Father Tyler is standing there. He has not visited her at her room before.

"I'm sorry, I didn't mean to interrupt you, but it totally slipped my mind at lunch today. You—*we*—have a dinner invitation."

"Dinner invitation?"

"Yeah. The Blakeneys. They're a couple of British expats. They live over in Sinzogoro. They heard about our

American guest, and they called Father Ubate to invite us to dinner."

She gives him a look that hints she's trying to conceal skepticism. "How'd they hear about me?"

"From Joe Kimbeta."

"Who?"

"Joe. You met him when you first came to town. He does business all up and down the river, and apparently he was in Sinzogoro today or last night and met up with the Blakeneys. Nigel and Agnes. Isn't that perfect, the names I mean? So British."

"Where is Sinzogoro?"

"Another town, like this one, to the west between here and Rundu. You probably passed through it on your way here. The Blakeneys have a really nice bungalow, and the food is always excellent. I can drive you. It's probably to your advantage to meet them. They might've seen that man you're looking for, or at least heard something about him."

"Yes, they very well might have. Why didn't you tell me there were other Western expats living in the area?"

Tyler shrugs. "Like I said, it totally slipped my mind."

"Okay. What time?"

"They told Father Ubate sevenish, and we should count on it taking an hour to get there. Can you be ready at six?"

"Sure."

"Okay. I'll leave you to it, then."

After she closes the door Brinson picks up her folio and reopens her notes. She scribbles down something about the Blakeneys and the name of the town, Sinzogoro. She hesitates as she fingers the photo of Ron Staley. Then she puts it back in the folio, zips it up, and begins getting ready for dinner.

The more or less official vehicle of St. Ambrose Parish is a 1980 Toyota Land Cruiser hardtop, in good condition despite its age. Two battered jerry cans are strapped to its rear door with red bungee cords. A small plastic statute of the Virgin Mary sits on the dashboard. The Cruiser sets off down Highway B10, Tyler behind the wheel—he's now in cargo shorts and a white button-up linen shirt—and Sarah Brinson in the passenger's seat. The sun is low in the sky and the whole landscape seems burnished.

The Cruiser has a tape deck, Tyler slides an old cassette into the slot. On its label, in blue ink, are scrawled the words *"AFRICA MIX."*

"I made this tape the summer before I came here." Tyler smiles with an air of nostalgia, or perhaps self-importance. "Did you make mix tapes when you were a teenager?"

"Nah. Different generation, I think."

The first song to come up on the stereo is Toto's "Africa." Gripping the steering wheel, Evan Tyler laughs. "You knew that had to be the first song I recorded, right? I mean, what would you do?"

She smiles thinly and nods. As she's about to turn away she notices a hint of a darker shape showing through the whiteness of the sleeve of Tyler's shirt. The very bottom of a tattoo is slightly visible under the hem of the sleeve. "Oh, you have a tattoo?"

"Oh, yeah." He pulls up the sleeve slightly and shrugs. It's an image of a heart, sheathed in barbed wire, with flames and a cross protruding from its top.

"When did you get that?"

He shrugs. "College."

"College, or seminary?"

"College."

She goes back to looking out the window at the scenery whirling by the side of the highway.

She has no awareness of it, but there is a gun less than twelve inches away from her, a 9mm semi-automatic pistol—a Vektor SP1—concealed in one of the baggy pockets of Tyler's shorts.

Chapter 4: Sarah

Eleven years earlier Sarah Brinson reached a milestone in her life. Carrying a hot M-16 that she never once fired, she was one of many shaven-headed soldiers —not many of them women—in tan suede boots and chocolate-chip camouflage, herding long columns of hundreds (eventually thousands) of Iraqi troops, most stripped to their underwear. She was not front-line infantry, but the war was over so quickly and there were so many prisoners to process, marching across the dunes, that all hands were needed to try to control the chaos. Not for the first time in her military career, she was essentially a policewoman. But two days after the

Iraqi surrender, while Kuwait was still ablaze from border to border with oil well fires, and it looked like the balance of power in the world had decisively shifted (it hadn't), Brinson was called into a modular office trailer in Dharhan and given the case that eventually made her. Or one of those cases, at least.

"We've received some intelligence. Illegal activity by a couple of rogue personnel." The bored-looking young captain spread a map of western Iraq out on the table. "We have reason to believe there is, or was, a network of Coalition personnel poaching valuables looted from the KTO." [*Kuwait Theater of Operations*] "There's rumors of a cache somewhere, maybe here, maybe somewhere over here, containing considerable contraband. Your mission is to recover said contraband and apprehend the personnel involved. Understood?"

"Yes, sir."

The caper was over by March 10, ten days after the surrender. Gwen Carrigan, Brinson's partner in later years, told her she should write a book about it. It was a real-life detective and adventure story. Brinson made seven arrests, of soldiers ranging from a PFC to a regular Army cavalry major, and located the mythical caches of stolen Kuwaiti swag which included plastic tubs of jewelry, three suitcases of American cash totaling $850,000, VCRs, cell phones, piles of designer jeans (worth serious bank in Arab countries) and lots of stolen U.S. Army radio equipment. She never got around to writing the book and never spoke to the press about the case, but rumors of it certainly got around. They were the loose basis for a Hollywood film called *Three Kings*, made in

1999. Sarah neither took nor sought credit, and in fact thought the film shallow and vapid.

The real life case should have made her career as a Criminal Investigations Special Agent. It looked like it was going to. But barely a year after Desert Storm she was discharged, and that promising career was scotched. She was a victim of bad luck and bad timing. Her discharge and the scandal that brought it on happened in 1992, still a year away from the policy, called *Don't Ask, Don't Tell*, that might otherwise have saved her military career. This bit of bad luck was a major vector in the course of her life.

She was born and brought up in Grand Rapids, an unusually stifling place in the '70s and '80s. It was the kind of place where people tended to hide their true selves. Her father, a sales executive who hopped from company to company, pissed away most of his money. on a succession of schemes uniquely home-grown in Grand Rapids. The area was the cradle and headquarters of Streamline, the multilevel marketing empire founded by the Van Cordt family. Like many middle-aged white men in Grand Rapids, Donald Brinson filled his garage with unsold boxes of protein bars, shake mix and skin cream and listened to hours of tapes of droning motivational speeches. Sarah's mother drank quietly but heavily. Sarah rarely heard words of affection spoken between her parents.

In middle and high school Sarah experienced a few romantic near misses. Sarah was attracted exclusively to girls from an early age, but this above all one hid from others in Grand Rapids. Upon her graduation from high school in 1982, at the very first possible moment, she seized the only obvious option that promised an escape from her physical surroundings: the Army. Young gays in that era were often attracted to the armed forces, believing either that they might find others of their preferred gender and orientation, or that the homophobic culture of the military might "straighten them out." Some believed both at once; the minds of teenagers can easily harbor contradictory motivations.

It took two years of bouncing around in dead-end Army vocations for Sarah Brinson to find something interesting that she was good at. On the recommendation of a commanding officer who noticed Brinson's clarity of mind behind her brusque manners, in 1984 she applied to the U.S. Army Military Police School at Fort Leonard Wood in St. Robert, Missouri. There, she achieved extraordinarily high marks. After graduation she was given an unusually glamorous destination for a new MP: Panzer Kaserne, a U.S. military colony in Kaiserslautern, West Germany. It was her first overseas assignment.

Germany in the mid-80s was a heady and adventurous time and place. Divided by the Cold War, foreseen by many to be the ground zero of the hot war that always seemed right around the corner, Germany provided a wealth of experiences Sarah Brinson of Grand Rapids, Michigan could previously only dream of.

It was steady work for military police. On the various American air and Army bases near Kaiserslautern, drug rings and embezzlement rackets, crooked kickbacks with West German military counterparts, as well as drunkenness, petty theft, bar brawling and rape kept a division of MPs busy full time. Within six months Corporal Brinson led her unit in arrests and convictions based on her arrests. The rate of crime committed in Kaiserslautern by American military personnel also dropped noticeably. That she was a lesbian was more a joke than an open secret but clearly many other MPs believed she was. It added, in a way, to her professional mystique.

On a personal level, for Sarah found fulfillment not in the work in Germany, but, eventually, in romance. She dated two Air Force women in quick succession: both relationships ended quickly and unhappily. Then, while interviewing witnesses after another drunken brawl, she met Beth Wycoff, an Army translator. Within a month they were spending raucous sexual weekends together in hotel rooms and Bavarian chalets, always far from the base. Being an investigator herself—and having worked on cases involving suspected homosexuals—Brinson knew how to be discreet. At least, no investigations were opened, and if there were suspicions, none made it to the level of appearing on official paper.

The military, though, has a way of breaking hearts with a couple of words computer-printed on a thin sheet of tissue paper. In September, 1987, Sarah was transferred—promoted, technically—to a position in Seoul, South Korea. At a final weekend in one of their rented Bavarian cottages they discussed what to do. Perhaps one or both of them would resign from the Army to remain together? In the end, Sarah made a choice. "I think I have to go for this. It could be my career." After they returned to Kaiserslautern and said an awkward good-bye, they never spoke again. Less than a year later,

Wycoff was discharged from the Army for homosexual activity.

If Sarah regretted her choice, she never told anyone. The Seoul assignment moved her slightly higher up the MP food chain, but she had no romances in Korea, at least no substantial ones.

When Saddam Hussein invaded Kuwait in 1990, the resulting military build-up drew personnel from across the globe to Saudi Arabia and Qatar. This great magnet brought her to those dusty dunes in western Iraq the following March, and into those prefabricated trailers lined with KTO loot.

The Gulf War also indirectly brought her into the arms of Rachel Garvez. Sarah's bust in the Gulf/KTO caper got her noticed by the head of the U.S. Army Military Police at the Pentagon, a man called Parham, who decided he wanted Brinson on his staff. Rachel Garvez—Navy, not Army—worked at the Pentagon on the staff of some low-level mixed civilian/military unit pitching aircraft carriers to Congress. Brinson met Garvez on her very first day at the Pentagon. What transpired between them in sunny apartments and motel rooms in Arlington and Annapolis seemed to bring back the glow of those romantic days in Germany half a decade before. Only now, someone found out, and this time it *did* hit official paper.

"This policy is asinine. I've always hated it. Think about what it says about us as a country, to our enemies. I'm ashamed to be in the Army today."

This was what Parham said to her when he heard of the charges brought against her. He tried to intervene, but his influence with CID—Criminal Investigation Division—was limited. The case was open and shut. Brinson and Garvez had each been interrogated for hours—never in the same room, of course—in front of CID inquisitors. Rachel Garvez had even gone on record saying that Sarah was the love of her life. This brought open chuckles from the CID panelists, who paged through her file between sips of stale coffee from styrofoam cups. During Sarah's own interrogation, she mostly confined her answers to "Yes, sir" and "No, sir." She was asked which of them pretended to be the man and whether she fucked Garvez with strap-on dildos. Her response to these offensive questions was a frosty, "It doesn't work like that, sir." The investigators snorted and laughed.

To Parham, who had faced reprimand in the past for speaking too freely in favor of gays serving in the military, Brinson said she thought the policy would be changed, and probably soon. "I may be back," she said.

"I wish that were true. I want you to know, Sarah, you've been a hell of an investigator."

"I appreciate that, sir. Thank you."

To his credit, Parham did use what influence he had to affect Sarah's case. She was discharged honorably, which meant at least she qualified for benefits and health care. That was the least the United States of America could do, Parham said, for a decorated Gulf War veteran, even if she was a lesbian.

This proved a lucky break. Had she been discharged other than honorably, the Washington, D.C. police force —her next job—wouldn't have taken her. Rachel Garvez was not so lucky. She got the dishonorable discharge, bounced between a few mindless jobs, lived with Sarah in the same low-rent apartment for three months, and ultimately went home to her parents in El Paso, Texas.

Sarah was once again alone.

Around the same time, and even more during the year after this event, Brinson's Grand Rapids family went to pieces. Her brother Ben became estranged from the family, and her mother was on her fourth or fifth round of alcohol rehab. Sarah's father, now a veteran of two bankruptcies, worked at a photo supply company. In 1993, just after a very stressed Sarah requested a transfer from D.C.P.D.'s robbery-homicide division to the financial crimes unit, her younger sister Paige was murdered by her abusive boyfriend. They found Paige's body on the floor of the garage of the house where she lived with him, her skull staved in by a hammer. He pleaded guilty to get a life sentence instead of lethal injection.

That wasn't the end of the family's troubles. Donald Brinson began experiencing, in the words of his psychiatrist, psychotic episodes. He could no longer work, and Sarah's mother Linda, still sodden with drink, couldn't take care of him.

In early 1994, Sarah resigned from the D.C. police department and returned to Grand Rapids. There, she worked on the police force only six months, until after her father was institutionalized. Striking out on her own, that year she launched her private investigation firm, which began, as most private investigation firms do, with the usual mainstays of asset tracing, divorce case support, and the occasional missing person.

She did not date in Grand Rapids. She was focused on taking care of her ailing parents and building her business. Perhaps she finally felt the pain of those prematurely ended romances, or perhaps she was too focused to dwell on the past.

Instead of a girlfriend, Sarah Brinson got a dog, an English bulldog she called Gribbs. The old irony is that love easily finds people who aren't looking for it. She met Gwen Carrigan at a dog park. Gwen's bulldog, Cracker, was French, not English, but the dogs—and their mothers—got along famously.

When they met, Gwen's son Vincent, whom she was raising alone, was ten, and she was only a few years out of the clutches of the abusive husband who had stalked her. Gwen was a radiology tech. They moved in together after only a few weeks and soon bonded as a family: two women, two bulldogs and a boy.

Sarah's parents passed away within a year and a half of one another, her father first. But by now the wanderlust was gone. Grand Rapids hadn't changed much in the decade and a half between 1982 and 1997, but Sarah Brinson had changed greatly. Through it all she carried herself as if she hadn't noticed it. She was not generally known as the reflective type.

In 1997 a Grand Rapids real estate developer named Jason Weintraub hired Brinson Investigations to look into the financial affairs of Marvin Kell, Weintraub's partner on a strip mall real estate deal. Weintraub suspected Kell of cheating him and the limited liability company that owned the mall. That Kell also happened to own several automobile dealerships and had bankrolled much of the campaign of Grand Rapids' new mayor, Paul Stenn, didn't seem to deter Sarah at all. She did her work quietly and discreetly. For months, Kell had no idea who she was or that he was being investigated. Kell was believed to have ties to Detroit-based Mafia figures, but more ominously, he was in the social circles of the Van Cordts, the founders of Streamline. For this reason no one else in town would touch the case. No one wanted to cross them.

A year later, Weintraub sued Kell for converting the assets of the strip mall LLC, and, largely on the evidence gathered by Sarah Brinson, the federal district attorney indicted Kell for racketeering. Kell's friendship with the Detroit mafiosi played big on the evening news and in the papers. The Van Cordts remained still and quiet, carefully not wanting to be tainted by association. Kell was dropped from all the boards and charities he served on, his car dealerships went into receivership, and Streamline cashiered him as a distributor. When he was driven away in a police car from the federal courthouse after being sentenced to 18 years, Kell curled up into a fetal position on the back seat and whimpered. He died of a stroke in prison in November 2000.

By then, Sarah Brinson was the most sought-after investigator in Grand Rapids, and the highest paid. Her firm now had three investigators on staff. The vast majority of private eyes were and are ex-law enforcement, but Sarah also preferred to hire people with military experience. She was now successful enough that the junior investigators handled the run-of-the mill asset tracings and divorce work. If a client came in with a truly unique or unusual case, as the Tyler family did in January 2002, Sarah would take the meeting.

Even at that, it was not like the movies. She had not carried a gun since that day the Iraqis surrendered in the desert. She spent most of her time staring at computer screens or calling banks, archives, or government agencies to verify this record or that. This was who Sarah Brinson was when she went to Namibia, in search of the thief who had stolen Barbara and Neil Tyler's son.

Chapter 5: Sinzogoro

As a town, Sinzogoro is no more than a small cluster of cinder block buildings—a school, a store and a church —fronting the river just off the main highway. The landscape is dotted with a few tiny homesteads, but most of the land is empty and rural.

Evan Tyler turns the Land Cruiser off the main road and starts down a smaller street, paved and dusty, heading south. The river recedes in the rearview mirrors.

Sarah has said little during the 45-minute drive. She asked Tyler about the Blakeneys, how long they've lived in Namibia, and what British expatriates might find to do in this part of the world. But the conversation really hadn't caught fire. He asked about the man she's searching for, Michael Kimmissee. "What was he doing in Africa? Where was he last seen? How long has he been missing?" Her answers have been as bland as Tyler's, casual lies. Kimmissee was a biologist. He was last seen in Windhoek for sure, but possibly also in Cuangar, across the river in Angola. A few months. This conversation, too, petered out. Now they are mostly silent. The tape deck provides a merciful diversion.

A mile or so away from the highway, the smaller paved road abruptly ends. A small copse of trees sprouts weathered trunks from the dusty tan earth. An old steel gate on rusty posts stands sentinel at the terminus of the road. Beyond that, an unpaved dirt road curves slightly as it heads into hilly country. A sign on the gate, its paint flaking, reads, *PRIVATE PROPERTY.*

Perhaps ten feet from the gate, Tyler brings the Land Cruiser to a halt. He does not turn off the engine.

"This is the Blakeneys' driveway. Would you do me a favor, get out and open the gate? It should be un-locked."

Brinson stares out the windshield at the gate. She looks at Tyler. "That doesn't look like a driveway."

"Excuse me?"

"You said this is their driveway. It doesn't look like one. Where's their mailbox, if it's a driveway?"

Tyler cocks his head and looks at her quizzically. "Um, what?"

"Where do the Blakeneys get their mail?"

"I have no idea. Why don't you ask them? After you open the gate."

"Something's not right here."

"What's not right? I don't understand."

"I'm not getting out."

"Jesus, you are suspicious."

"Do the Blakeneys really exist? I think it's bullshit." One of Sarah's eyes suddenly twitches. "Wait, what did you just say?"

"I don't understand. I asked you to open the—"

"You said *Jesus*. You took the Lord's name in vain. You, a priest? I think we should go back to Tondoro."

He motions at the gate. "We have a dinner invitation. You want me to stand the Blakeneys up?"

"I don't think the Blakeneys live at the end of this road. I don't think there *are* any Blakeneys."

Tyler sits, griping the steering wheel, not looking at her. He gives a little sigh.

"You're paranoid, and you're being rude. We're going to see the Blakeneys. They're perfectly real. But if you don't want to open the gate, fine. I will."

He turns off the car engine and pulls the key out of the ignition. Opening the door, sliding out of the driver's seat, Tyler climbs down from the high car and steps toward the gate. He leaves the driver's side door open. Sarah watches him carefully. In the dusky glow of sunset his shadow is impossibly long, stretching into seeming infinity.

He unlatches the gate—which indeed is unlocked—and swings it open. He turns and walks back to the car.

She sees nothing until it's almost too late. His hand comes up, arm outstretched, something small and dark in his palm. Sarah yelps and grabs for the handle of the passenger's side door. The sound of the gun is a short crack echoing across the African landscape.

The shot catches her in the top of her left shoulder. Crying out, she stumbles out of the car. Blood is splattered on the inside of the windshield on the passenger's side. Tyler walks calmly around the front of the Land Cruiser. Brinson tries to flee, but another crack of the

Vektor plants a shot in the lower part of her left calf. She collapses into the buff-colored dust.

"Who hired you?" He is now standing directly above her, the short barrel of the gun inches from her head. *"Who hired you? Dubo or O'Cuinneagain?"*

Her answer comes as a hiss through pain-clenched teeth. "Fuck you."

The pistol makes a third crack. Her inert form, skull shattered, lies still on the dusty ground.

After a while he walks back to the gate, closes and refastens the latch. Brinson was right. The Blakeneys do not exist. This road did once lead to a small farm once owned by expatriates—Germans, not British—but they left the country and their house was torn down long ago. No one lives on this road anymore.

Anyone observing the scene—no one does, since it occurs so far off the main road in the bush—would quickly realize that Tyler came well-prepared. He walks round to the back of the Land Cruiser and opens its rear doors, revealing a large red picnic cooler. Tyler unbuttons and removes his white linen shirt, which he hangs over the corner of one of the open rear doors. He opens the cooler and fishes out a large canvas tarp, olive drab in color, neatly folded. He unfurls it, covers Brinson's body, and drags her six feet or so to the side of the car. Then he crouches down on the driver's side, reaches under the car and pulls her body directly underneath the Land Cruiser's high wheel base. He makes sure the tarp is covering her all the way, stands up, and brushes dirt from his shorts.

Brinson's black leather folio is still on the passenger's seat. Tyler takes it, sits in the driver's seat and carefully pages through it. He finds Sarah Brinson's passport, her Michigan driver's license, and the travel documents for her trip back to the States from Windhoek. While examining the documents, Tyler whispers: "Grand Rapids, Michigan."

He finds her notes, too. He laughs. "*Star Trek* fan!" Something else catches his eye. "Seed questions. The zoo. I should've known that was a trick. And the goddamn tattoo." Zipping the folio back up, he seems to speak to the body under the car's floor. "Very clever, Ms. Brinson. The Tylers will never know they got their money's worth."

Tyler sits in the driver's seat of the Cruiser for a long time. Dusk flattens into quickly-falling darkness. Not long after, a single set of car headlights is visible farther up the small paved road, but no one comes down this far. The sky, free from light pollution, is a mantle of glittering stars. The Milky Way arcs overhead. Crickets make the only sounds.

When it is fully dark, he gets out of the car and goes around to the rear door. The picnic cooler contains a kerosene lantern, a Boy Scout-style folding camp shovel, several folded towels, a jug of water, a bar of soap and two plastic squirt bottles of cleaning fluids. He takes the lantern and the shovel, closes the cooler, and sets his linen shirt on its lid. He closes the rear doors of the Toyota and walks through the small copse of trees to its far side. He unfolds the shovel and begins probing the ground with it.

The burial process takes close to two hours. Tyler works with minimal light from the lantern. When his pit is about four feet deep, he returns to the car, reaches under it and tugs the tarp away from the body. Rolling Brinson onto it, he drags her body on the tarp across the dirt to the side of the hole, and dumps her corpse into the pit.

Once the grave is filled in, he carefully goes back over the ground, using the shovel to scratch at patches of darkened dirt illuminated by the lantern to conceal, as much as can be done, the traces of recent disturbance. He rearranges a few rocks and fallen branches. He moves the car, backing it up into its own tire tracks, exposing the spot where the body lay. He digs up the bloodstained earth, turns it, refills the shallow holes, and pats them down with the back of the shovel.

Next, he cleans the car. Using the cleaning supplies, he wipes away every spot of blood on the inside of the Cruiser, and for good measure swabs everything under the dashboard and the floor carpets. He then washes himself as best he can. The bloody towels go in a small hole he digs some 25 feet from the body. He makes one last careful pass with the torch, shining its beam to and fro. At long last he returns to the car and puts his shirt back on. It is spotless, not even fouled with dust. He gets back in the driver's seat. Tyler starts the engine and slowly drives—in reverse, headlights off—back up the small paved road toward the main highway.

It is 10:30 PM when he returns to St. Ambrose Parish in Tondoro. There are only a few vehicles parked in the small gravelly lot behind the main compound, shielded from view of the main thoroughfare by the edifice of the church. One of the vehicles parked there is the SUV Brinson drove to Tondoro two days ago. He has the keys; of course he stripped Brinson's pockets before burying her. He waits a long time in the Cruiser, lights and engine off, waiting for the compound to grow quiet and for as many window lights in view to wink off as he dare wait for.

When the parish is dead silent, except for the crickets and the distant babble of the Okovango River, Tyler visits Brinson's guest room. It is a simple matter to gather up what few belongings she had there, which were already packed in anticipation for her early-morning departure for Windhoek. He brings her suitcase and carry-on bag to the SUV, locking the door of the guest room behind him. A few minutes later the car is racing down the B10 highway in a westerly direction, away from Tondoro, putting even more distance between the car and the lonely place where its driver is buried.

Just outside of Kahenge, 20 minutes from Tondoro, a small dirt road branches off from the B10 highway and leads northeast to the Cubango river. The river is the border between Namibia and Angola. At the end of this road, Tyler gets out of the SUV. He is careful to leave the windows rolled up, but the sun roof open a crack. With the gear set in neutral, he rolls the car across the sand at the end of the unused road and into the scrubby reeds leading into the water. Soon, it floats. The current begins to push it away from the bank. Water begins to pour through the crack in the sun roof. In minutes, the car sinks, far out of sight now in the darkness, and there is again no sound but the crickets and the river lapping at the shore.

Tyler is careful to walk back to Tondoro along the unlighted riverbank, not the highway. When he returns to his own room in the St. Ambrose compound it is nearly two AM. He sleeps soundly.

The next morning, Saturday, February 16, the absence of the SUV—and of Sarah Brinson—raises few eyebrows. She had told Father Ubate that she was leaving at the crack of dawn on Saturday. At brunch, however, the aged father asks Tyler about it: "What time did our guest leave this morning?"

"She left late last night, actually. We had dinner in Rundu and at the restaurant she talked to somebody who thought he'd seen that man she was looking for. She made me drive her right back so she could pick up her car and take off. I didn't even see her leave."

"Oh, so that American *was* here?"

"Not here in Tondoro, but apparently he might've been in Rundu."

No more is said about Brinson's absence. The parish settles back into its normal routine. There is no school today.

But despite that, after they meet at breakfast, Tyler tells Moses Mbwele to come see him later that afternoon. The meeting occurs in Father Tyler's office, which is just off his small apartment. On the wall is his framed certificate of ordination, a photo of John Paul II, and a banner for the Detroit Lions. A picture of Neil and Barbara Tyler, framed in silver, sits on the corner of his desk, which is otherwise cluttered with papers and file folders.

"Moses, I hate to tell you this, little buddy, but the day has come." There's a slightly regretful tone in Tyler's voice. Mbwele sits in the small old chair next to Tyler's desk.

"You're leaving?"

"Don't say anything to Father Ubate yet. I'll break it to him in my own time. And I'm going to have to notify the Vatican and OMI, so they can send my replacement."

Mbwele's eyes are starting to moisten. "How long, then?"

"I don't know. I have to go to Windhoek to take care of some business, probably next week. I'll be back after that, but not for long."

Moses wipes his right eye, but keeps his composure. "Take me with you?"

"I can't. Not right away. When I get settled, I will, I promise. I'll send for you. You'll have to think of something to tell your mom."

"I'll tell her I'm joining your new ministry."

"Well, we'll see if that's feasible." They are silent; Tyler glances at the floor and then back at Mbwele. "You can't tell anyone anything. You know that, right? People wouldn't understand. We'd both get in trouble."

"I won't say a word."

"You really won't? I mean, really, not a word."

"I obey you, Father."

"We'll see each other tonight, then."

They both rise from their chairs. Mbwele turns to leave, but suddenly reverses, steps toward Tyler, and they crash into an embrace.

"It's all right, buddy." Tyler's voice is barely a whisper. "It's going to be all right. I'll send for you." Moses Mbwele can no longer hide that he's crying.

Chapter 6: Marcus

Sarah Brinson never knew the name of the man impersonating Evan Tyler, but she had scrawled accurate impressions of him in the notebook in the little leather folio now in that man's possession. He was not from Grand Rapids, but had grown up in a middle class family in Saugerties, New York. His father had been a lawyer. He had grown up watching *Star Trek* as a kid and young teenager; the shtick he sold his class in Tondoro about "the Preservers" was the backstory of an episode of that show called *The Paradise Syndrome*. But Brinson could not easily have ferreted out his real name, which was Marcus Holcomb, nor could she have done more than guess at the twisted skein of events that had brought him to Tondoro. That story may occupy us for some time.

Holcomb had begun his criminal career in his early 20s, scamming colleges and universities. At first it was for relatively low stakes. He cheated university housing departments out of free room and board, squatting in college dormitories, by taking—by agreement with such persons—the places of students who told their parents (who paid the bills) that they were living in dormitories but who were actually living off-campus with others, usually girlfriends of whom the parents disapproved. Eventually Marcus's *modus operandi* became more sophisticated: he transferred from college to college with altered or misleading transcripts and phony recommendation letters, applied for financial aid with fraudulent loan applications, and lived—for precarious stretches of time—on the proceeds. By the time he ripped off his final college, University of California at San Diego, the authorities still had not quite caught up to him, though his actions after that time seem to indicate he thought they would, and soon.

Then there was that business aboard the cruise ship, the *M/V Norse Star*, in Alaska. Holcomb, then 26, went aboard with a young man called Rafael Moreira, only 18, an exchange student from Brazil whom he met at UCSD. Holcomb and Moreira were lovers; Moreira was not out to anyone else including his family. Official records indicate that Moreira vanished from the ship on June 12, 1997. He was presumed to have fallen overboard, but Holcomb, who initially reported his boyfriend missing in the first place, abruptly jumped ship when the *Norse Star* docked in Vancouver, British Columbia. At that time, he had only a few thousand dollars in cash, mostly Moreira's, which dissipated quickly. But the money got Marcus Holcomb as far as London.

In London, Marcus began to position himself on the fringes of the criminal underground. His main objective seems to have been to ingratiate himself with someone who would forge him a work visa or other immigration document whereby he could remain in the UK indefinitely—beyond the reach of police departments in

Alaska, Vancouver, and Seattle, who might want to question him about Rafael Moreira.

Terrorists can more readily forge international documents than run-of-the-mill gangsters. It was no accident, then, that he fell into the orbit of a Belfast-born businessman called Michael O'Cuinneagain. To be sure, O'Cuinneagain himself was much more of a gangster than a terrorist, though he'd been deeply involved with financing the Irish Republican Army since the early 1970s. By 1997, the tail end of the conflict known as The Troubles, O'Cuinneagain ran numerous criminal rackets in London, including a pub that was the front for one of his many money laundries. Eventually Marcus worked there. Instead of a fake student visa, he got a real work visa. And O'Cuinneagain began to take a liking to him.

The seed of both Marcus's temptation and his undoing was a one-off transaction O'Cuinneagain arranged with an Iraqi agent in France, a distant contact of O.C.'s old IRA friends. O'Cuinneagain facilitated the smuggling of a cache of microchips out of a tech firm in the UK and had them sent surreptitiously in UPS and DHL packages to Iraqi moles on the continent. Marcus was unwittingly one of the couriers of the microchips.

In return for the microchips, the Iraqi mastermind arranged for an athletic bag stuffed with £806,450 in cash [*about $1.34 million USD*] to be dropped off at a train station locker in Calais, France. O'Cuinneagain assigned Marcus to travel to France via the Chunnel, pick up the bag and bring it to O'Cuinneagain's country cottage in South Mimms, in Hertfordshire, about an hour's drive outside of London. Marcus was only recently engaged to

Shannon O'Cuinneagain, age 18, his employer's daughter. This was why the gangster trusted him.

He shouldn't have. The moment he heard about the transfer of the gym bag of cash, Holcomb was angling to steal it and flee the country. He enlisted an unlikely ally: a Brazilian mafia hood, unknown to O'Cuinneagain, called João Broka. He proved important to how and why Marcus wound up in Africa.

Broka, age 28, was sent to the UK as a tool of private vengeance. He was hired by Anchieta Moreira, Rafael's older half-brother. Their father Daniel, known as Dubo, had in the '80s been one of Brazil's most prominent pop stars. He had no thirst for revenge against the American scam artist they believed—but could not prove—had murdered Rafael, but Anchieta, who had acquaintances among Sao Paulo's criminal syndicate, sprang for the caper on his own. Dubo himself didn't know of the plan until later.

Broka's loyalties were suspect. Shortly after he tracked down Marcus Holcomb in London in the spring of 1998, he supposedly made a deal with him: he'd help Marcus embezzle the gym bag, they'd pretend that Marcus was killed and the bag stolen in an ambush by rival gangsters on a country road outside of South Mimms, and they'd secretly split the money and go their separate ways. Marcus laid elaborate plans for his escape. He stole the wallet and UK driver's license belonging to a friend, Gavin Grove, a fellow employee of O'Cuinneagain's syndicate. Marcus even put his own photograph on Grove's license using a plastic laminating machine. With Grove's ID, he booked passage on a ferry from

Weymouth to the island of Jersey, one of the Channel Islands. The escape was set for a Friday morning in June.

On Thursday evening, June 11, 1998, Hertfordshire police found a silver BMW abandoned on the side of Trotters Bottom Road, just adjacent to a traffic circle a few kilometers outside of South Mimms. Inside the car was the body of a young girl, identified as Shannon O'Cuinneagain, who had been shot once through the gut —there was a bullet track going through the trunk and back seat of the car—and once in the head at point-blank range. These wounds had been made with different guns. Next to the car was another corpse of a man in his late 20s, who had been shot four times, including, as with Shannon O'Cuinneagain, an execution-style round to the head. It took the police two days to identify the man: João Broka, a Brazilian national who had entered the UK via Heathrow Airport a few weeks before. Marcus Holcomb had vanished. The police never knew anything about a gym bag full of £806,450 in £20 notes, but Michael O'Cuinneagain certainly did.

The South Mimms Traffic Circle Murders, as they came to be known (briefly) in the press, may even have involved a third victim. The following day the body of Trevor Munford, age 23, a low-level car thief connected to a gang called the Battersea Boys, was found in a trash dumpster in a car park across from Brookmans Park train station only a few minutes' drive from South Mimms. Munford had been killed sometime on Thursday: somebody had jammed an ice pick into the base of his skull. In the absence of any other evidence the police could only guess at what had gone down.

It is worth sparing a few words for Marcus Holcomb's appearance, as it is relevant. He was 27 years old, just under six feet, and considered handsome. He had gray-blue eyes and very long blond hair falling down past his shoulders. He sometimes wore glasses, but the lenses were plain glass with no prescription. With the right clothes and mannerisms, he could pretend convincingly to be nearly ten years younger than he was. After the murders, photos and a description of him were circulated to police forces all over the UK, including customs and border officials, but not outside the borders. Law enforcement computer databases, somewhat rudimentary in 1998 by modern standards, identified him as a person of interest in an open case, but no charges were filed against him.

Chapter 7: Deauville & Ventimiglia

No one knew it—at least not for a while—but Holcomb had gone to France.

He caught the Weymouth-St. Helier ferry on the morning of June 12. He'd spent the night in a sleeping bag stashed in a small knot of trees near a truck stop and a cluster of petrol stations on the outskirts of Weymouth. The authorities did not yet know that the name Gavin Grove was connected to the man they would eventually seek for questioning, and as Jersey was part of the UK, one did not need a passport to board a ferry headed there; a driver's license would do. Neither was carry-on luggage, called hand luggage in Europe, X-rayed. Marcus Holcomb walked aboard the ferry, and off again on the quay in St. Helier, burdened by the blue Umbro bag which weighed 40 pounds and had, in the preceding 48 hours, cost four people their lives.

He remained in Jersey only a few hours. Literally weighed down with cash, he had only to flash a wad of it in the presence of a local fisherman on one of the working docks. "I need to get across the Channel to France, this afternoon, no questions asked. I'll give you the money right now, but we have to leave right away. Are you game?" By four o'clock that afternoon, he was trudging along a lonely beach just outside of Créances, France, the strap of the Umbro bag digging into the flesh of his shoulder. In one hand, he carried a much smaller knapsack containing one change of clothes and a little plastic bag of travel-sized toiletry items he'd bought at a drugstore in Weymouth just before the ferry departed.

Soon he was in Caen, which he reached by hitching a ride with two young women he encountered at a petrol station. He spoke no French, and they understood only a few words of English, but he managed to tell them he was a student from England and he needed to get to Paris by the end of the weekend. At the Caen railroad station, he also convinced one of the girls who had a credit card—he did not—to buy, from a machine, a train ticket for Deauville. Neither of the young women suspected the blue bag he was lugging contained nothing but bricks of cash. When he reached the train station in Deauville, Holcomb put the bag in a locker and went promptly to a currency exchange booth in the station, changing £500 into its equivalent in French francs. Then he went shopping at a nearby department store.

He never checked into a hotel in France. It is sometimes customary in Europe—more so in Italy than in France—for a foreigner to have to show or even surrender his or her passport to the desk clerk upon check-in, so that the names of visitors can be reported to police. Holcomb was then carrying two passports. One was his own American passport, with his real photo and real name. The other was a British passport belonging to a man named Stephen Trask, a graduate student from Leeds. Trask resembled Marcus Holcomb only to the extent that both had long hair, but Stephen's was dark and wavy, while Marcus's was blond and straight. Holcomb also possessed various other documents belonging to Trask, including a copy of a sublease of a small apartment in Rome where Trask was expected to arrive on July 1. He had a fellowship to conduct research for his thesis at the Vatican Library, but no one in Rome had actually ever met Stephen Trask.

Unbeknownst to anyone at the time Holcomb entered France, Stephen Trask was also dead. His body was discovered in his subleased flat in the Fitzrovia neighborhood of London that Sunday, June 13. His throat had been slashed and he'd been dead at least three days. This murder was never connected to the South Mimms slayings and was a dead end for the police. It remained officially unsolved into the 2020s.

On that Sunday morning, the day Trask's body would be found in London, Marcus Holcomb awakened in a small tent at a campground just outside Deauville. He washed himself in a public bathroom at that facility.

Later in the day, in the same bathroom, he worked crude black dye into his blond hair; he'd ventured out to a drugstore on foot to get it. Next to the drugstore, by chance, was a shop with a MoneyGram outlet. From this outlet he purchased, with French francs, three Money-Gram transfer slips. On the Sender line he wrote a ficti-tious name, *Nigel Blakeney*, and on the Recipient line he wrote *Gavin Grove*. These transactions cost him all the cash in his pockets at the time.

The Chinese have a proverb: "Building a mountain starts with a single bucket of dirt." Laundering over $1.3 million in stolen cash through petty currency exchange transactions and MoneyGram slips is something of a similar endeavor. But Marcus Holcomb was patient and resourceful. Time, however, was his enemy, as was any official at a border crossing, hotel or train station who might ask him to present a passport. And he was as afraid of X-ray machines as a vampire is of daylight. These factors drove his actions over the next three months.

To understand Marcus Holcomb's process, it is help-ful to have an understanding of how MoneyGram—and its chief alternative and competitor Western Union—are supposed to work.

Imagine this situation: you are on vacation in a for-eign country, run afoul of the traffic laws, and wind up in jail. You can't afford the bail. You call me, a friend in your home country. I go to a MoneyGram outlet at a lo-cal supermarket or drugstore, give them $500 plus a small fee, and write my name (Sender) and your name (Recipient) on the form. The MoneyGram clerk types it into their system and writes down an 8-digit number, called a Money Control Transfer Number or MCTN, in a series of boxes at the top of the slip. I call you and give you that number. You go to the MoneyGram or Western Union outlet in the foreign city where you're located, give the clerk that number, and they pay you $500 in cash from their store's register. Because they involve international funds transfers without waiting times and without the record-keeping or involvement of financial institutions, MoneyGram and Western Union are the main ways in which advance fee scammers—such as the purveyors of infamous "Nigerian prince" emails—conduct their business.

Both systems have a rule that funds sent must be picked up by the recipient within 90 days or the MCTN on the transaction expires. Thus, to Marcus Holcomb, these services were not merely a money laundry, but also a temporary bank. Within two days of his arrival in Deauville—which was all the time he stayed—he had visited every MoneyGram and Western Union counter in the city, and had already begun to accumulate what would become a thick sheaf of transfer slips that he kept on his person or in his knapsack. Eventually, when they became unwieldy he dispensed with the slips entirely. All one really needed to collect a MoneyGram or Western Union transfer was the Money Control Transfer Number. Few would have guessed the significance of the long column of 8-digit numbers that Marcus scrawled down in a small leather Moleskine notebook.

He also visited casinos. The first was the Casino Barrière in Deauville. He spent several hours there, on two successive nights, playing slot machines and sitting at blackjack tables. Security checked his ID upon entry, but only for proof of age; Gavin Grove's driver's license was genuine and valid, even if it showed Marcus Holcomb's picture. Pit bosses or other security functionaries did not notice him. He won no more or more often than any other patron of the casino; in fact, on his second night he lost nearly 3,000 francs. The purpose was not to win but to launder. At the end of each night, when he cashed out, instead of having cash paid back to him he requested a casino check in the name of Gavin Grove. The true risk was leaving the Umbro bag in train and bus station lockers, which he did frequently, but it was never discovered.

After two days in Deauville, Holcomb, now again with the Umbro bag against his back, used cash to purchase a Eurail pass good for three months. He began a trek across France, headed mostly in a southeasterly direction. He usually chose night trains, where he could sleep in train compartments with his head on the Umbro bag. The surface of the bag began to accumulate a dark stain from the cheap black dye on his long hair. Other times, as in Deauville, he slept at campgrounds, or sometimes even on train station benches. He wore a Nine Inch Nails T-shirt and baggy jeans riven with holes; he painted his fingernails black. No one could or did suspect that a serial murderer carrying nearly a million dollars in cash would present the image of a vagabond goth kid in his late teens. He was questioned by police only once, in Valence, but only because he was sleeping on a bench and the town had a curfew for young people. The gendarmes left him alone when he showed them Grove's driver's license. Grove was 26.

On Holcomb's trip across France, he visited various casinos and nearly every MoneyGram and Western Union outlet between Normandy and Alpes-de-Haute. This was not difficult. Many such outlets were located in railroad stations, or in central districts within walking distance of railroad stations. He never checked into a hotel; he never rented a car. Remaining within France, he never came to a border checkpoint where he would've had to show a passport. Slowly, day by day, town by town, the Umbro bag grew lighter, less unwieldy, and less dangerous. The sheaf of casino checks and transfer slips grew thicker. Within ten days of his arrival in France he'd laundered more than £100,000 of his booty. Though both the British police and the organized crime syndicate of Michael O'Cuinneagain were hunting Marcus Holcomb, none were yet close to his trail.

At Menton, on the Riviera at the southeast corner of France, Marcus crossed the border into Italy, on June 25, 1998. He couldn't do it in any conventional way. He bought a mountain bike and some more camping gear in the city and then went up into the scrubby rugged hills to the west of Menton, in a hiking area called Plan du Lion. There are some high chain-link fences along the border here, but in the steeper and more inaccessible areas, off trail, there are no such barriers. He camped in one of these areas, shivering without a campfire for fear of attracting attention from rangers. In a grueling and dangerous night hike, wearing a miner's lamp, pulling the mountain bike and with the Umbro bag across his back, he crossed the unmarked border. In the morning, he hiked down to the small town of Ventimiglia, Italy.

From there, his continued his pattern: night trains, sleeping in stations or pitching his tent in campgrounds, and endless trips to MoneyGram and Western Union outlets. Had anyone been tracking his movements on a map—no one was—they would have seen Holcomb inch and hop from town to town in northern Italy, arcing above the Ligurian Sea and working his way down into the boot: Cuneo, Alba, Asti, Alessandria, Tortona, and a burst of activity in Genoa, where there were many opportunities to launder cash. Then Rapallo, Pistoia, Grosseto, a zigzag to Terni, and west to Civitavecchia. Rome was drawing him like a magnet.

Marcus by now carried a dog-eared Frommer's tour book, a travel guide for Italy, marked and annotated with pencil scrawls and colored tape flags like the case book of a law student preparing for exams. In fact, the University of Arizona law school was one of the institutions Marcus had scammed before he met Rafael Moreira. His habits reflected his dip into a legal education. Though he was a millionaire now, Marcus did not spend much. His meals were often from small cafés or McDonald's. Methodical as he was, it seems doubtful there was a master plan in his mind, at least not one with a high level of detail or granularity. When he made the decision to steal O'Cuinneagain's money he probably didn't envision this would be the result. But we cannot know for sure.

On July 2, 1998, trailing Umbro bag and French mountain bike behind him, Holcomb appeared at an apartment building in central Rome. He put on a phony British accent as he punched the button on the intercom to talk to the super. "Hello, you speak English? My name is Stephen Trask. I'm subleasing a flat in this building for a few weeks?"

This move was something of a gamble. All Marcus knew about the Rome sublease was from the documents he'd stolen from Stephen's flat in London, and what little Stephen had told him about the arrangement. He had no way of knowing if the building superintendent or the sublessors—a married couple who worked for Sapienza University—had been told that Stephen Trask was dead. This was the gamble. It paid off; they had not been. But he also had to know that it was only a matter of time before they found out. The sublessor couple was, in any event, on vacation in Norway. Marcus knew Trask had deliberately arranged the sublease so they wouldn't have to be bothered or even notified when he arrived.

In this apartment, stacked with books and lined with framed prints of photographs of Rome from decades past, Marcus had a proper shower for the first time in a long time, and he slept in a real bed. The Umbro bag was relatively safe. Aside from visiting restaurants and some necessary shopping trips, his first ventures in Rome were to the campus of Sapienza University, where he familiarized himself with the foreign exchange student program. On July 13, eleven days after his arrival, he appeared at an orientation event for English-speaking exchange students who were to spend a week touring the university and getting to know the campus before classes began.

He didn't even bother to check in at the registration desk. He slid one of the orientation packet folders off the table when the women sitting at the desk were distracted. The folder contained a little decal label with *"Ciao, Il Mio Nome E"* printed at the top. With a pen beneath this he wrote *KYLE BARNES*, peeled the sticker off its backing, stuck it to his Nirvana T-shirt, and walked into the lecture hall. No one questioned him.

Chapter 8: Rome

Two young men, foreigners, unknown to one another, in Rome that summer, became useful to Marcus Holcomb's schemes. One of them physically resembled him. The other did not. Both were purely targets of opportunity.

The one who bore no resemblance to him was Jeffrey Elgin Wright, age 20, from Boston, Massachusetts. Slightly heavy-set—the word "chubby" perfectly described him—he had short dark hair and dressed and looked very much like the frat boy he had been at Boston University, up until he was accepted as a JYA (Junior Year Abroad) exchange student at Sapienza. Wright suffered from social anxiety; the junket to Rome was the first time he'd been outside the orbit of his usual friends. He struck up a conversation with Marcus in the lecture hall at the start of Sapienza's Open Days, the orientation

period for international students. They had lunch together that day.

"How easy is it to get laid here in Rome?" The young
man who'd introduced himself as Kyle had already remarked on several attractive women in eyeshot at the
restaurant in Sapienza's student center. "The women in
Italy are scorching."

"Shit, man, I don't even know where to start."

"Well, maybe we an advantage. Do Italian chicks like
guys with American accents?"

A group of four or five American students stuck together at orientation, and Kyle Barnes was one of them.
At the end of the week there was a party in the flat on
the Via Ticino of an American expat who was dating one
of the girls in this circle. Wine, beer and booze flowed
copiously; at one point the group decamped to a dance
club, then returned to Via Ticino after 2:00 in the morning. Party nights in Rome run late.

Jeff Wright awoke in that flat the next morning,
shirtless, slumped on a couch with a plastic wastebasket
underneath him, its bottom covered in dried vomit.
Penises and swear words were drawn on his face in
Sharpie marker. "Oh, Jesus Christ, man, what happened?" His hangover was so severe that he couldn't
move for several more hours, but after finding his
clothes and shoes, he discovered his wallet was missing
from the pocket of his cargo shorts. One of the other
Americans gave him a ride back to the international student dormitory. As he was severely hung over and clinging to the back of a motor scooter in Rome's chaotic
traffic, that ride was itself an ordeal.

The following Monday morning, Marcus Holcomb walked into a branch of a UniCredit bank in central Rome. He wore Dockers shorts, hiking boots and a rugby shirt, all crisply new, and his long dark hair was invisible, gathered up under a white baseball cap embroidered with Greek letters. He sat down at a desk in front of exactly the kind of bronzed young Italian woman he'd pointed out to Wright.

"Hello. I'm a student at Sapienza, an American exchange student. I want to open an account. Do you speak English?"

The woman did not speak English, at least not very well, so the transaction proceeded haltingly. Holcomb, who had brought the Sapienza orientation folder, produced from it a paper describing how foreign students at the university were entitled to open local accounts with UniCredit, a perk of the relationship between the bank and Sapienza University. He was able to open an account and received a passbook on the spot. They did not question Jeffrey Wright's passport or his Sapienza University ID card when Holcomb casually placed them on the woman's desk.

When he was asked if he'd like to make a deposit into his new account, he said, "Yes, please." He then produced several thousand dollars' worth of cashier's checks, issued by casinos in France, made out to Gavin Grove but endorsed over to one Jeffrey E. Wright. These too were deposited without inquiry.

"Can I get an ATM card, too?"

The Italian woman, when she finally understood, nodded, smiled, and drew another form out of a drawer of her desk.

Marcus spent the rest of the day visiting nearly every MoneyGram and Western Union outlet in Rome. Both of these services had a function whereby one could transfer money, not to another individual, but to a bank account. Presenting—as Gavin Grove—many of the slips and MCTN numbers he'd sent to himself in France and northern Italy, he now initiated new transfers, directing all of the proceeds to the UniCredit account of Jeffrey Wright. He ran out of MoneyGram and Western Union outlets, so the next morning, using the same Eurail pass he'd bought in Deauville, he caught a train to Naples, a fast 90-minute ride, and exhausted the transfer outlets in that city. He was back in Rome by nightfall.

The day after that, he paid a visit to the international students' dorm at Sapienza and rang Jeff Wright's room. When the frat boy appeared in the lobby, Marcus handed him his wallet and passport. "I found these. I'm so sorry, man. They were in the pocket of the hoodie I was wearing the night of the party. I guess someone found them and put them in my pocket, maybe they got us confused. I didn't even find them until I went to do laundry."

Wright was suspicious—though he said nothing to Holcomb and pretended to believe him—but when he looked in the wallet he found all of the cash that he'd been carrying the night of the party, and after calling his bank, he verified that neither his credit cards nor his U.S. Bank ATM card had been used. Wright had no idea that he now had a bank account in Rome in his name, which had in it over $70,000—the amount of money Holcomb had managed to launder in his name in less than 48 hours.

***

The second young man, the one who resembled Holcomb at least at first glance, was one Gunther Dortgard, age 18, a German citizen from Rostock. He never once saw Marcus or spoke to him. He did, however, lose his passport in an ice cream shop near the Spanish Steps. Dortgard was on vacation with his parents and younger sister. He was a tall thin youth with long hair dyed crudely black and he tagged along after the family with a surly manner. He didn't even know his passport was gone until the next day, when the family, on a package tour, were about to board a train for Venice.

The theft occurred two days after an incident on the Sapienza University campus. Holcomb frequented the library and the student center, and because of his regular presence during orientation he was assumed to be a student. A professor who led some of the orientation session events, however, had checked the official rosters and found no evidence of an American named Kyle Barnes admitted to the university. The exchange department notified campus police, and the next time Marcus appeared at the building he was met by two uniformed guards. In heavily-accented English, one of them challenged him to produce his Sapienza University ID card. "I guess I left it in my room," he told the officers. They warned him never to set foot on university property again.

He did not. Curiously, it was not until a week or so later, after classes had begun, that anyone in the cohort of American students noticed that Kyle Barnes was missing. Those who did asked Wright, who had been his closest friend, what happened.

"Fucked if I know," the Bostonian shrugged. "Just as well. There was something not quite right about that guy."

Marcus began to haunt the tourist traps of Rome: the Colosseum, Trevi Fountain, Piazza Navona, and the Spanish Steps. He spent long hours sitting at tables in sidewalk cafés near these sites, paging through his Frommer's Italy tour guide and slowly nursing a limonata or a Peroni beer. By complete chance, the Dortgard family walked by him. He paid his check quickly, put on sunglasses, snatched up the tour book and followed. Even bobbing in a throng of tourists, tall Gunther's black-dyed head was easy to spot.

The acquisition of Gunther Dortgard's passport prompted Marcus to buy a German phrasebook and dictionary, which, along with the Frommer's guide and the Moleskine containing the MoneyGram MCTNs, were seldom out of his reach. In this period, he also visited a pawn shop where he bought an acoustic guitar and a guitar case. The same afternoon he exchanged the guitar —sans case—for a smaller one. He went to an art supply store and a fabric shop and bought sturdy cardboard and several yards of red velvet. In the evenings, at Trask's apartment, Marcus set to work on a craft project while watching Italian-dubbed American shows, including *Star Trek*. With the cardboard and velvet, he modified the guitar case with a false back and sides into which the smaller guitar fit perfectly. The gaps between the false and real contours of the case were papered solid with thin stacks of £20 bank notes.

He also left Rome, again on a night train, for a city with as-yet untouched Western Union and MoneyGram outlets. This time he chose Ravenna, a four hour train journey away up the peninsula. In addition to the usual Grove-to-Wright bank account transfers he also created a few fresh transactions, paid for with Italian cash, in the name of Gunther Dortgard. They totaled less than $10,000; curiously, Marcus never collected these transfers, allowing the 90-day deadlines to lapse. He may have done this as a form of last-ditch insurance, a sort of rainy-day fund which he either forgot about or perhaps decided not to use.

Toward the end of his stay in Rome, Holcomb seems to have feared that someone was on to him. He never answered the phone in Trask's apartment but left an answering machine on. He carefully reviewed every call, sometimes looking up words he'd heard in his Italian dictionary. He entered or left the flat only during times of darkness, and would pause before opening the door, listening to make sure no one was in the hallway or stairwell. He had small amounts of cash, in nylon knapsacks bought from tourist gift shops, stashed at the main train station and in a locker at Fiumicino Airport. He also checked the mailbox at the flat obsessively.

On July 27, 1998, what he was apparently waiting for arrived: an envelope from UniCredit Bank, addressed to Jeffrey E. Wright at Trask's flat address, which contained a stiff rectangular flat object. Marcus tore the envelope open and peeled the ATM card off the paperboard backing. He used the pay phone at a nearby café to call the bank to activate it. Then he immediately returned home, packed his bags, sealed up the guitar case, and used baby wipes to swab down nearly every exposed surface in the flat. He locked the door behind him, left the French mountain bike chained to the bike rack in front of the building, and from a bridge he tossed the flat's keys into the Tiber. He caught the subway to Fiumicino Airport, collected his knapsack of cash from there, then took the subway back to the main train terminal. He used the Eurail pass to board a train to Naples and, presenting Gunther Dortgard's passport as identification, at a travel window in Naples bought a ticket for the overnight ferry. Within a day he was in Palermo, still not having crossed a national border at an official checkpoint.

Chapter 9: Sicily

The weeks that Marcus Holcomb spent in Sicily were strange and empty. On the day he arrived in Palermo, he spent the evening at a club frequented by young people. With their language translated by an English-speaking girl named Monica, he struck up enough of a friendship with a young man, Simone, such that Simone allowed him to sleep on a sofa in his flat. Simone also knew some people outside the city, in the countryside. Within a few days, through these contacts Marcus found a small family-owned flat for rent in the town of Torretta, a few miles outside of Palermo. This was where he spent most of his time.

Torretta is a small settlement thrown onto the jumbled scrubby hills of Sicily. Its streets are narrow, some still covered in cobblestones, and ancient stucco buildings loom over them, festooned with tiny balconies supporting clotheslines, drooping with drying laundry, strung between the houses. Almost no one in Torretto spoke English. Marcus had to improve his rudimentary Italian rapidly so he could be understood at all. But there was little else to do there. He read a book he bought before leaving Rome, a paperback biography called *Bare-Faced Messiah: The True Story of L. Ron Hubbard* by Russell Miller. He walked the streets and ate in Torretto's few cafés. In one of them he met the serving girl, Emiliana, age 19, dark-haired and beautiful, if provincial. After he was in Torretta a week or so they began a sexual affair.

Another detail about Torretta: there are no Money-Gram or Western Union outlets there. In 1998 there was not even an ATM machine. A bus went to Palermo multiple times a day, and Marcus rode it often, but the mechanics of the money laundering business were much more difficult here than they'd been in cosmopolitan Rome. Maybe Emiliana was the main reason he stayed. They fucked nearly every night, in a variety of adventurous positions. She also brought him regular baskets of bread, cheese, meats and wine from the restaurant, owned by her uncle, where she worked.

Torretta did have a major advantage. It was very much off the grid. Unless someone was very creative or comprehensively thorough, no one was likely to find him here. None of the various groups actively chasing him or interested in questioning him knew the name Gunther Dortgard.

The question remains, though: was anyone chasing him?

The simple answer is yes, but none of Holcomb's enemies were making much headway. The Hertfordshire police were still focusing their efforts on locating him within the UK, on the assumption—or perhaps the hope —that he was still there. His name was added to a tepid list kept by the U.S. State Department of American nationals abroad who were wanted for questioning by foreign authorities, but they expended no investigative resources to actively trace him. Interpol was notified, but they, too, did nothing more than add him to a list. As no Marcus Holcomb had crossed the border into another country according to passport records, he was universally regarded as the problem of the Hertfordshire police, the main force investigating the Traffic Circle Murders.

The Hertfordshire constable did not know that Gavin Grove was an alias of Marcus Holcomb. O'Cuinneagain could have given them that information, perhaps via an anonymous tip that wouldn't have incriminated him, but he did not. As Grove (the real one) was still an employee of Michael O'Cuinneagain, giving his name to law enforcement in connection with the South Mimms slayings—even to suggest that they search abroad for someone using that identity—would've brought down scrutiny on O'C.'s operations, which Scotland Yard was now already looking into as a result of his daughter having been murdered. O'Cuinneagain also figured that the name and identity of Gavin Grove was the flare which would draw his organization's attention to Holcomb so he could be terminated, wherever he was found in the world, before any police could get to him.

Over the course of his investigation, conducted mostly by his right-hand man, Hamish Laerner, O'Cuinneagain did learn a name he hadn't known before: Daniel Moreira—Dubo, the now mostly-retired Brazilian pop star. O'C. guessed correctly that the mysterious Brazilian, found dead next to his daughter, was dispatched by someone seeking to hit Marcus Holcomb for the murder of Dubo's son. Driven by the notion of joining forces, an Irishman and a Brazilian, both of whom were mourning children murdered by the same man, Laerner tried several times to contact Dubo surreptitiously, but he never returned any of these entrees. O'Cuinneagain and Laerner never knew that Broka was hired by Anchieta, not Dubo, and news of Broka's death spooked Anchieta sufficiently for him to drop the whole matter immediately. Anchieta Moreira had friends who were gangsters, but he was not a gangster himself. Dubo had no knowledge that his older son had tried to hire a hit man. There was a mysterious hole in the accounting of the Moreira family's real estate business, where some sum had been siphoned off for reasons unknown. Dubo himself knew the ways of shady business dealings enough to recognize them. He never asked his son about it. Rafael went unavenged. Even 20 years later, his mother cried uncontrollably at the mere mention of Rafael's name.

* * *

In the middle of August 1998, two black-uniformed Carabineri officers—Italy's semi-military police force—appeared at the café run by Emiliana's uncle in Torretta. They were not looking for Marcus, but rather inquiring about someone connected to local Mafia who had some dealings with the uncle. Nevertheless, Marcus witnessed the police emerging from the café. That day he hastily grabbed his camping gear, the guitar case, and the Umbro bag, and caught a bus to Messina. He did not say goodbye to Emiliana.

It's quite possible that the Carabineri truly panicked him, because, for the first time in the chase, Marcus's travels and decisions show no clear plan or pattern of movement. From Messina he took a ferry to Villa San Giovanni, just across the strait on the southern toe of the boot of Italy. He then took a train to Bari, where the ankle of the boot meets the heel on Italy's southeastern coast. He spent several successive nights on trains shuttling between Bari, Brindisi and Taranto. Each of these nights he fell asleep in a train compartment wearing Walkman headphones and listening to a tape that included Toto's song "Africa." During these nights he traveled in circles. He might have been trying to clear his head and figure out what to do. That he kept returning to Bari gives a clue as to his possible intentions: there is a car ferry that runs from Bari to Patras, Greece. Doubtless he spent many hours on those trains weighing whether crossing a border with Gunther Dortgard's German passport, by now certainly reported stolen, was a risk worth taking.

It seems likely that about this time he reached some point of decision. He may have felt overwhelmed, exhausted and strung out; he'd been on the run for nine weeks now and he can't have slept or eaten well while train-hopping after fleeing Palermo. He did not try the Bari-Patras ferry. On the early morning of August 21, 1998, he boarded a train back to Rome.

Upon arriving there, Marcus did not leave Termini Station for many hours. He left his camping gear, Umbro bag, and guitar case in a large locker, and parked himself in a café in the station with a stack of newspapers and his Italian dictionary, studying classified ads for rooms for rent. The next day—he camped again overnight—Marcus appeared at a house owned by the Rietti family in the small town of Campolimpido, a suburb to the northwest of Rome proper. He did his best to communicate in a goulash of English and rudimentary Italian. "Hi, um, I'm here about the room to rent. *Stanza in affitto? La pubblicità?* My name is Nigel Blakeney."

The room in Campolimpido was actually the detached garage of a larger estate, little more than an outbuilding made of cinder blocks at the end of a street that looked surprisingly rural for being part of an administrative division of the City of Rome. The room had a bed, a dresser, a chair and a one-quarter bathroom; a hose jury-rigged to a sprinkler head behind the building served as its shower. Marcus rented the room for cash. As it was not a hotel there was no check-in record or paperwork. He pretended to be Nigel Blakeney of Dubuque, Iowa, but Mrs. Rietti, the broad-shouldered matron who rented the room, did not ask for ID. He stashed the guitar case and the Umbro bag under the bed, took a shower out in the yard, and then slept for the better part of three days.

* * *

His next purchase was a motorbike, secondhand, which he bought a few days later, again after consulting classified ads. Indeed, after a few more trips into urban Rome, the little garage flat was soon cluttered with newspapers, many in English. At a gift shop in the shadow of St. Peter's Square, he simply asked the attendant, in his slightly improving Italian: "I want to buy all the English language newspapers you have, please." Several of the papers he bought from that location were published in the Vatican, or had something to do with the Catholic Church.

In his little room in Campolimpido, Marcus pored over these papers. He does not appear to have been searching for something specific, but perhaps—most likely—gaining a feel for the daily pulse of life in the Vatican, in which he was clearly interested. There were announcements of conclaves and conventions, priests arriving from various parts of the world or going out again, and of course exhaustive discussion of Pope John Paul II's every move. Tellingly, on the second day of this project of study, when he went into the city on his motorbike Marcus purchased a Bible and an English language version of the *Catechism of the Catholic Church,* promulgated by that same Pope.

The newspaper study stopped abruptly when he found a story buried on the announcements page of one of the English Vatican newspapers. It was a short posting about a convention that was due to begin in the Vatican City the next day, at the headquarters of the Missionary Oblates of the Mary Immaculate. The article noted that attendees of the convention were Post-Novitiates about to go claim their assignments at various OMI missions in the developing world. Though the article did not name any of them, it did state that several attendees were recently-ordained priests from the United States.

Chapter 10: Confession

On that Monday, the first day of the OMI convention for Post-Novitiates, the tree-dotted compound at No. 290 Via Aurelia in Rome, barely more than a kilometer from St. Peter's Basilica, was given a thorough going-over by a little white-haired Italian priest, fluent in English, named Father Guglielmo Bertholdi. As he toured each building, office and chapel of the Oblates of the Mary Immaculate headquarters, his shadow was a young man in a new-looking rugby shirt and Dockers slacks, his long dark hair bound up in a tasteful ponytail, who took obsessive notes in a small Moleskine book. They were together for many hours, and Father Bertholdi, bubbling with excitement, showed him everything.

"These are our administrative offices. Just been remodeled! Do you see that portrait there? That's St. Eugène de Mazenod, who founded our order in 1816. This map shows where all our missions and projects are around the world. Every six years the Order holds a General Chapter with delegates from all over the world. I wish you could be there to see that! Hearing the firsthand stories of our brothers in the field is the best way to learn about what we do."

The young dark-haired American, who said he was Jeff Wright from Sapienza University (and from the Archdiocese of Boston, where he said his father knew Cardinal Law), asked few questions but soaked up information. Father Bertholdi was so excited that he went beyond the brief of plugging OMI. "Would you like to see the Vatican? I mean, the *real* Vatican. Not just the areas the tourists see—but behind the scenes. This is the perfect time to go. The crowds will be much less right now."

"Yes, absolutely! That'd be wonderful."

"Why don't we step into my office? I'll call the visitors bureau and let them know we're coming, and arrange a visitors' pass for you."

So by this process the man who had, at various times in the past few weeks, been known as Gunther Dortgard, Jeffrey Wright, Nigel Blakeney, Stephen Trask and Gavin Grove—but definitely *not* Marcus Holcomb—gained access to some of the most secret grottoes of the Vatican. He saw the elegant carved stone animals on the way to the Cabinet of the Masks, the Vatican Gardens, and the tomb of St. Peter and the necropolis beneath the basilica. Father Bertholdi also took him into the Niccoline Chapel in the Apostolic Apartments, and they had a light lunch in a private cafeteria frequented by cardinals and sometimes (but not today) His Holiness. When the old man grew tired, they returned to the OMI campus. It was now four o'clock and the first day's sessions of the Post-Novitiates' convention was just getting out.

"Oh, look, there's Father Tyler! This is who I wanted you to meet."

Bertholdi introduced them in the lobby of one of the OMI complex's meeting room areas. He was almost the same height as Marcus, crisply dressed in priest's cassock and collar, and his blond hair was brushed back from his forehead.

"Father Tyler! I'd like you to meet Jeffrey, from Boston. He's here from Sapienza University."

They shook hands. The young priest smiled. "Evan Tyler. Nice to meet you."

"Great to meet you."

"Jeffrey is writing an article on OMI for the Sapienza University newspaper for international students," said the old priest. "I thought he might appreciate the chance to interview a fellow American."

"I don't want to impose," said Marcus.

"No, not at all. I'd love to talk about it. Do you have plans for dinner?"

"Just the cafeteria at the international student dorm." He laughed. "I'd jump at a chance to eat somewhere else, frankly."

There are certain moments, which often pass unnoticed at the time, that shape people's destinies. The last such moment in Marcus's life before this one was when he saw Rafael Moreira reflected in a mirror at the University of San Diego dorms in January 1997. This meeting in Rome on a Monday afternoon 20 months later would prove momentous to Sarah Brinson, too. It was largely the cause of her death.

* * *

Evan Tyler and Jeff Wright quickly got along famously. They went to dinner at a small trattoria a few blocks from the Vatican that had been recommended by a friend of Tyler's from Catholic Theological Union in Chicago, where he attended seminary. Though they talked about church affairs and Catholic theology briefly —Tyler did most of the talking, with Marcus occasionally nodding or interjecting—their conversation really caught fire when it wandered to purely secular subjects. They talked about Spider-Man and *Star Trek*, the Trans-Siberian Orchestra, their families' Christmas traditions, an obscure mid-80s cartoon show called *M.A.S.K.*, *The Muppet Show*, the Clinton and Lewinsky scandal, and their own travels in the U.S. and Europe. They each consumed several glasses of wine. Tyler spoke as if he hadn't had this sort of conversation in a long time. In fact, he mentioned as much.

"I've wanted to be a priest, and do missionary work, since I was 12. I've been working toward that goal all my life since then. In that time, I guess I kind of forgot about what it was like to be a real kid."

Marcus smiled. "Is there a hint of regret there?"

"Oh no, not at all. This is exactly what I want to do."

"Even going to...what was the name of that place they're sending you?"

"Tondoro."

"Right. What country is that in? Angola?"

"Namibia."

"Oh, yeah, I remember." Marcus sipped from his wine glass. "I gotta ask. The celibacy thing. Does it suck as much as it sounds?"

Tyler laughed. "I bet you never asked a priest that before."

"I've never known any priests, at least as anything other than priests. I mean, sure, I know priests, but I've only interacted with them when they're acting in their official duties. You know what I mean."

"Well, honestly it's not something I think about. I guess I just don't miss it. Sure, I guess it'd be nice to be married, but I don't think my life would be any less, you know, because of it."

"You never missed it, I mean, growing up and stuff?"

The priest shrugged. "I was kind of shy in high school. I never really had a chance with girls anyway. By the time I was out of high school I'd decided to become a priest, so it was just something I couldn't have."

"I bet you had more chances than you think you did. A good-looking guy like you."

A slight flush came over Evan Tyler's face. "Thank you."

For the next several days the two young men saw much of each other. Tyler's days were mostly spoken for; he was in meetings and activities at the OMI convention, but Marcus would meet him at the end of the day for dinner, and often they would hang out after that. Though they hadn't known each other long, the truths they shared with one another—at least it was Tyler who spoke truths—grew increasingly intimate.

At dinner mid-week, Tyler talked about the incident in his childhood when he'd been kidnapped after being mistaken for another boy, the son of a rich family. "That was when I decided to be a priest," he told Marcus. "When I was in the hospital after that. I knew God saved me, and I would devote my life to Him."

It was also on that night, in the little lounge of the rectory on the OMI campus, that something else occurred. Tyler had begun to ask Jeff Wright about his own faith and his own journey as a Catholic. The answers he gave were evasive and non-committal. He spoke of being an altar boy and enjoying the majesty and pageantry of the church, but he had no deep connection to God.

"When did you last confess?" Tyler asked him.

"Oh, I don't even remember the last time I went to confession. It was a long time ago."

"You've got something on your conscience, don't you, Jeff? It seems like you're, I don't know, burdened by something. I *am* a priest, you know. I can hear your confession."

"I thought it had to be anonymous."

"It doesn't have to be. I mean, in the booth or whatever. Do you want to confess?"

It was Marcus's turn to blush. "Um... I don't know."

"If you want to, I'll hear it."

After a while Marcus knelt down, his face turned away from Father Tyler. He began slowly, haltingly. "I, um...whoo. This is hard. Um...I've done, uh, some things."

"What things?"

Marcus sighed. "I stole some money."

"A lot?"

"Nothing that would make life hard for anybody. I was at the end of my rope. If I didn't—"

"Don't justify it. I don't care why you did it. Anything else?"

"I hurt someone. A friend. His name was Rafael. We were friends, and I said some things I shouldn't have. He made me angry. I broke his guitar on purpose. His father had given it to him. It was his favorite. I broke it to hurt him."

"I see. Go on."

"I, uh… I felt lust."

"We all feel that."

"But my lust, it's sometimes.. you know…um, for men. Rafael was one of them. I wanted him. Partly why I was mad at him."

"Did you act on this lust for this man?"

Marcus was looking at the floor. "Yeah. I did."

A silence stretched between them. Eventually, Tyler made the sign of the cross in the air in front of the penitent. "God, the father of mercies, through the death and resurrection of the Son has reconciled the world to himself and the Holy Spirit among us for forgiveness of sins. Through the ministry of the church may God grant you pardon and peace. And I absolve you from your sins in the name of the Father, and of the Son and the Holy Spirit."

Marcus Holcomb was technically Catholic; a priest in London converted him, as Michael O'Cuinneagain required that he could not marry Shannon unless he was also Catholic. Perhaps it is an irrelevant detail, but three of his four victims—Rafael Moreira, João Broka and Shannon O'Cuinneagain— were practicing Catholics.

* * *

Evan Tyler's stopover in Rome was intended partly as his formal entry into the missionary world, and partly as a vacation, though the leisure aspects of it had a heavy religious tinge. He was booked to attend the OMI post-novitiates convention at the time the organization assigned him to St. Ambrose Parish in Tondoro; the convention was scheduled for the last week in August. Then, after a few more days in Rome to soak up the sights, Tyler was to fly to Tel Aviv and depart on a five-day tour of the Holy Land, including Bethlehem, Nazareth, the Dead Sea and Jerusalem, from which he would fly to Cape Town in South Africa. After a few days there, he was scheduled to fly to Windhoek, Namibia, where someone from St. Ambrose Parish would meet him and travel with him to remote Tondoro. The start of the school year—Tyler was always intended as a teacher for the parish children—was September 25.

During their week together Tyler showed Marcus these elaborate arrangements. There was a thick sheaf of travel papers, including plane tickets and itineraries, which Tyler kept on his person most of the time, in the folder OMI had given him at the start of the convention. On the last day of the convention, Friday, that morning Tyler and Holcomb had breakfast together in the restaurant of a hotel not far from the OMI campus. When breakfast was finished and Tyler got up from the table, he found this important folder was missing.

"Where is it? Did you see it?"

"See what?"

"The folder, the OMI folder. I know I had it with me."

For several minutes of increasing panic, they searched for it. Holcomb called over the waiter and spoke some broken Italian to him. They looked under chairs and picked up napkins. The waiter promised to look in the kitchen in case the folder was accidentally taken there on the tray where he whisked away the breakfast dishes.

"You don't understand, Jeff. That folder's got everything—my travel documents, my bank stuff, even my passport. We've got to find it." He glanced at his watch. "And I'm late! The final sessions are starting. I've got to be there..."

"I'll stay behind and look for it. Go to your convention. I'll bring the folder to you when I find it."

Tyler departed, nervous, but Marcus insisted he would find the folder. After the priest was gone Holcomb and the waiter continued to search. While the waiter's back was turned Marcus suddenly produced it; he'd scooted it across the carpet with his foot from under Tyler's chair and hidden it. "Oh! Here it is. Thank you for your help." He left several tens of thousands of lira notes on the table, and was soon off.

Marcus was busy that day. His first stop after the restaurant was a copy center. He Xeroxed everything in Tyler's folder: not just the passport, Social Security card, Michigan driver's license and the paper on which Tyler had written down his bank information and credit card number (he only had one), but all the tickets, itineraries, reservations and brochures, and even the convention schedule, the materials supplied by OMI, mostly promotional materials, and the handwritten notes Tyler had been taking during the convention sessions. After this, on the motorbike, he went to another copy center in a different part of Rome, and made Xerox copies of some of the Xerox copies—specifically, the passport and identity documents.

At lunch time he returned to the OMI compound. As the post-novitiates streamed out of one of the conference rooms Marcus stood in the lobby, smiling, and held up the folder as Tyler approached. The priest heaved a sigh of relief. "Where was it?"

"Under one of the chairs. It fell and the waiter accidentally kicked it across the floor without noticing. Found it less than five minutes after you left."

Tyler paged through the contents of the folder. "I can't thank you enough."

"Why don't you let me take you out tonight? You're leaving on Sunday. We'll go out—dinner, a drink, maybe a club. Not as a priest. Don't wear your collar. Two American dudes on vacation in Rome. Okay?"

Tyler smiled. "Okay."

When Tyler went back into the convention after the lunch break, Holcomb mounted his motorbike again. He drove to a hardware store whose address he'd previously looked up. It was incongruous with the tourist vision of Rome, a shop selling wrenches and fan belts inside an 18th century stucco-faced building. He spent a great deal of money there, all in cash. He purchased bolt cutters, pliers, a hammer, a folding shovel, a few tarps and several yards of heavy-duty plastic. He let the salesman, who spoke English, think that it was he who talked Marcus into also buying a small pull trailer that could be attached to the motorbike, in which to haul his purchases home. With these transactions done, he returned to his rented garage in Campolimpido and showered in the cubicle behind the building. He read *Bare-Faced Messiah* until it was time to go back into the city again for his final date with Evan Tyler.

Chapter 11: Evan

The Tyler family was Catholic, but none of them were especially devout, at least until Evan came along. They were what one might derisively call "cafeteria Catholics," picking and choosing the doctrines and rituals they agreed with. Evan was the second of four children, all born between 1968 and 1976, the most intense phase of prosperity and happiness the family enjoyed. That was the time Neil was on his way up in the Grand Rapids law firm of Novak & Porter. Nineteen-sixty eight, the year Neil and Barbara's oldest son Greg was born, was also the year Roger Van Cordt came to that firm seeking a tax lawyer. It was largely a fluke: Van Cordt's normal outside lawyer, who handled business affairs for the then-young Streamline multilevel marketing empire, had decided he was conflicted when it came to Roger's personal taxes. He was having a minor dispute with Streamline Corporation over a tax matter. That minor conflict changed the fortunes of the Tyler family, four years before Evan was born.

Evan had no memory of the house his family was living in when he was born. When he was three, the family moved to the house he would consider home, a spacious Tudor affair on the west side of Grand Rapids, near Reeds Lake. The boy's childhood was not especially tumultuous—in fact not at all. Their lives changed when Michael, the Tylers' youngest child, was born with Down's syndrome. At that time, Greg was eight, Evan six and Zoë two. Michael required more patience and attention than the other children, but none of them seemed to resent it. The baby was also born with a heart condition, but that was not discovered until years later, a ticking time bomb that would explode in due course.

From early on, the Tyler children associated with the many young progeny of the Van Cordt clan, who by the mid-70s had entrenched themselves as the royalty of Grand Rapids. It didn't hurt that the Van Cordts' hand-picked politician and hometown hero Gerald Ford was now sitting in the White House. Karen Van Cordt, Roger's wife, knew Barbara socially and their children were roughly the same age; she recommended day cares and preschools to Barbara, the same ones to which she sent her own children. This was how Evan Tyler came into the orbit of Brent Van Cordt, a boy almost exactly his age.

It's not often that a person's young childhood friends have an appreciable effect on the course their adult lives will take, but this rarity was true of Evan Rodgers Tyler. For years he and Brent were inseparable. They played war, fort and *Star Wars* in the woolly acres that stretched behind the Van Cordts' mansion. Evan spent a hundred nights sleeping over and was pampered vicariously: the Van Cordt children had a VCR in 1982, compact disc players in 1985 and Nintendos in 1986, long before they were common among other kids. Many of the obsessions Evan would discuss with Marcus Holcomb a decade and a half later in Rome—*Star Trek*, the best G.I. Joe toys, *M.A.S.K.* and *The Muppet Show*—were consumed in these settings.

In some ways the friendship was uncomfortable, at least to some. The Van Cordts weren't born into wealth, but now that they had it, they were quite conscious of class. Brent would soon be leaving Grand Rapids to attend Philips Exeter Academy. His parents were much more comfortable with his friends who were the sons of bank presidents and politicians, not merely a hardworking tax lawyer. But Brent and Evan remained locked to each other as if genetically attached. They even looked and dressed somewhat alike. This too was to have unforeseen consequences.

On May 20, 1984, a Sunday, Brent Van Cordt and Evan Tyler, both 12, spent much of the afternoon at Woodland Mall, a frequent hangout where they often played video games at the arcade or saw movies at the cinema. This particular afternoon Brent had to go home earlier than usual, but Evan, absorbed in a game of Zaxxon, remained. Less than 20 minutes after Brent had left, Evan was approached, coming out of the arcade, by an overweight man in a maroon jacket and blue stocking cap who surreptitiously pressed a butterfly knife against Evan's stomach and growled, "Come with me, or you're fucking dead."

The kidnapper took Evan to a van disguised as a carpet cleaning service vehicle idling outside the mall entrance. Evan screamed and struggled in the back of the van as they bound his hands and mouth with silver duct tape. He continued to fight. He landed a savage kick to the groin of the man who'd taken him. "You little fuck! You fucking little fuck, you kick *me* in the balls? Fuck you!" The man in the stocking cap beat and kicked Evan savagely, especially in the groin. He was so unhinged that the man behind the wheel—a skinny greasy-haired fellow in gray coveralls—had to calm him down. "Don't hurt him. We need the fucking brat intact. You want the money or not?"

Evan had no idea where they took him; in fact, they merely parked the van beneath a viaduct and remained there for several hours. The man in the boiler suit got out of the van periodically and was gone for 20 or 30 minutes at a time. In fact, he was walking to various pay phones in the area—the viaduct was chosen because it was equidistant from several gas stations—to call in ransom demands to the Van Cordt family. Evan's mouth was taped; he sat in the back of the van, quaking in terror and pain. The fat man in the stocking cap smoked weed and listened to heavy metal on the stereo. Occasionally he taunted Evan. "Your mom's shittin' her pants right about now. Dad too. Seriously, I bet your dad put a big stinking load right in his pants. Oh no, our little shithead is in danger!"

The boiler suit man got back into the van after a while. "Something's wrong. They don't believe we got him."

"What? I don't understand."

"The family. They think I was lying. They said I couldn'ta got their brat because he's there at their house."

"Are they fucking with you?"

"I called three times. First time they think it's a prank. Second time they say the kid is sitting right in front of them so I'm a liar and they gonna call the cops if I don't stop calling. I tried a third time but no answer."

"You told him we'd cut the kid's fingers off if they called the police?"

It took the men several minutes to figure out they'd nabbed the wrong captive. Evan had his middle school ID card in his jeans pocket, but neither of the kidnappers had bothered to check, until the skinny one wondered aloud if the family was telling the truth. When they finally did look at his ID, the man in the boiler suit was consumed with rage. He leaped into the back of the van and began beating and punching his compatriot. "You moron! How could you be so fucking stupid? You're gonna get us killed! I ought to fucking kill you right now!"

They debated—right in front of Evan—whether to kill him. The fat man with the butterfly knife was clearly in favor, but his companion was not. "I'm not going to the fucking gas chamber because *you* fucked this whole thing up." They did not finish the debate while he was conscious. The thin man brained Evan with a tire iron; he was unconscious for three days.

He woke up in a hospital. He had suffered a severe concussion. His right leg was broken when the kidnappers threw him out of their van—evidently at full speed

—on Chicago Drive southeast of town, where he was eventually spotted by a highway clean-up crew. Worst of all, both Evan's testicles were severely swollen from the beating the fat man had given him. The doctors told his parents that his testicles might have to be removed. The kidnappers nearly castrated him.

The injury to Evan's genitals and the totally coincidental timing of the kidnapping worked a freakish twist into the fabric of the boy's life. Three days before the attempt, Evan had discovered masturbation for the first time. We cannot know what went through his mind, but given that he was a closeted homosexual in adulthood, it stands to reason that during this first sexual experience he thought about a boy. It might even have been Brent Van Cordt. That he interpreted the kidnap attempt as a message from wrathful God is at least a fair inference. A week after he recovered and got home from the hospital —fortunately the swelling subsided and a double orchiotomy was not necessary—Evan asked for a Bible and told his parents he wanted to go to church.

As a result of the failed kidnapping, Evan brought devout Catholicism into the household. He'd had his first communion at age seven, but now insisted on attending Mass every week, sometimes more often. He told his father he wanted to go to a Catholic school. Eventually he did: Sacred Heart Academy, to which his sister Zoë was also eventually sent. Evan prayed dutifully every night and read the Bible daily. He began reading the catechism and Catholic inspirational books. When people asked him what he wanted to be, the answer was always the same: a priest.

The friendship with Brent Van Cordt did not survive Evan's religious transformation. Roger Van Cordt, still Neil Tyler's law client, felt terrible about what had happened and quietly paid for all of Evan's medical expenses that were not covered by insurance. The two men involved in the kidnapping, Gaigen and Mantaseru, were eventually caught, but not for this crime; after they were imprisoned each of them confessed separately. At first, Brent Van Cordt remained friendly with Evan, but their friendship never regained its former intensity. Within two years of the kidnapping, they ceased to have any contact. Brent was a freshman at Exeter Academy in New Hampshire, Evan the same at Sacred Heart. Neither family ever spoke of the kidnapping, but it was a deep wound on both clans, whose association now, as it had been at the beginning, was purely professional.

Evan Tyler was an excellent student, a very high achiever. While at Sacred Heart he became a National Merit Scholar, was elected president of his class, and led the swim team to a regional championship. He was always popular and well-liked. He never had a girlfriend in high school, but that was usually ascribed to his intense religiosity. The truth was never known, at least not publicly. He once made out with another boy on the swim team, and for about two weeks had a regular mutual masturbation session with a boy who went to another school, but this was as close as he got to any sort of romance. He did not look at pornographic movies or magazines, and of course he never spoke of his sexual orientation.

During high school Evan's brother Michael died. The heart condition, discovered at age eight, claimed the boy's life at eleven. Evan spent many days in his room, crying and praying, but the ordeal strengthened his faith. It seemed to have the opposite effect on his parents, or at least his mother. She was proud of him and vocally supportive of his ambition to enter the priesthood, but an air of sadness entered the Tylers' house after Michael's death that never fully went away.

Evan's desire to serve abroad, particularly in the developing world, began at about the time he started university at Aquinas College in Grand Rapids. He had by this time become friends with Ronald Clarendon, the Bishop of the Diocese of Grand Rapids. Indeed, Clarendon functioned as sort of a mentor to Evan. They had lunch together frequently, and often engaged in deep philosophical or theological discussions. Clarendon was sometimes a guest at the Tyler home for dinner.

Excelling at college much as he had in high school, Evan secured admission to the Catholic Theological Union in Chicago where he would attend seminary. It was his time here that he became acquainted with the Missionary Oblates of Mary Immaculate. Father Owen Roteman, one of his professors and his latest mentor, had been a missionary for OMI back in the '70s and the order maintained a student group on the CTU campus. By Evan's second year in seminary, his trajectory toward missionary work abroad with OMI was firmly fixed. He never wavered from this goal or seemed to question it, at least not out loud.

But he did falter once in his personal life, if he considered it faltering. One evening in November 1995, he went to a gay bar in Chicago, his first time ever in such a setting. What sparked this act we cannot know, but that day was, coincidentally or not, the eighth anniversary of his brother Michael's death. At the club, Evan met a young man named Andy, an artist, guitar player and computer programmer. Andy brought Evan to his apartment late that night. After Evan's embarrassed and tearful confession that he was a seminary student—he'd originally told Andy he was a grad student studying sociology—and also a virgin, they made love.

Evan stayed the whole weekend with Andy. It might have been the beginning of a long affair, or even a major inflection point in Evan's life. It was not. After he returned to his own apartment late Sunday night, Evan showered for a long time, read St. Thomas Aquinas, and prayed. He did not return Andy's calls and never saw him again. Notably, Evan did not mention the affair when he had his next confession, and in fact never spoke of it to anyone. Shortly after the weekend with Andy, Evan went to a tattoo parlor in Chicago and got a traditional sacred heart of Jesus inked on his right arm.

In early 1998, as his seminary study was nearly finished, Evan Tyler received a conditional posting to an overseas assignment from OMI. Originally, he was scheduled to be sent to Thailand, but a month or so later OMI notified him he'd been reassigned to St. Ambrose Parish in Tondoro, Namibia. He told his family that the day he was ordained a priest, in late May 1998, was the happiest day of his life. It probably was. He packed up his belongings, decamped from the little apartment where he'd lived all during seminary, and spent a lazy golden summer at his parents' house in Grand Rapids before he departed in late August for Rome. He had never been out of the United States before. His passport was crackly new. The worst luck of Evan's life—even more damning than having been mistaken for Brent Van Cordt—was to encounter Marcus Holcomb, whose real name he never knew.

Chapter 12: Campolimpido

For one evening at least, this Friday night in late August, Evan Tyler no longer had to be a priest. The man he knew as Jeff Wright took him out to dinner, to a club with some middling punk band, and to an Irish-style pub where they drank Guinness. Tyler wore a polo shirt and jeans, Marcus a rugby shirt and baggy cargo shorts. When they rode from place to place on Holcomb's motorbike Tyler clung tight to him because he drove fast, clearing the sides of parked cars and mirrors on trucks by mere millimeters. The young priest never complained.

Finally, Marcus said that he had a surprise for him, "This next place is a bit wild." They were in the street outside the Irish pub while strapping on their motorbike helmets. "This is your last weekend in civilization. Maybe you'll have to say an extra rosary or something, but trust me, you need this."

"This sounds ominous."

"No, it'll be fine. Just follow my lead, let me do any talking that needs to be done."

Marcus brought him to a narrow cobblestone street in Testaccio, a block or so from the Tiber River. It was a club that pulsed with dance music and there was a line to get in. Holcomb paid for them both and they walked into a room of ancient brick arches and columns lined with glowing blue lights. Tyler looked around nervously. As they approached the bar, he noticed two young shirtless men gyrating in a pool of orange light on the dance floor. Several other men nearby were kissing.

"Hey, Jeff, I don't, ah, I don't know if we should be here, man."

"It's totally okay. This is the Alibi Club, it's world famous."

"I'm really not comfortable here, Jeff."

"Let me get you a beer."

They took their drinks to a table in the corner. When they sat down, Holcomb leaned forward, grasped the nape of Evan Tyler's neck, and pressed their foreheads together.

"Look, Evan, I understand. I get it." His voice was not a whisper, but with the pounding of the club music he was just barely intelligible. "You're a priest. You became a priest because you were trying to cure yourself, didn't you? I know that had to be what happened. I thought about that, too. A long time I thought about it."

Tears were welling up in Tyler's eyes. "I don't want to have this conversation."

"Do you think I'd let you get out of Rome without having it? Don't you get it? We're the same, you and me. You've never told anyone in your whole life that you're gay, have you? You didn't even have to tell me. I understand it that much."

Tyler wiped his eyes. He took a sip from his Peroni bottle. "Did you have this conversation with that friend of yours, Rafael?"

Holcomb gently grabbed Tyler's chin and forced him to look at him, deep into his eyes. "Look at me. *Look at me.* Yes, I did have this conversation with Rafael. Right before I fucked him."

"Oh, please don't say that."

"I'm saying it. You need this, Evan." He let go of Evan's chin and neck, and drank from his own bottle. "I have a friend who has a place, a room, outside the city, in Campolimpido. He's out of town this weekend and he gave me the keys. It's way out of town. No one knows about it. We can go there any time. Right now, if you want."

The priest shook his head. "No. I can't. I know you think you're being kind, but you're not."

"I think you need this. It'll be safe with me. You know I won't tell anyone." Marcus reached across the table and clasped Tyler's hands. "You can make a different choice, you know. About Africa. I know you think you want to go there, but I also know how scared you are of it. If you go to Namibia, it'll be too late to make another choice. I'm just saying that because no one else in your life will."

After a long time, Tyler said: "I *am* scared. The whole thing scares me to death, actually. But it's too late to get out of it."

"No, it isn't. You don't have to go."

"I do. It's all arranged."

"Nothing that can't be undone. I'm just saying, you *do* have a choice."

They sat there in the Alibi club, holding each other's hands, for a long time.

They reached Holcomb's room in Campolimpido at nearly one AM. Tyler was woozy, not quite drunk, and it was obviously an unfamiliar feeling to him. So, too, must have been the sensation, once they were in the room and each stripped to the waist, of kissing another man.

His protests were only token ones. Once, the priest said, "I don't know if I can go through with this, Jeff." A moment later, Marcus slid Evan's penis into his mouth and his resistance was at an end. They coupled twice. Then they slept.

An hour or so before dawn, Marcus Holcomb sat naked on the edge of the bed, which had no frame; it was merely a box spring and mattress set on the floor. Tyler slept beside him, naked, snoring. Holcomb remained a long time, occasionally looking over, seeming as if he was going to do something, but unable to do it without a measure of courage or self-fortitude.

Finally, he just did it. He reached over, took his own pillow, dropped it onto Tyler's face and then literally sat on him, weighing him down. The priest twitched and thrashed, but only toward the end did he truly fight. Marcus held down his left wrist; Tyler's hand was balled into a fist. His right arm flailed and reached out, but ultimately he could do nothing. After a minute or so, he stopped moving, but Marcus remained, sitting on the pillow, for a full ten minutes, long after there should have been no doubt.

When he got up, he left the pillow across Tyler's face. He reached for a pair of boxer briefs and pulled them on. He turned on the light and took his Moleskine notebook from his stack of belongings on the small dresser. Marcus sat on the edge of the bed, put Tyler's right arm at his side, and calmly sketched a copy of Evan's tattoo into a page of his notebook, life-sized, extraordinarily detailed. He then closed the notebook, put it back on the dresser, urinated, washed his hands and his genitals, and then began the grisly work began.

He spread the heavy duty plastic on the poured cement floor, and rolled Tyler's corpse onto it. Using the bolt cutters, Marcus snipped off the ends of Tyler's fingers, collecting them in a rusty coffee can. Holcomb knelt on the plastic next to Tyler's head, propped the priest's mouth open and used the pliers he'd bought that afternoon to pull out every one of his teeth, which he dropped into a pile next to the corpse. These he eventually collected into a Ziploc plastic bag.

Holcomb wrapped the body in three layers. First was the plastic which collected the blood while he was working on the corpse. He then wrapped this in one of the nylon tarps, taped it up with duct tape—he bent the body double at the waist—and wrapped that bundle in another nylon tarp. He half-dragged, half-rolled the bundle outside to where the motorcycle trailer already sat open. He dumped the coffee can and Ziploc bag of teeth into the motorcycle trailer, which he slid into a corner, and loaded the body in. Once he closed and locked the trailer he returned to his room and packed up the camping gear and tools. He Bungee-corded the sleeping bag, bedroll and knapsack to the top of the trailer carrier, and secured the guitar case and the Umbro bag to the back of the motorbike. Tyler's jeans, shoes and polo shirt were in the knapsack, but Holcomb had put on his boxer shorts, over his own boxer briefs, under his clothes. He tidied up the room, which was not very messy, went outside, strapped on his helmet, and started the engine.

He drove to a campground on the far northern fringes of the Rome area. Base Carpegna was a forested glen off a narrow one-lane road winding through the Roman hills. There were a few families staying there, but most of them were Romani and kept to themselves. Marcus parked his motorbike and the trailer and set up camp on the farthest edge of the campground. He'd left Campolimpido in the early morning; soon it was high noon and quite warm, over 80 degrees. He pitched his tent and stayed the whole day there, shirtless, drinking water from the campground's spigot which he poured into a 2-liter plastic bottle. He spoke to no one, and alternated reading *Bald-Faced Messiah* and trying a few rudimentary chords on the guitar. None of the Romani made any attempt to speak to him.

At the hottest part of the day an odor began arising from the motorcycle trailer, but he'd parked far enough away from the rest of the campground that no one— other than him—noticed it.

When nightfall came, he packed up the camp site and was on the move again. He stopped briefly at a petrol station, bought some salami and cheese in a plastic package, and then continued on to Parco Naturale La Corona Sant'Andrea, a nature park 45 minutes or so out of Rome. He drove the motorbike as far down the remotest unpaved trail as its terrain and the tires would allow. Finding himself in a thicket of trees, he walked a distance into them, shining a flashlight, and selected a spot for Evan Tyler's grave.

This burial was more elaborate and lengthy than the funeral he would give Sarah Brinson nearly four years later. He buried Tyler in a hole seven feet deep, narrow, and slightly angled into the earth. He did not bury the coffee can. After refilling the grave—the process of excavation, burial and refilling took nearly six hours—he sat near it on the ground, doused the bottom of the coffee can and its contents with lighter fluid, and set it ablaze. While it burned, he began working on Tyler's teeth, which he poured out of the Ziploc bag onto a rock. He thoroughly smashed them all with the hammer. He collected as many of the broken pieces as he could find with the flashlight, but it didn't matter if a few were scattered. The floor of the thicket was cluttered with leaves and brush; it was unlikely fragments of human teeth would be found or recognized.

The Tiber River wound through this part of the countryside, and after he left the grave site at Parco Naturale La Corona Sant'Andrea, he took a side road through farmland to reach the riverbank. Dawn was just starting to tinge the eastern sky. He flung the burned coffee can into the river, and also sprinkled the broken teeth into the water. The motorcycle trailer still retained a disagreeable aroma, but Holcomb stopped at a highway truck stop on the way back to Rome and washed it out with a hose. Then he went back to Base

Carpegna and camped another day. He was so tired that he slept most of it, even in the stuffy overheated tent.

When night fell again—it was Sunday night, August 30—Marcus at last returned to his rented room in Campolimpido. He slept heavily again. By this time, there was not a single trace of the murder in his room, and no evidence that Evan Tyler had ever been there, except for his underwear, which Marcus wore for two more days before tossing those, too, into the Tiber. According to Tyler's itinerary, he was supposed to be staying at the Hotel Barocco. Obviously, he never checked in, but aside from forfeiting his room deposit, nothing else happened and he was not missed.

Chapter 13: Florence & Bologna

The next morning, Marcus Holcomb got on a train headed for Florence. With the new fast trains across Italy, it was almost a straight shot, taking barely an hour and a half. He was there, in the shadows of campaniles, by the open of business.

Florence was one of the last two large cities in Italy he had not yet visited. He was very thorough this time, having made a list in his Moleskine notebook of the exact addresses of MoneyGram and Western Union outlets to visit, and in which order. Most of the cash he brought with him on the train he used to buy transfer slips made out to Evan Tyler. Some of the earlier transfer slips, the ones he bought in France made out to Gavin Grove, he re-sent to Evan Tyler without withdrawing any cash. He did not use—and outside of Rome still had never used—Jeff Wright's UniCredit ATM card. The Florence-Rome train ran every 40 minutes or so, and he was back in the capital by three PM.

At 3:30, dressed in baggy jeans and the Nirvana T-shirt, he sauntered into a tattoo parlor on a narrow street not far from Termini Station. He unfolded a page of notebook paper torn from the Moleskine, pulled up the right sleeve of his T-shirt and tapped his shoulder. The man behind the counter, who did not speak English, took the paper, looked at it, glanced at Marcus and quoted a price in lira. Holcomb laid a stack of Italian notes on the glass counter. The attendant said something in Italian to the tattooist—a woman with a silver bull ring in her nose, working in the room behind the lobby—and Marcus was told (in Italian) to wait. He returned to Campolimpido in pain, with his upper right arm swathed in a bandage and Saran wrap.

That evening was also the end of one of Marcus Holcomb's more distinctive characteristics. He'd had long hair since his sophomore year in high school. Using an electric razor he'd bought at a drugstore on the way to his little flat, his very long, formerly blond locks, fell across the basin of the tiny sink in the Campolimpido garage-room bathroom in wispy black fibers. He did not have to wash the dye out. It had been long enough since he dyed his hair that the blond roots had grown back; he simply shaved his head to 1/8-inch stubble. When he was done, he resembled Evan Tyler less than he did a fresh U.S. Army recruit, but he was blond again. Not coincidentally, he did not use the Gunther Dortgard pass-port again. It happened that the real Gunther Dortgard also cut his hair at the end of that summer. His new passport sported a photo of a short-haired lad who looked nothing like Marcus.

In the morning he went to the Hotel Barocco, which had a business center. He wore a black polo shirt and khaki slacks and looked at least slightly professional. The door to the business center was propped open; no member of the staff challenged him. He made two phone calls using one of the telephones there. The first was to the rectory at the OMI headquarters campus. Marcus paused a moment before he punched in the number, his eyes closed; then he sprang into confident action.

"Hi, this is Father Tyler. Who is this? Marabella—you remember me. Look, something happened, and my plans got all messed up. I know I was supposed to leave yester-day morning, but my passport and all my papers and reservations, they all got stolen. Yeah! I'm tied up at the American Embassy and I'll be here all day. I know you need the room for somebody else. So would you do me a huge favor? Could you have somebody pack up my stuff, all the stuff I left there, and send it someplace? Okay. Yeah, I canceled my trip to the Holy Land—well, not can-celed, but I can't go. Without a passport, I can't check into a hotel. So I'm going up to Bologna, I know some-body there who got me a hotel room. You can ship my suitcase and my shoulder bag. You can ship them DHL. I'll be staying at the Hilton in Bologna. Yes, I have the address. I will reimburse OMI for the DHL ticket as soon as I get to Bologna. Okay, you ready? The address is..."

The second call he made was to the American Embassy in Rome. That building was only a few blocks from where he sat at the Hotel Barocco.

"Hello, uh, my name is Evan Tyler. I'm an American citizen here in Rome. I'm a priest. I was pickpocketed last night. They got away with everything. Where do I report this, and how do I get my passport reissued? I'm supposed to travel to Israel in a few days."

Later, on the same call:

"Okay. Well, here's the good news: I have copies of all my stuff. Passport, driver's license, credit card, everything. They're Xeroxes, but I do have them. Hm? Okay. Yes, I can come down. I'm not very far away. Really? That would be incredible. Thank you so much."

When he arrived at the American Embassy, less than ten minutes later, he presented the folder of second-generation Xeroxes—the copies of the copies—that had the effect of morphing the real photos of Evan Tyler into indistinct monochromatic blobs. The secretary who examined the copies did not question them. For instance, the fact that the nose on the man in the picture was wider than Marcus' went unnoticed.

"I'll need you to fill this out." She passed a clipboard across the counter. "That box there, for identity documents, I'll fill that in. It was certainly smart of you to keep copies. Your new passport will take about 48 hours—do you have someplace to stay 'til then?"

Three hours later, with a temporary ID form, stamped with the official and genuine seal of the U.S. State Department, Marcus Holcomb was able to check into a hotel in Rome, legally, with no challenge or police trouble. And Tyler's replacement passport—with Marcus

Holcomb's photo on it, genuine and unaltered—was in process, fast-tracked, and entirely above board.

The final major Italian city he had yet to visit was Bologna. By the time he arrived there, two days later, he had a hotel reservation in the name of Evan Tyler, and the hotel staff knew he was coming because a suitcase and shoulder bag tagged with that name had arrived via DHL the day before. In his hotel room, Holcomb carefully unpacked and examined all of Tyler's belongings. He tried on his clothes, most of which fit reasonably well, and began to wear them around Bologna. He also studied the tantalizing evidence of Tyler's family and personal life: an address book, an envelope of cherished photos, and a prayer book inscribed by someone called Fr. Roteman. Marcus used the computer in the hotel's business center to research this name and discovered he was on the faculty of Catholic Theological Union in Chicago, where Tyler had gone to seminary.

The next day, Marcus visited a shop in Bologna that specialized in men's hairpieces. The owner spoke fluent English. "I'm in the early stages of cancer," he explained. "I'm going to have to shave what I've got or lose it all when I start chemo, as soon as I get back to the States. I've been in Europe for over a year. My friends back home will be shocked to see me with short hair. I used to play in a rock band, if you can believe it."

The wigmaker could not help him with his main request, which was for a very long blond hairpiece. But he did refer Holcomb to a woman's wig shop that could. Instead, he sold him a respectable short-cut toupée, blond, the kind a middle-aged man would wear. Holcomb paid cash for it. He went to the woman's shop and bought a blond wig off the shelf, as well as makeup to properly conceal the attachment points. That night in his hotel room sink he dyed the short toupée dark using hair color from a drugstore. The blond wig did not look much like his former hair, but at least it was long, and with a baseball cap worn backwards over it, it looked well enough.

On day three in Bologna, Marcus visited a travel agency. He inquired specifically about cruises from Italy to the Holy Land, Israel, or even Alexandria. After looking at the brochures, he vetoed several options, but told the woman at whose desk he was sitting that he might consider Greece as an alternative. She gave him a sheaf of new brochures.

"How about this one?" He tapped a booklet for a line called Mt. Olympus Cruises. "Do they have anything leaving in the next week?"

"To be honest, sir," said the agent, "we've had some customer complaints about that line. Their ships are kind of, how do you say...*sciatto, sporco.*"

"Well, why don't you book me first class, then. They've got to keep *that* up, right?"

The rest of that day was a flurry of activity. He had a list of all the Western Union and MoneyGram outlets in Bologna; he hit them all systematically. Much of the money that had been sitting in suspension in these systems all summer drained away. Every transfer was directed to Evan Tyler's bank account. Just before the end of business, as Holcomb sat back in his hotel room, he called the UniCredit mobile banking line. "I'd like to make a transfer to a bank in the United States. My name is Jeff Wright, I'm a student. My account number is..."

He also called the Venice offices of Mt. Olympus Cruises. With some difficulty, due to a language barrier, he was able to make *una prenotazione* on the *M/V Golden Isle*—a second reservation—in the name of Gavin Grove. Though he did not say he was Jeffrey Wright, he gave them Wright's UniCredit debit card number. With this business done, Marcus went to an expensive restaurant in Bologna and treated himself to a bottle of wine. He paid cash for the meal, went back to the hotel and went to bed early.

It is difficult to quantify, in dollar terms, the success of Marcus Holcomb's entire enterprise that summer. Of the more than $1.3 million in cash he stole from Michael O'Cuinneagain at the South Mimms traffic circle, he was ultimately able to transfer $284,953 in laundered funds to Evan Tyler's bank account. He left Bologna for Venice on the morning of September 15, 1998, carrying the Umbro bag and the guitar case, which together held approximately $400,000 more, some in Italian lira, some in the original British £20 notes that were delivered to Calais. He also brought Evan Tyler's suitcase and athletic bag. With the exception of the Catholic catechism, everything in Campolimpido, including the motorbike, he simply abandoned. This was, by now, his pattern.

Chapter 14: Venice

The *Golden Isle* was a small, antiquated cruise ship, 20,000 tons, which had started life in the 1950s as a transatlantic liner, just before that trade was decimated by the coming of jet aircraft. She lay low and surly at the Venice passenger terminal, patches of rust showing on her blue-painted sides. The lounge furniture surrounding the small pool on her lido deck was dilapidated. Most of the plates that turned up in the dining saloons, even in first class, were chipped. The crew was a Babel of nationalities: Albanians, Palestinians, Greeks, Turks, Cypriots and Filipinos. Mt. Olympus Cruises, in 1998 teetering on the brink of bankruptcy, was the lowest-rated cruise company in Europe in terms of customer satisfaction. The ship was a holdover from another era, manifestly unfit to exist in the same epoch as email and fiber optics. In the 1990s, you could still find ships like this in the back corners of various European ports.

It is difficult to understand all of Marcus Holcomb's actions on the day he boarded this ship, September 16, 1998. Specifically, we can't know how much of the sequence of events was planned and how much can be ascribed to lucky accidents. When it came to taking the occasional risk, Holcomb often preferred to machinate events and conditions on the front end of a risky gamble, to improve the odds of a favorable outcome. It is possible that he regarded boarding the *Golden Isle* in Venice as the single most dangerous choice he made in his entire odyssey. Or he might have regarded it as a small everyday risk, like running a red light when no other cars were around.

Before going to the passenger ship terminal, he locked the guitar case and the Umbro bag in a locker at the central Venice train station. The Umbro bag contained not just what was left of the cash, but also some clothes he hadn't worn since he was in England: jeans and a Manchester United football jersey. The blond wig, dyed toupée and the baseball cap were also in the bag. From the Santa Lucia station, dressed in Evan Tyler's clothes and carrying his luggage, he walked across the Ponte degli Scalzi over the Grand Canal, then took a leisurely stroll to the Venice cruise ship terminal. The windows for Mt. Olympus Cruises had just opened. He was smiling and easy as he presented his reservation. "Hi, I'm Evan Tyler. I have a first class cabin on the cruise to Piraeus." It is noteworthy that he had not shaved in several days. This was before passengers on ships were routinely photographed upon boarding, or at least before that practice became universal; that was largely a 9/11 legacy.

Once in his cabin, Holcomb drew the drapes, took off Tyler's clothes, and shaved. He donned a set of workman's coveralls which he'd also bought in Bologna. Pausing until the corridor outside his stateroom door was quiet, he crept out and locked it behind him. He found a companionway at the end of the corridor and descended to a lower deck. Something of a comedy of errors ensued as he wandered into a crew space where pallets of supplies were being wheeled aboard through a hatch: a crew foreman, mistaking him for a genuine crew member, shouted at him in Greek and Marcus helped load several of the pallets or at least went through the motions of doing so. At a moment when the crew's attention was focused on the next pallet darkening the hatchway, he slipped out and emerged on the unguarded crew's gangway to the dock.

Hands jammed deeply in the pockets of the boiler suit, he walked, retracing his steps from the cruise ship terminal back to Santa Lucia Station. He fetched the Umbro bag and guitar case and locked himself in a toilet stall. In this station, the toilet cubicles were fully enclosed closet-like spaces. The toupée ended up in the toilet. He put on the jeans, the Manchester United jersey, and the blond wig covered by the baseball cap. It was now barely more than half an hour before the sailing of the *Golden Isle.* The passenger boarding door would be closed very soon.

Notably, this time he came to a different window at the terminal than the one he'd visited as Evan Tyler. He presented, for the first time in over a year, his genuine, unaltered, non-fraudulent American passport bearing the name Marcus Holcomb and a photo of a young man with long blond hair. "I travel under a different name," he told the Mt. Olympus desk agent. "The reservation is in the name of Gavin Grove. But here's my reservation number. My *numero di prenotazione.*"

For the first time during the chase—or at least one of the few times—someone finally questioned one of his artifices. The agent, a young Italian man with thick eyebrows, squinted at his computer screen. "I don't understand. Who made the reservation? Grove, or Hol, Hul, Hul…"

"I made the reservation, but I used my traveling name, Gavin Grove. Look, I've got valid ID."

"Traveling name?" The young Italian man furrowed his brow. "Don't understand. *Non capisco.*"

The digital clock behind him blinked to 11:29 AM. "Please, I have to get on. This is my reservation. This is my passport. What's the problem?"

"The name does not match the reservation. I'm not allowed..."

For the third time Marcus handed over his passport. Now there were six 100,000 lira notes inside its front cover, sticking out.

Those who knew Marcus Holcomb said he could turn on a piercing stare with his grayish-blue eyes. At this moment he fixed such a stare on the young Italian.

"This is my reservation. I've *got* to get on. You understand me? *I've got to get on.*"

The clerk quietly swept the banknotes out of his passport and under the counter. He tapped a few keys at his computer and handed over a small cardboard folder containing a hotel-style room key. He gave him back his passport, and said nothing more.

Unlike Evan Tyler's first-class room, the one that had been booked under the name Gavin Grove was small, windowless and cramped, hot and noisy from proximity to the ship's engines. When he reached it, Holcomb immediately locked and chained the door, drew the curtains across the porthole and lay down on the bed in the darkness. He was breathing heavily and shaking all over. He did not get up or even turn on the lights until after the *Golden Isle* had cleared the spits and barrier islands on the outer boundary of the Venice lagoon.

Several days later, when the *M/V Golden Isle* docked at the Port of Piraeus in Greece and all the passengers disembarked, the ship's second officer, a man called Constantaros, was summoned by a steward to a room on the lowest passenger deck toward the stern. It was the cabin that had been reserved for Gavin Grove. The room was empty, but the passenger's luggage was still there, the bed unmade, and the steward who had come to make up the room said the lights were on when he entered. An open guitar case lay on the bed. On the bed, the dresser, and the floor were stacks of cash, British pounds and Italian lira. The only thing in the guitar case was a sealed envelope, addressed simply, *POLICE*.

Constantaros in turn called the customs and border officers from the disembarkation station; they eventually summoned Greek federal police. The cash, the guitar case and the passenger's belongings were impounded and carefully analyzed.

The letter addressed to the police was handwritten in English. It read:

Sept. 18 '98 / To whoever finds this letter:

I cannot be part of this world any longer. It's too exhausting. I can't even put into words what I've been through.

On June 11, 1997, I killed Rafael Moreira. We were on board the Norse Star off Alaska. We had a fight, I lost my temper and threw him overboard. We were both drunk. Rafael was my boyfriend. I cannot live with the guilt of having destroyed him, he was so beautiful and sweet. I apologize to Rafael's family. I know I can't make up for what I did. That's why I'm doing what I am going to do tonight.

I also admit that I shot and killed Shannon O'Cuinneagain and João Broka in South Mimms, England on June 11, 1998. It was about this money, some of which you'll find with this letter. I'm not sure the money really belongs to anyone. It's illegal cash from an illegal deal (not mine, I merely stole it). The person who thinks they own this money will not stop until I am dead. I made it easy for him. Today he will get his wish, but I doubt you (police) will let him keep the money. I hope it goes to someone who can use it. I spent the rest by the way. Stealing this amount of money isn't worth it. I learned that the hard way.

I decided to end my life aboard a ship because that's how Rafael died. I want to experience exactly what he experienced when I killed him. I heard drowning is an awful way to go. Guess I'll find out. Anyway, that's all. If it makes anyone feel better, I regret everything.

Marcus Holcomb

The investigations that followed, principally conducted by Greek police, turned up very little additional evidence. The ship's manifest was checked against the

Greek border guards' records, and every one of the passengers who boarded the *Greek Isle* in Venice got off and was cleared through Piraeus, with the exception of one passenger listed as Gavin Grove. The Greek police concluded this was a stolen identity of Marcus Holcomb, who had helpfully left his American passport behind in the same envelope as the letter. Inquiries to Interpol by the Greeks quickly turned up the British police's interest in Holcomb.

An internal investigation by Mt. Olympus Cruises could tell the Greek police, the Hertfordshire constabulary and the U.S. State Department only that, while they had no direct evidence that Holcomb jumped overboard somewhere in the Mediterranean between Venice and Piraeus, they believed this was what happened. For a brief time, a previously unidentified body that washed up on the western shore of the island of Zakynthos was suspected of perhaps being Holcomb's—it was found September 22—but ultimately it was determined to be the body of a Greek fisherman who had fallen off a boat a week before. No remains determined to be Marcus Holcomb's were ever found. He had that in common with Rafael Moreira, whose body was also never found.

The case opened a row over the money between the governments of the UK and Greece. The Greek government claimed it under international maritime law. Her Majesty's Government contended it was hers, as proceeds of a crime that had occurred on British soil. In October 1999, a low-level office of the European Union ultimately awarded the sum to Greece. Michael O'Cuinneagain, whose criminal empire had steadily unraveled since his daughter's murder, had by this time fled to

Panama, which lacked an extradition treaty with the United Kingdom. He never saw a shilling of the money, but he remained a free man. For the record, he did not believe that Marcus Holcomb was really dead, but there was nothing he could do about it.

On December 2, 2001, a court in upstate New York, where Holcomb's father still lived, declared Marcus Holcomb legally deceased. The order specified the date of his death as September 18, 1998, the date on his purported suicide note. All police agencies in Britain that had open files on the Traffic Circle Murders closed them. The real Gavin Grove, arrested later in 1998 for an unrelated crime, was by December 2001 out of prison, married and living in Wigan, UK.

On September 23, 1998, a middle-aged woman named Sarah Kurzweil, who wore a nun's habit and bright white sneakers, stood at the gate of the international flight arrival hall in the airport at Windhoek, Namibia. She held a cardboard sign with *"FR. E. TYLER"* written on it in black magic marker. She worked for the Missionary Oblates of Mary Immaculate, and was stationed at Tondoro; she was the person whom the Vatican was replacing with Tyler.

A tanned, handsome young man of about thirty, dressed in a priest's collar and carrying an athletic bag, walked out of the gate, saw the sign, smiled, and went up to Sister Kurzweil. He shook her hand warmly.

"Father Tyler! It's wonderful to meet you at last." The nun had a slight German accent.

"It's wonderful to meet you."

"Did you have a good flight?"

"Yeah. It was just a short hop from Cape Town. It was the one from Athens to Cape Town that was grueling."

"Well, let's fetch your luggage, and we'll get to the hotel. It's too late to start up to Tondoro tonight."

They departed Windhoek for Tondoro in the morning in the very same Toyota Land Cruiser that Marcus Holcomb himself would drive three and a half years later. Neither Sister Kurzweil, who would soon be leaving Tondoro for good, nor Father Ubate, nor any other of the people who met Evan Tyler for the first time that week noticed anything odd about him, except that he was often forgetful of the various Catholic prayers that he should, after years of seminary and a lifetime of devout worship, have known by heart. But no one suspected him of not being anyone other than Evan Tyler, or if they did, they never said anything to anyone. As for the five people in three countries that Holcomb had murdered by this time, they, of course, were silent forever.

Chapter 15: Okovango West

In the first week of March 2002, an envelope bearing numerous stamps and international postmarks arrives at the headquarters of the Missionary Oblates of the Mary Immaculate on the Via Aurelia in Rome. It is addressed to the director of personnel for mission place-ments in the Africa/Asia region. It is only a few lines long, and it reads:

"I hereby tender my resignation as Director of Outreach and Charities of the Parish of St. Ambrose in Tondoro, Namibia, from the Missionary Oblates of the Mary Immaculate, and from the priesthood of the Catholic Church, effective immediately. I thank you and His Holiness for the opportunity to serve. God bless you and keep you. Fr. Evan R. Tyler."

At about the same time as the letter reaches the Vatican, there occurs a splendid and unusual event in St. Ambrose Parish. On a Saturday evening, much of the town—at least its residents who interface with the mission—turn out for a banquet, in the garden behind the church, honoring Father Evan Tyler. A banner of foil letters reading *"FAREWELL!"* is tacked to the wall of the church. The dishes brought to the picnic are simple, a lot of mahangu pap—porridge made from millet flour— and various grilled meats. They are served at pine picnic tables. A group of children from the school sing a Latin hymn. Father Ubate, propping himself up on a cane as he stands, gives an address.

"The day the Lord our Holy Father sent Father Tyler to us was a blessed and happy day. For the past four years he's been the light of our church, the backbone of our school and a dedicated friend to the community of Tondoro. What he has accomplished for our parish is almost incalculable. We wish him the best in his future life back in the United States, and Lord, we give our most humble thanks to you for the time he was with us."

During the adulation Tyler merely smiles amicably, nods, occasionally presses his hands together in a humble gesture. The evening sky glows rose gold above the trees and the roof of the church. After the banquet is over a line of townspeople move through the garden. Some of the women embrace Tyler. Joe Kimbeta gives him a handshake which eventually becomes an embrace. A few of the smaller children wipe away tears.

When a woman from the village approaches—she wears a colorful red blouse—she too grasps Tyler's hand. "Thank you for being such a friend to my son. He will never forget you. God bless you."

"Thanks so much, Mrs. Mbwele. I don't see Moses anywhere around, did I miss him?"

A strange look— perhaps shame, perhaps awkwardness—crosses Anika Mbwele's face. "He did not want to come. He refused to come. When I told him it was time to leave, he burst into tears and hid in his room and wouldn't come out. Please accept my apology, Father Tyler, on his behalf."

Tyler smiled. "You don't need to apologize, and he doesn't either. I'll write."

"I hope you do. Moses has never been as devoted to a teacher as he is to you."

This is Tyler's last night in Tondoro. In the morning he rises early, loads his bags into the Land Cruiser and Father Hague drives him to Windhoek via Rundu—a drive Tyler himself has made twice since the departure of Sarah Brinson nearly two weeks ago. That night he stays in a hotel in Windhoek, the very same one he stayed in four years earlier. On this Sunday he makes that same journey in reverse, catching an early morning flight to Cape Town, South Africa. As he walks through the Cape Town airport, Marcus Holcomb no longer looks to be a priest at first glance. The clerical collar is packed in his—Evan Tyler's—suitcase. He wears ordinary street clothes. He also carries himself slightly differently. Unlike the desperate weeks following his flight from England, this time no one is chasing him.

Three weeks later, a white SUV rolls into the town of Tondoro and drives up to the main entrance of St. Ambrose Parish. It is a police vehicle, its doors painted with the seal of the Namibian Police Force, Okovango West region. Two men get out. One is in uniform; the other is in jeans and a white sport shirt. Their names are Victor Urikhob and Henrik Isaacs.

Within a few minutes the officers are standing in the garden before the church. Urikhob, the uniformed officer, takes notes on a pad while Isaacs asks the questions. Father Ubate is, as always, cooperative and affable.

"We are investigating the disappearance of a woman, an American." Isaacs's tone is matter-of-fact, devoid of any emotion. "We believe she came to, or passed through, Tondoro on or about February the 14th."

"Miss Brinson?"

"She was here?

"Yes, she stayed with us for two...yes, I think it was two days. And it was around that time."

"What did she do here?"

"She told us she was looking for someone, also an American. Did you say she's missing too? You'd better come to my office."

The interview lasts an hour. Ubate tells the officers everything that transpired with Sarah Brinson's visit, at least everything he knows. Oddly, the interview has been going for nearly 15 minutes before he even mentions that Father Tyler left Tondoro a few weeks ago.

"He spent the most time with Miss Brinson of any of us. Sadly, he was recalled by the OMI and had to return to America. If you want to talk to him, he might be back there by now." Ubate's hands are quaking violently. They shake all the time now.

"That probably won't be necessary," says Isaacs, "but thank you for telling us. Can we see the room where Miss Brinson stayed, please?"

The officers look around St. Ambrose thoroughly, and return to their station in Rundu that afternoon. Isaac writes an email to his superior on the police force —who had dispatched the officers in the first place—reporting that they verified Sarah Brinson visited Tondoro but apparently left there on her own initiative. This is an error, but it is not Isaacs's. Ubate told him that Brinson left Tondoro the Sunday morning, early, following her Friday arrival, and that he knew she left because he heard her drive away in her rented SUV before dawn. Ubate had indeed heard the engine of an SUV, but he didn't look out his window to see it and had no independent knowledge that it was Sarah Brinson driving away; when he left his room that morning he noticed her car was gone and thus he told the officers he was sure she'd left at that time. He had evidently forgotten that Tyler told him she left the previous night.

This email from Isaacs becomes the basis of a telephone call from the Namibian Police Force, West Okovango Region, to the U.S. Consulate in Windhoek. That office had begun the whole investigation after they got a call from a woman in the United States, one Gwen Carrigan, reporting that Brinson had failed to return from her trip to Namibia. The consul relied on the word of Isaacs's superior that she was confirmed to have departed Tondoro, which meant something happened to her between there and Windhoek, where she had a hotel reservation but failed to check in. The Namib police carry this as an open case and several more inquiries are made to police stations in every sizable town between Rundu and Windhoek. But because of elderly Father Ubate's error—his false certainty that the investigator had left Tondoro under her own steam—the parish, and Evan Tyler, and Tondoro are all excluded from the scope of the investigation. Predictably, the Namibian Police find nothing, and report truthfully to the U.S. State Department that they have no evidence that Sarah Brinson met with foul play or accident within the borders of Namibia.

Chapter 16: Cape Town

It is a brilliant fall day in Cape Town. The waters of the Victoria & Alfred Waterfront glint gold and green at the feet of floating piers, brick-lined walkways, and luxury condominiums that front its inner channels. The marinas are busy. It is nearing the end of tourist season and the day sailers, whale watchers and boat tour operators are fully booked. Low clouds are visible on the horizon beyond Robben Island, but no storm is threatening yet.

A sailing ship is tied up to one of the piers, a two-masted schooner painted dark blue. Her sails are stowed. She was probably a looker in years past, but now seems a bit run-down, with lines of rust along her hull plates, and peeling paint on her lengthy raked white bowsprit. Her home port—*Cape Town*—is painted beneath her name curling around the cruiser stern. The *Sea Diamond*, 120 feet long, is nothing close to a derelict, but she seems almost forgotten at the quay.

At 10:30 in the morning, two men board the *Sea Diamond*, one a tall, lanky, dark-bearded, white South African called Martin Beyer, the other an American with short-shaved blond hair, blue deck shoes, jeans and a rugby shirt. Beyer unlocks the gate at the end of the gangplank. Evan Tyler follows. No one else is aboard; the hatches are locked and shades are pulled over most of the windows and portholes.

"She's been kept in fairly good order, though not perfectly, I admit." Beyer speaks English with a South African accent. "She's been scrubbed down every couple of weeks, and taken out of the water once since you bought her. No damage or incidents, so far as I know."

Tyler stands on the rear deck, paces, and runs his hand along the railing. "Funny, I've never actually been aboard in person. I saw tons of photos, but I couldn't get away to come tour her before the deal closed."

"She's in pretty good shape for not having been sailed regularly in such a long time."

"Did you use her for tours?"

Beyer shrugs. "'Bout three times a year. She's not really a luxury yacht anymore, you know—oh, she's comfortable enough, but most of the clientele that wants a sailing experience expects fine cuisine and a dance bar, y'know? We've got two newer ships better suited for that sort of charter. And the business has changed a lot, which is why I 'spect Krueger listed her for sale and leased her to us in the first place. No, what we've mostly used this one for is training, and she's right good for that. The employees don't expect much in the way of luxury accommodation, so she's the perfect training vessel. Be sorry to lose her, truth be told."

"Can we go below?"

"Of course." Beyer begins unlocking the rear hatch and they go down the companionway.

Their thorough tour of the schooner lasts nearly an hour. Beyer points out item after item of repair and refurbishment. "You've got some floor rot here. Prob'ly have to take up the floor and replace her." He shines an electric torch into dark curved nooks and corners. "See here, there's some water damage in the bulwarks. This will be quite a bitch for you. It's not just replacing the toe rails—you might have to put in a few new deck beams." In the galley Beyer wrenches the control knobs on the propane stove. It clicks and hisses, but nothing happens. "This has been giving us trouble for months. Prob'ly replace this too. You'll want to test out all the electrical—if you're lucky that can stay." Tyler interjects questions, but otherwise says little.

The crew foc'sle is a large space forward with angled walls, each side of the ship fitted with double berths, top and bottom, for a total of twelve accommodations. The wooden berths are stocked with thin mattresses of the kind found in low-rent dormitories. Urine stains are visible on one of them. Beyer lifts the corner of one of the mattresses. "These are shot, I'm afraid. If you remodeled the foc'sle, you could turn it into a nice stateroom. Mind you, your chain locker is just forward, so you'll have to leave this hatchway clear."

"I'm not going to remodel this. It's perfect."

Beyer chuckles. "We use this for the crew. We kept it raw so they get a taste of life at sea. If you're gonna be carrying cruise passengers—"

"I'm not. This is going to be a floating school."

"A school?" Beyer sounds surprised.

"Yes. My company, Oceans for Christ, is an educational institution. That was always my plan, to sail her as a floating boarding school. This space would be perfect for the students. I like that you left it raw. Half dorm, half prison. Exactly what I need to teach them some discipline."

"Well, good luck, then."

"What about the captain's cabin?"

They venture aft and are soon there. It's a small room paneled in polished oak. It has a built-in desk and a dedicated head. Tyler opens the door to the bathroom, looks inside, nods with satisfaction and closes the door. "Perfect."

"This is traditionally for the skipper. The *owner's* stateroom is the one we saw further forward, on the port side."

"No, this is perfect."

"You have, er, sailing experience?"

"Not a bit. In fact, I could use your help. I could use someone with some good sailing experience to run the ship for me, and probably help with the refit too. Someone with a master's license who knows their way around a ship like this. I'm not a sailor myself, and I don't have the connections that you do in the community. Can you help? I'd pay you a finder's fee."

Beyer crosses his arms in front of his thin but muscular chest. "Well, that's pretty irregular. We're not in the business of staffing the competition, are we?"

"I'm not competition. You're in the business of charter sailing and passenger cruises. I have no interest in that. I'm running a school, remember?"

"Well, there *is* someone you might think about. May Pinder is a good sailor and she's got a skipper's ticket. She's done a few cruises for us, in fact one or two on the *Diamond* herself, here. I'd love to have hired her, but we don't have enough work to keep her busy full time. I can give you her number."

"A lady captain. Sounds perfect."

"We have some paperwork to finish back at the office anyway—wind up the lease and that sort of thing."

They start back up the companionway. Once on deck, Tyler again nods with satisfaction. "I'm happy with the way your outfit has taken care of her while I've leased her to you."

"Well, it was better than just leaving her sitting at a dock without using her. That was what Krueger thought when he first leased her to us."

Once they're back on the quay, headed for the V&A Charter Rentals office within walking distance but not line-of-sight of the old blue schooner, the *Sea Diamond* is again quiet and deserted, though not for long.

The next few weeks and months are, for Marcus Holcomb, a period of intense grueling activity like nothing in his life since the chase across France and Italy, four years before.

The work that must be done to refit the *Sea Diamond* is staggering. A small construction crew descends on her at the quayside and soon she is alive with sound and activity: the shearing noise of sanders, the splinter and crackle of planks being removed, the clang of metal tools against her steel hull and the hiss of acetylene welding torches. Holcomb is constantly among the hired crew, asking questions and giving orders as often as he is taking them, swinging a crowbar or holding steady a beam or the end of a rail being sawed. But there's only so much that can be done while the ship is afloat. In the first week of April, she's towed into a small dry dock and put up on blocks. For the first time in months, the South African sun touches the thin colonies of barnacles on her hull. Holcomb begins to curse a whole host of new problems just revealed: rudder damage, anti-fouling paint in shreds, dents in the keel. The costs are mounting.

Early in this process, May Pinder makes her first appearance at the dry dock. She is a petite woman with dreadlocks and an air of can-do about her. She often wears Carhartt dungarees, steel-toed boots and a dark gray cable-knit sweater; within days most of the orders given aboard or around *Sea Diamond* are given by her. One bright April morning she stands next to Marcus in the main salon. A blueprint of the ship is spread out on the table and she marks areas of concern with a pencil. "These bulwarks here. These two here. This one looked bad. This one, this one. Deck plates here. This section comes out. We'll need to tear this out to get the new V-drive in. This Dorade box has to be rebuilt. We'll have to take down the masts, both of them, to re-wire them. New spreaders up top."

"How long?"

"You're asking how *long?* You should be asking how *much.*"

"She's got to be ready to make a transatlantic crossing in August."

"Four months." May looks down at the plans. "It's possible, but I can't promise anything."

"Why don't you do this? Start by making a list of anything kids can do."

"Kids?"

"Teenagers. Boys. Anything they can do—sanding, varnishing, painting, any sort of grunt work that doesn't require skill. I can shoot for getting a class together, a temporary one, at the winter break in June and July. We'll put them to work doing anything that's still undone at that time."

"It's not going to be that easy."

"Well, let's give it a try."

Marcus spends long hours at the dry dock, sanding, sawing, welding, cleaning, measuring, and doing all manner of other tasks. He's there seven days a week. He has rented a small furnished apartment in Kensington, a 90-day rental, and he sleeps only a few hours a night. Sometimes—often, in fact—the work on the *Sea Diamond* stretches so late that he sleeps overnight in the captain's cabin aboard the ship. He carries a laptop computer in a bag that he shuttles between Kensington and the Victoria & Alfred waterfront in the small beater car he bought. The work begins to pay off. As time passes the old schooner begins to show signs of life, like an old bear stirring at the end of winter hibernation.

But there are many tasks to be done besides readying the ship. Evan Tyler is constantly creating flyers, writing ad copy, building and tweaking the Oceans For Christ website, and placing telephone calls to school administrators and guidance counselors all over South Africa. "Yes, hello, my name is Father Evan Tyler, and I'm the headmaster of the educational program for Oceans For Christ here in Cape Town. Can I talk to you for a few minutes?" He repeats many of the same lines on these calls, such as: "The program is faith-based, and I *am* trained as a Catholic priest, but we accept students of all denominations, and our religious instruction isn't Catholic-centered..." And: "At my parish school in Tondoro, we graduated students from secondary school at twice the statistical rate of graduation in the country of Namibia overall." He tells many lies on these calls, but this particular claim happens to be true. He reads from scripts, working from a long list of potential contacts written on many pages of yellow legal paper. It's perhaps noteworthy that Marcus Holcomb's first job for the gangster O'Cuinneagain in London also involved phone work, calling long lists of contacts day in and day out. His lists then looked very much like the ones he's working from now.

Eventually more humans begin visiting the *Sea Diamond,* especially after she's liberated from dry dock and again seaborne, or at least tied up at the pier. On a Saturday morning in late May, a group of schoolboys from a Cape Town high school storms the quay and files aboard the schooner, where they are handed paint brushes or scrapers by May Pinder and put to work on the grunt tasks. Tyler does not pay these boys directly, but the labor isn't free. Instead, he bought a stack of entry tickets for Ratanga Junction, the popular amusement park in Century City, and gave them to the guidance counselor at a Catholic school who promised to help round up volunteers for a day's worth of labor in exchange for the tickets. It is a group of these boys, dispatched in the ship's brand-new inflatable Zodiac dinghy, who bob beneath the overhang of the *Sea Diamond's* stern, painting out the old name and replacing it with the ship's new moniker: *GLOBAL REDEEMER*. Each of these boys goes home with an Oceans For Christ T-shirt and a glossy folder full of promotional literature about the OFC program. Tyler was at an all-night copy store at four o'clock this same morning finishing their printing and bundling.

Eventually, as the *Global Redeemer* turns white, her brightwork begins to shine again, and brand-new sails begin to be hoisted up her repainted masts, the first telephone call from a parent clicks on to the voice mail at Oceans for Christ's telephone number. It's a woman's voice. "Hello, I'm calling for Father Evan Tyler. My name is Gertie Weyrenga and I'm calling about my son, Lucas. He's 16, level 10 in school. Lucas has had a lot of difficulties, especially in the last year. He's been suspended for fighting and also for marijuana. My husband and I are at wit's end in dealing with him. I saw on the web site that you specialize in troubled youth, and I wonder if your program might be a good fit for him. Please call me at…"

* * *

In the first week of July, not long after the winter break has begun in South African schools, Marcus Holcomb and May Pinder spend the night together in the captain's cabin aboard the *Global Redeemer*. Their first coupling was in mid-May, somewhat impulsive, and they did not speak of it to one another, but merely went back to work the next morning as if nothing had happened. Now it's a more frequent activity. They have dinner aboard the ship in the main salon, where the galley has been stocked with food and other stores in anticipation of the shakedown cruise that will begin tomorrow. Then they retire to the captain's cabin. On voyages, May will have her own cabin—the owner's stateroom Martin Beyer spoke of—but they have only ever slept together in his room. She gets up on all fours and he takes her from behind, but when their grinding becomes particularly intense, he takes himself out of her and instead penetrates her buttocks, which seems to drive him insane with desire. After it's over, he lies panting in the double berth. The water laps gently against the *Redeemer*'s hull. May lights a joint. The only light in the cabin is a small reading light over the desk, whose little yellow bulb gleams off the combination dial of the small wall safe that Marcus had installed only today.

"Did you violate your vows when you were a priest?" May exhales these words with a cloud of pot smoke and passes the joint to him.

"Sometimes I did, yes." He smokes. "It's hard to be celibate. One reason why I'm not a priest anymore."

"I have a real hard time thinking of you as a priest. How did you decide to become one?"

"To be honest, I just sort of fell into it."

She giggles. "How do you *fall into* being a priest?"

He takes the joint back from her after she's had another drag. "Can I tell you a secret?"

"Sure."

"I'm not really a priest. I mean, I am *sort* of, but I was never technically ordained." He smokes, and smiles up at her; she's propped above the pillow on one elbow. "It's bullshit."

"I knew it." She traces the sacred heart tattooed on his arm. "This is a good disguise."

"It is."

"So why do it? Why *pretend* to be a priest?"

"Well, do you know who L. Ron Hubbard is?"

"No. Keep in mind I grew up here in South Africa, and apartheid only ended nine years ago. They kept the townships pretty cut off from the world."

He smokes again. "L. Ron Hubbard was a science fiction writer who founded a church. He said once, 'You don't get rich writing science fiction. If you want to get rich, you start a religion.'"

"Is that what we're doing? Getting rich?"

"That, and the occasional ass fucking."

They laugh. The joint is about down to the roach.

The next day the *Global Redeemer* leaves the Cape Town waterfront on its first business voyage. It's been advertised as a shakedown, an orientation cruise, three days at sea specifically timed to take advantage of the second term school break: the ship will sail northward along the coast, visit Port Nolloth Harbour on the northwest coast of South Africa, and then return. Five students are on board, Lucas Weyrenga among them. In addition to Father Tyler and May Pinder there are two temporary crewmen, Donduras and Blum.

As the ship leaves the Cape Town waterfront behind a mantle of glinting water—the wind sweeps through the lines and causes the sails to draw—five young men, ranging in age from 14 to 18, stand in a line on the aft deck of the ship. They wear jeans or shorts and blue Oceans For Christ T-shirts. May Pinder is in the cockpit, tending the wheel. Father Tyler, who has not been seen on deck until now, emerges from the main cabin at the forward companionway, walks aft—clinging to lines and railings—and stands before them like a drill sergeant.

"Welcome aboard the *Global Redeemer*." His tone does not sound welcoming. "You're here because you're all fuck-ups."

"Hey, fuck you," says one of the students, a surly-looking youth with curly hair.

Tyler is immediately in his face. "If you dare speak to me like that again you're going over the side. You think I won't do it? I've done it before. I know all about you, Lucas Weyrenga. I know you're about to be thrown out of school. As I was saying, you're all fuck-ups. Your parents are desperate. Well, you're now crew aboard my ship, and for the next three days you'll do everything I tell you and listen to every word I say. Because there's nowhere for you to go, unless you want to try to swim back to Cape Town. Would you, Lucas, like to be the first example of what happens when a member of the crew doesn't obey his captain?"

The boy is silent, but continues to wear an indignant expression.

"Over there, next to the railing, you will see five neat little sets of buckets and brushes—one for each of you. Each of you miserable little shit stains is going to grab one of those buckets, get down on your hands and knees and start scrubbing the deck. This is no longer the 21st century. You're in the Napoleonic navy for the next three days, and I'm Napoleon. Any of you who refuses to do your duty will be severely punished. Each of your parents signed waivers saying I can do whatever the hell I want to do to you. This is not like any other school you've ever been to. Do I make myself clear?"

Within five minutes the *Global Redeemer* has indeed gone back in time two centuries. The five students are knelt over, scrubbing with wire brushes, soap suds oozing from repurposed paint cans. The sails snap in the breeze; the rigging creaks. May Pinder, her nose covered in zinc oxide, spins the wheel to turn the schooner leeward. The South African flag flying from the stern beats in the wind.

Father Tyler wanders about the deck, holding a small leather-bound Bible. "Since it's clear none of you wastes of flesh know a single thing about God, we're going to start right at the beginning." He turns the first few pages of the Bible; the sheets are so thin they're almost tissue paper. "Genesis. Chapter one. *'In the beginning God created the heavens and the Earth. Now the Earth was formless and empty, darkness was over the surface of the deep, and the spirit of God was hovering over the waters.'* Greg! You're Greg, right? You call that scrubbing? Put your shoulders into it. *'And God said, Let there be light, and there was light. And God saw the light was good.'*"

Chapter 17: Civitavecchia

Heat rises in shimmers from the concrete streets and tile rooftops of Civitavecchia, Italy. On this intolerably hot afternoon—so hot that even tourist spots like the Spanish Steps in Rome, 37 miles away, are mostly deserted—a car with Vatican City plates pulls to an old 19th century building retrofitted as a modern office complex, a door opens and a priest in a bright red cassock emerges. He hurries into the building to escape the heat. The bishop, sixtyish, portly with gray hair, looks like an Italian cardinal, but Leonard Vitacchi was born in New York City and still holds American citizenship, despite having lived in Rome for decades. He knows this building well; as a courtesy, a secretary escorts him to an office.

The man whose office it is, Giuseppe Colvino, is 49, completely bald, thick-necked, powerfully-built, and well-dressed. He greets the man in the cassock warmly. "Bishop Vitacchi! Wonderful to see you again." He speaks Italian. He motions to two leather chairs, set on a Persian rug some distance away from Colvino's desk. The bishop inquires after Colvino's wife.

"She's very well, thank you. She went up to Tivoli a few days ago to escape the heat. I can't say I blame her. Would you like a drink? Water? No? Very well. What can I do for the Vatican today?"

"We have an unusual situation that has just come to the IOR's attention." IOR—*Istituto per le Opere di Religione,*

Institute for the Works of Religion—is what the rest of the world refers to as the Vatican Bank. "It involves a strange little matter down in Africa. It may be nothing, or it may be something. We don't know."

"Africa!" Colvino wears an easy smile. "You do reach the corners of the globe, Bishop."

"This isn't a direct IOR investment. In fact, we don't know if any IOR money is involved in it at all, which is why I said it may be nothing. Either way, we'd like you to find out."

The office in which they are sitting is part of the headquarters of Banco Catolico di Civitavecchia, of which Giuseppe Colvino is head of the compliance and forensic accounting department. This bank is, at least ostensibly and officially, completely independent of the Vatican, though it is well known that the Vatican Bank owns 61% of its stock. This arrangement is typical of how the Vatican's finances work, and it's why it is inaccurate to call any one entity, even the IOR itself, the "Vatican Bank."

"What's the situation, Leonard?"

"A few months ago, a young priest, an American, resigned his post at a small missionary parish in Namibia run by the Missionary Oblates of the Mary Immaculate. The priest there, one Father Ubate, was very elderly. He asked OMI for a replacement, and they sent one, a Mexican called Suarez. By the time Suarez reached Namibia, though, Father Ubate had died. Suarez did his best to review the financial records of the parish, St. Ambrose, which the American priest had handled pretty much by himself. Apparently, the parish received considerable donations and they were able to build a lot of improvements. But Suarez found the financial records an incredible tangle—lots of missing documents and such. When he talked to the bank in Namibia that handled money—all those donations—Suarez learned that the American priest told them, the Namibian bank, that part of the funding they were handling came from the IOR. Apparently this priest even took out a loan from a bank with fraudulent papers listing IOR as the guarantor on the loan, which was to buy some kind of property."

"And let me guess: in reality IOR wasn't involved at all."

"Exactly. We haven't put a single coin into St. Ambrose Parish in Namibia, and IOR clearly would not have guaranteed a mortgage on Namibian real estate. At least not officially. However, we can't rule out the possibility that IOR money was somehow used, perhaps diverted illegally. Suarez called us, and I've already had three examiners look at what records he was able to show us, but we can't figure it out."

Colvino rubs his shiny scalp and thinks for a moment. He rises from the chair. "I'm going to have a bottle of water. Sure you don't want one?"

"Yes, I'm sure, thank you."

Colvino walks back to his chair from the sideboard, bottle of water in hand. "What do you think happened?"

"We don't have much of a clue, I'm afraid. The man who should have been minding the store down there, Ubate, evidently wasn't—he delegated everything to the American priest from OMI. And in any event, Ubate is now dead. The records are incomplete and probably untrustworthy. We need someone to figure out what happened, whether any IOR money was involved, and, if so, where it is now."

"Why isn't this the problem of the missionary association, Oblates of—what were they called again?"

"The Missionary Oblates of Mary Immaculate owes no fiduciary duty to the IOR. Your bank, on the other hand, does. If resolution of this matter involves facts or practices that put the Vatican in a bad light, OMI would simply deflect by claiming it was malfeasance by the Vatican Bank or something like that. You, on the other hand, can be trusted to keep any such embarrassing disclosures, should they exist, confidential."

Colvino drinks from his water bottle. "Do you expect there to *be* disclosures? It sounds like the IOR is innocent in this matter. Someone appropriated your name to obtain money under false pretenses. How is that the Vatican's fault?"

Vitacchi pauses a moment. His lips move but at first no sound emerges. When he does speak his tone is lower, almost reticent, or perhaps slightly secretive.

"This is a time of maximum danger for the Church, Giuseppe. The abuse scandal that broke in the United States seven months ago is rocking the Vatican to its foundations. The pressure is incredible. More than that, the Holy Father, who's been on the throne of St. Peter for a quarter century now, is advancing in years and declining in health. Since I have no idea what happened down there in Namibia, I have no understanding of the potential magnitude of the scandal, if there is one. If the abuse scandal widens, or His Holiness dies, the Church will be placed under even more intense worldwide scrutiny than it already is. I can't allow another potential scandal to land on His Holiness's desk. You understand, yes?"

Colvino nods. "I understand completely. I've never been to Africa. I suppose this is my chance."

"I have a file with all the relevant details. I'll have it messengered over this afternoon."

"It sounds like all roads lead to this American priest. What do we know about him?"

"Very little. His name is Tyler and he's from a diocese called Grand Rapids. I think that's near, I don't know, Chicago?"

"Where is Tyler now?"

"No idea. He resigned from OMI in March. He told someone there he was going back to Grand Rapids, but I had one of my people call the diocese there inquiring about him, and he's not shown up there. His letter of resignation reads as though he considers himself as having resigned the priesthood entirely."

Vitacchi uses the words "considers himself"—*si considera*—because the Catholic Church does not typically recognize such a thing as self-resignation from the priesthood.

"That could be dangerous." Colvino pauses a moment, and drinks again. "A rogue ex-priest is not likely to listen to commands from the Vatican."

"One of our problems, precisely. You're going to have to locate him and determine whether he ran off with funds belonging to the IOR."

"And once I find him, what would you like me to do with him?"

Vitacchi looks momentarily puzzled. "Excuse me?"

"I want to be perfectly clear, Leonard, on what my mission is. Of course, you want to know what happened. I assume that's not all. If IOR funds were stolen or misused, is recovery of the stolen funds my primary mission? If this American, Tyler, is behind it, do you want him to be made an example of? If he's guilty not of theft but merely misappropriating the name and reputation of the IOR, do you want that dealt with, in a demonstrative way, a retributive way, or...?" Colvino allows his voice to trail off.

"Revenge is not a Catholic virtue. If this man is guilty of crimes, it is for the secular authorities, and the Lord, to punish him, not you and not the Church."

"Very well. That's clear enough. It sounds like you want the money back, if the IOR has been robbed, and if it's able to be recovered."

"If monies were stolen, yes, we'd like them back."

"And you want this done without involvement of the authorities?"

"Right. Nothing that would trigger negative publicity for the Church or the IOR."

"Very well."

"Will you require a retainer?"

Colvino shakes his head. "I know you will pay. When the job is done."

"You've always been easy to do business with." Vitacchi stands. "I'll be sure to send that file over."

"I look forward to it. Blessings to you, Bishop."

"Give my best to your lovely wife."

Once Vitacchi has left, Colvino strides to his desk, which is a vast sea of polished mahogany, on which sit only a computer monitor and keyboard, a notepad and pen, and a photo framed in silver of Colvino's wife and daughter. They are close in age. Melina, his second wife, is 29; Sofia, his daughter, is 25.

He taps the keyboard of the computer; the screen jumps to life. Colvino brings up a browser window and begins searching for information on the country of Namibia. He also does a Yahoo search for "St. Ambrose Parish" and "Namibia," and brings up the same antiquated web site, nearly two years old, that Sarah Brinson also accessed on the day she accepted the Tylers' case. The page contains a small photo, slightly blurry, of a good-looking blond man with gray-blue eyes. He wears a clerical collar. The caption beneath reads, *"Fr. Evan Tyler, Director of Outreach & Charities."* Colvino right-clicks his mouse to save the photo to his hard drive, just as Sarah Brinson did, seven months ago.

Chapter 18: Woods Hole

Two women sit across from one another at a table in a mid-range Italian restaurant in Grand Rapids, Michigan. Over tortellini alla panna, garlic bread and a bottle of Chianti, they have been discussing events that occurred across the world, and which neither of them witnessed. Gwen Carrigan, blonde, with glasses and a piercing stare, has a diamond stud in her nose and carries herself with a confidence that borders on arrogance. The other woman, much heavier, brunette, has deep blue eyes, long fingers and a bright sunny smile, when she chooses to display it. This woman, Zoë Tyler-Petrick, is, at 28, the younger of the two; Gwen is 35.

"My husband thinks we should just let this thing go." Zoë's face is not exhibiting her bright smile, but rather careworn concentration. "He didn't even want me to come on this trip. Says I'm getting obsessed."

"I've *been* obsessed for a long time. Speaking only for myself, I'm long past the letting-it-go stage."

"How has Vincent been handling it?"

Gwen shrugs. "He's devastated, but he won't show any emotion. If I thought it'd work, I'd get him into ther-apy. But he wouldn't go. He's even more surly than most teenagers. He's going to do what he's going to do."

The two eat some more of their pasta. Several threads of the conversation have gone on since the be-ginning of dinner. Zoë resumes one of them randomly: "What should we do about the police in Namibia? What's the next step?"

"The police are controlled from a central govern-ment agency. I got some names, some members of their parliament. I'll write letters, but you know what we'll get back—'We've done everything we can do, sorry.'"

"We should still send the letters. And to the State Department too." Gwen nods, and reaches for her wine glass. "Did you hear back from that producer at CBS, *48 Hours*?"

"He said they'll look into it, but I don't think they're serious."

"What about your Congressman? I can't pronounce his name."

"Blagojevich. *Blah-goy-oh-vitch.* Got a letter from a staffer saying they'd contact the State Department. What about yours, Ehlers?"

"No response. He's a Republican, though, so I didn't expect one. I called his office, got an intern. Contact State Department, she said."

"Do we know anybody who can influence Colin Powell?"

Gwen laughed. "Bush doesn't even listen to him. Besides, as long as this Iraq thing is on their plate, I don't think the State Department is going to be paying attention to anything else."

Their conversation continues in this vein throughout the rest of dinner, on the ride home to the house on Juneberry Avenue where Gwen lives and Zoë is staying for the weekend, and over the dining room table in this house which is strewn with papers and Gwen's laptop computer. It's an endless disputation about which bureaucrats and politicians to lobby, which law enforcement agencies to pester, and which media outlets to pitch. Gwen's laptop contains a spreadsheet with a long list of these tasks, letters to write and phone calls to make. Gwen opens another bottle of wine. It's more mutual bonding now than strategy. The disappearance of Sarah Brinson—and the apparent indifference with which the rest of the world is treating it—has brought these two very different women together into a friendship that didn't exist a few months ago.

Amid the papers cluttering the kitchen table is a letter, a piece of laser printer paper folded in thirds, sticking out of an envelope. This evening neither Gwen nor Zoë has glanced much at it. They both know it well. It arrived at Evan Tyler's parents' house in Grand Rapids in early April. It was postmarked from Windhoek, Namibia. Its text is computer-printed; only the signature, in blue, is freehand. It reads:

Dear Mom, Dad and Zoë:

I have made several changes in my life recently. I've decided to resign from OMI, from the priesthood and give up my position in Tondoro. I have found a new and very compelling spiritual calling. I am going to follow it. I cannot be burdened by family obligations. For this reason, I am cutting all ties with you. Please do not pursue me or try to contact me. I'm thankful for all you've given me, but the time has come to move on. I will not speak to you again in this life. God bless.

Evan

After they've gone through the list on the spreadsheet and exhausted the to-do list, the women sit at the kitchen table, silent and dejected, nursing their glasses of wine. After a sip Gwen finally speaks.

"We've been dancing around the central issue. Somebody's going to have to find this son of a bitch, and get him to say what he did to Sarah. That's not gonna be easy, not gonna be cheap, and probably not gonna be legal."

"Who are we going to send? Who's going to want to go after him, after she never came back?"

Gwen sighs. She runs her finger along the rim of her glass. "Let's not beat around the bush. I think we hire somebody to hit him."

"You're drunk, Gwen."

"Tell me you haven't thought of it."

"I'm not out for revenge."

Gwen scoffs. "Speak for yourself. *I* certainly am! If he killed Sarah, I want him to pay for that. Especially if the authorities won't help."

Zoë shakes her head. "I don't think that way. I know you're hurt and angry—"

"Aren't you? He may have killed your brother."

"We don't know that. I refuse to give up hope. You shouldn't give up on Sarah."

"I have hope. That doesn't mean I'm not realistic."

"We don't even know what this man's real name is. I think we should stay focused on finding out what really happened."

Gwen clearly does not agree, but she doesn't argue. The women sit in silence. Zoë finally takes a sip from her wine glass. The awkwardness of the moment is palpable.

A few moments later sounds come from the front room, the squeak-slam of the storm door followed by the front door opening. The entryway is visible from the table where Gwen and Zoë sit. Vincent steps inside. He is tall, lanky and still in that awkward phase of adolescence, though at 16 he is starting to resemble a man. He has broad dark eyebrows and fleshy lips. His eyes are narrow slits, and his cheeks are dotted with acne. His teeth are sheathed in gleaming braces. He barely waits before the door is closed to begin stripping the red polo shirt, emblazoned with the logo of Regal Cinemas, off his knobby shoulders.

"Hello, Vincent." Gwen doesn't turn to look at her son, who pauses in the entryway at the sound of her voice.

"Hi, Mom. Hi, Zoë."

"Zoë's staying with us for the weekend again, so keep your stereo or your video games or whatever on low volume."

"Okay." A few moments later, after he's kicked off his shoes, Vincent disappears into a bedroom down the short hallway.

Gwen reaches for her wine glass again. With a twitch of her head, she motions slightly in the direction Vincent went. "Talk about someone who wants revenge." She drinks. Zoë says nothing.

Ten days later Zoë Tyler-Petrick is back home in Chicago; the new batch of letters and phone calls they agreed upon during her visit to Grand Rapids have gone out. On a Tuesday afternoon, an hour before her shift ends at Helen Van Cordt Children's Hospital, Gwen Carrigan calls in to check her voice mail and finds a message, left 20 minutes ago, marked urgent.

"Hi, Gwen, it's Zoë. Please call me as soon as you can. Better make it my cell phone, I'll keep it on. I got some new info just today. Not about Sarah. About *him*. Call me."

She does not call before her shift is over, but she drives home from the hospital faster than usual, cursing at every stoplight and traffic slowdown. When she reaches the house at Juneberry Avenue, she doesn't change out of her scrubs, and does not stop to feed Cracker. The bulldog circles her feet expectantly as she reaches for the kitchen phone.

"Hello? Oh, Gwen, it's you."

"What have you got?"

"A line on him. He's back in the country. Or at least he's been back."

"Where?"

"There's a company recently registered with the Secretary of State of Massachusetts. It's called OFC, Oceans For Christ. It's a foreign company but its U.S. headquarters is in Woods Hole, Massachusetts. Chief executive officer is Evan Tyler."

"Oceans For Christ? I've never heard of it."

"Neither had I, until today. Some automatic alert triggered on my search browser and it brought up the web page for this company which apparently just went online. Gwen, it's him. The company is headquartered in South Africa, right next door to you-know-where. OFC is some kind of school for troubled teens."

"A school?"

"I've got it up on my laptop right now. It's some kind of boot camp program, but it's at sea. They hold it on board a sailing ship called the *Global Redeemer*. Web site has a bio of Father Evan Tyler. That's what triggered my search alert. Ordained priest, Chicago Theological Union, St. Ambrose Parish in Tondoro, Namibia. That's what it lists as his credentials."

"Is there a photo?"

"Same one that was on the St. Ambrose site for years. If you know Evan well, you can tell it's not him, but it looks enough like him that you sound like Oliver

Stone explaining JFK photos if you try to point out what's different."

Gwen sighs. "All right. What do we do?"

"I don't know. I want you to see everything I've got. I'll email it to you in a couple of minutes. Read it all and we'll talk."

Gwen spends that evening on her laptop computer, reading the Oceans For Christ website and the other assorted press mentions that Zoë has managed to collect. There aren't many: an article on a website about teen boot camps, an advertisement that ran in a newspaper in Woods Hole, Massachusetts, and OFC's own promotional literature. There are lavish photos of the *Global Redeemer* and many pictures taken at the Cape Town quay by Evan Tyler, the day he hosted the kids he paid with Ratanga Junction tickets.

There's also a section of the site called *"Testimonials."* One shows two photos, before and after, of a curly-headed lad about 16. In one, taken at a party, he holds a bottle of beer and has a cigarette dangling from his lips. In the other, a professional studio shot, the same boy glows and smiles wearing a suit and tie.

TESTIMONIAL: LUCAS WEYRENGA

"I spent my Year 10 in school getting drunk and high. I was arrested three times. I was about to be sent to reform school. I'm sure I would've ended up in prison. After two summer tours with OFC, I've turned my life around. Father Tyler opened me up to His love and the forgiveness of the Lord. I couldn't have done it without

OFC. Thank you, Jesus, and thank you, Oceans For Christ!"

(LUCAS'S MOTHER): "We were very skeptical of OFC when we first heard about it. But we're believers now. When Lucas came home after his first tour, he was like a new person. Kind, considerate and conscientious. I'm so happy to have my son back! All he could say was, 'When can I go back?'"

Still at her desk, Gwen calls Zoë Tyler-Petrick. Without any antecedent she says, "One of us has to go there, to Woods Hole. Confront this guy."

"We can't be hasty, Gwen. It may be harder to find him than you think. Woods Hole is just the ship's port of call, or, I don't know what you call it, port of registry or whatever. This thing is a ship, it's on a ship. He probably did that so it's harder to track him down, the authorities or process servers or whatever."

"Yeah, but he's obviously recruiting kids in Massachusetts, so he has some presence there."

"I can't go. All he has to do is find out my name and he'll be onto us. He's got to be expecting someone to come after Sarah."

"He probably doesn't know *me*."

"We have no idea what he knows. He obviously had access to Evan's private information—ID, bank accounts, probably lots of personal information. And he might have learned a lot about Sarah. We can't assume he won't know you. Besides, what would you do? Corner him and ask him pretty-please to tell you who he is and what happened to Evan and Sarah?"

"Well, we have to do *something.* If nothing else, we have to get some information on him."

"I certainly agree with that."

The conversation continues for a while; it does not end in any decision or resolution. What Gwen Carrigan does not know is that it—or at least her half of it—has been overheard. Vincent spends most of his time, when he's not at work at the cinema, in his room playing video games. Long ago, their noise was declared by his mother distracting enough that he was obliged to play while wearing headphones. As a result, however, she doesn't know when he's playing or not. There is a cordless phone in his bedroom that displays caller ID. He has been listening, perched at the top of the stairs, quiet and unmoving. When his mother hangs up, Vincent creeps back into his room and puts on his gaming headphones, but before he dives back into *Halo* he takes an atlas from a shelf of haphazardly-stacked books and looks up where Woods Hole is.

The next afternoon, Vincent is off work at the cinema earlier than usual, and returns home more than an hour before the end of his mother's hospital shift. Her laptop remains on the dining room table, just where she closed and left it last night. This is the era before computers had default settings where a user had to enter a password before unlocking the system; in any event Gwen probably wouldn't have bothered for her home computer.

He is able to see everything she was looking at the previous night: Zoë's email, the browser links, and the entire Oceans For Christ website. Vincent reads it all, chin in hand, elbow on the table, slowly scrolling through the digital dope on the murderer of the person he considered to be his mother.

Chapter 19: Gwen & Vincent

Unlike the Van Cordts, who were already wealthy by the end of the '60s, or the Tylers, who were solidly middle class, Patricia Gwendolyn Carrigan grew up in a version of Grand Rapids so different from theirs it is difficult to believe it occupied the same physical space. She didn't know comfortable suburban houses or backyards. Her mother, Ellen—a single mother, as her daughter later would be—moved on average every 18 months, usually from one low-rent apartment to another, sometimes into or out of her own parents' home. Ellen Carrigan did not have anything resembling a career. She waited tables, worked at a laundromat and a supermarket, and once as a secretary at a car dealership. Patricia's father, a construction worker named Ben Franko, deserted his pregnant girlfriend after living with her only a few months. She was 16, he 18. This was not so far from the pattern Patricia's own life might have taken, and almost did.

Rosanna, Ellen's mother, at least took an interest in the child and did her best to help raise her. Ellen was not disinterested, to be sure; merely exhausted. Being raised in part by a grandmother, Patricia would later say, was both a blessing and a curse. Rosanna was no substitute for an involved father. But things certainly could have been worse.

Patricia grew up troubled and surly. In 1980, age 13, she wore ripped Ramones T-shirts to school and had a shock of her hair dyed green, a look some years ahead of the time it would become trendy in the wealthier suburban schools. That same age was when she had her first taste of Wild Turkey and her first drag on a marijuana cigarette. It seems impossible to believe she didn't know by this age that she was a lesbian, but she certainly never told anyone until years later. Booze, drugs and partying were simply occupational hazards of being that age in the crowd she ran with.

She lost her virginity with a boy named Matt Laramie at age 15 in a grimy Dodge Monaco parked in the lot of a mall where kids sometimes went to do such things. Matt was three years older and was Patricia's principal supplier of weed. For a brief time, she acted as though she was his girlfriend, but that phase didn't last long. What she principally wanted from him was marijuana, and what he wanted from her was sex. Eventually it became a bad trade, and on a final time in the Monaco, parked at the edge of the mall lot beneath the trees, she told him no. He forced himself on her, then opened the car door and pushed her out onto the asphalt, clutching her jeans, panties and shoes.

A few weeks later her period was late. Instead of telling her mother, Patricia told her grandmother.

Eventually Ellen did know, but there wasn't much she could do. Every penny she earned in tips or starvation wages went to food, rent or bills. Rosanna—her husband, Patricia's grandfather, had been dead several years—dipped into her own meager savings and set aside part of her Social Security to pay for an abortion. There was a complication and Patricia was sick for two weeks. Her mother thought it prudent for her to change high schools yet again. Patricia would later tell others, including Sarah Brinson, that the abortion her grandmother paid for saved her from the grinding life of poverty to which a teenage pregnancy had sentenced her mother.

One further incident from her childhood is worth relating. That same summer, 1980, that she began running with the boozers and stoners, she happened to be at a carnival in Grand Rapids with her friend Simone, who was dating one of the ride operators. Walking by a concession stand, not looking where he was going, an 8-year-old boy crashed into her with a full cup of Coke; it splashed down Patricia's front. She gave him a tongue-lashing and shouted, "I'm gonna kill you, you little shit!" The blond boy scampered away. She never saw him again. She forgot this incident a few months later. As adults neither of them would remember encountering each other, but the boy who'd spilled Coke on her at the carnival was Evan Tyler.

The rape and the abortion had a profound effect on Patricia Carrigan's life. They were terrifying near misses with a future she did not want. Starting over at a new school where no one knew her—Union High—offered her an opportunity to change things. She began studying and applying herself. She dressed differently. She even began using her middle name, Gwen; as an adult she would legally switch her first and middle names. She had no contact with her previous friends. Slowly, she became a different person.

Two months before Gwen's 1985 high school graduation, Ellen Carrigan was diagnosed with breast cancer. She had no health insurance at the job she was working at that time, and thus had avoided seeing a doctor until she began feeling wretched. It had already metastasized. She died on the 4th of July, age 35. Gwen was in shock for several weeks. By then, she was living with her grandmother. After a period of mourning (and heavy drinking), she enrolled at Grand Rapids Community College. She told the college's career counselor that she wanted to work in health care so that she could be reasonably assured to have health insurance. But there was no money, of course, for traditional college, much less medical or even nursing school. She chose a vocational program to become a radiology technician. This was largely a strategic choice: the college offered it, and she could get a decent job right after certification.

Gwen, who probably believed at this time that she was a lesbian, seems to have been surprised to meet a man to whom she was attracted. In any event, there doesn't seem to have been any artifice about her relationship with Jeremy Truax, another student at GRCC. He was a lanky, dark-haired, doe-eyed lad with a wispy mustache and a kind smile. When they met during

Gwen's first term, they became inseparable. He was also in a vocational program, auto mechanics. They liked and even loved each other, but did not plan, at least at first, to have a long-term attachment. But Gwen found herself pregnant again, and emphatically did not want to have another abortion.

Shortly after the discovery of her pregnancy, Jeremy dropped out of GRCC and took an entry-level auto mechanic job. Both he and Gwen's grandmother insisted that she stay in school and finish her tech program. She took her final exams while nearly seven months pregnant. She and Jeremy were married in March, but there was no ceremony or celebration to it. They did not even live together at first; he lived in an apartment with his brother, and she was still living at Rosanna's house. Vincent was born in June, a few weeks after finals. He was a month premature.

For a few years, the young family managed. They did eventually move into an apartment of their own. Gwen was conscientious and attentive to Vincent, and also to her studies. Jeremy wasn't as focused, though he did spend time with his son, and did what he could to be a good father. He was susceptible to drinking binges, however, and in a town founded on and famous for pyramid schemes—Streamline and its many imitators—he also tended to fall for get-rich-quick cons. He worked several successive mechanic jobs at various garages, but the family wasn't really stable until Gwen secured her first radiology tech job at Mercy Health St. Mary's Hospital.

In 1990, Jeremy Truax was hooked by the latest of Grand Rapids's shady enterprises, a company called ReJu that sold dodgy anti-aging cream through means of wildly exaggerated claims about its powers. ReJu was started by a disgruntled ex-Streamline distributor who was burning to get revenge on the Van Cordt family for some long-ago slight. Truax quit his mechanic's job and even sold the classic car he'd been restoring, a 1953 Cadillac Series 75, which he'd said was "Vincent's college fund," to buy ReJu inventory. Six months later, the FTC banned most of ReJu's advertising and the company was consumed by lawsuits. Unemployed now, Jeremy hit the bottle hard.

At about the same time of Jeremy's decline, Gwen rediscovered her lesbian side. She began having an affair with a nurse at Mercy Hospital, Christina Kirk, six years older. Christina helped Gwen work through her years-old trauma from the rape and her troubled childhood. She also sounded the alarm about Jeremy, especially when, one rainy night, he hit Gwen. "Get out," Christina told her. "Take Vincent and leave, now."

Gwen did not listen to this advice. She stuck it out for several more months, trying to validate four years of more or less unhappy marriage. There were several more abuse episodes; Jeremy was eventually charged with battery. On another rainy night, Gwen finally did take her lover's advice. She brought Vincent, now a toddler, to Christina's apartment. The next day she both filed for divorce and confessed to Jeremy that she was a lesbian.

Jeremy had been twitchy and unreliable before, but now he became dangerous and unhinged. He left bizarre messages—some threatening, some groveling, some pornographic—on Christina Kirk's answering machine and Gwen's voice mail at work. He staked out the hospital to shout at her in the parking lot as she walked to her car after her shifts were over. He once abducted Vincent from his day care, an episode that ended with the police being called and Gwen as frantic as she'd ever been. A string of court dates began to appear on the big calendar tacked to the wall of the kitchen in Christina's and Gwen's apartment. Some of the many restraining orders she filed against him worked, but Jeremy was arrested twice for violating their terms. Vincent once woke up from a screaming nightmare and said, "I dreamed that Daddy got me!" This was the lowest time of Gwen Carrigan's life up until that point.

Then it abruptly stopped. For one blessed weekend in April 1992, the phone did not ring and Gwen was not told about someplace Jeremy had been seen, or a threatening note he left for one of her friends or at the hospital. After several days passed it seemed that no one had seen Jeremy Truax at all.

On a Tuesday afternoon his car was found at the bottom of a drainage ditch leading into the Grand River. The autopsy showed he was drunk and on drugs, and apparently drove his car right off the overpass into the river. A .38 revolver was found in the glove box but had not been fired. There was talk of suicide but it was officially classified an accident. Gwen told both Christina then and Sarah Brinson later that she was sure he'd bought the gun with the initial plan to use it to kill both her and Vincent. Whether it was a drunken accident or a deliberate suicide, Gwen and her child had been delivered from calamity.

* * *

Vincent was a boy who grew up in the company of strong women, and, dreading and fearing his father at such a young age, did not generally connect with male authority figures. By the time he turned ten, in the summer of 1996, things were very much more tranquil for the family. Gwen had by now left Mercy St. Mary's for a position at Helen Van Cordt Children's Hospital. His surname (and his mother's) had gone from Truax, to briefly Truax-Carrigan, and eventually just Carrigan. He had some early childhood memories of Christina Kirk, but she wasn't a mother figure to him, and in any event she went away when Gwen's relationship with her petered out. Then there was that fateful meeting at the dog park between Gwen and Sarah Brinson, which also happened in the summer of 1996.

Gwen was fond of telling a joke: "What does a lesbian bring on a second date? A U-Haul." It was a joke, but it was almost literally true in the case of Gwen's and Sarah's relationship. By the end of the summer Gwen and Vincent were living in a Grand Rapids apartment with Sarah Brinson, but that lasted less than a year, and together, the women bought the house on Juneberry Avenue. Two women, two dogs and a boy: by all appearances it was a stable and gratifying situation.

Sarah rubbed off on Vincent in subtle and unsubtle ways. He always seemed more like her, the mother to whom he was biologically unrelated, than like Gwen. He was fascinated by her stories of the military, the Gulf War, and her travels abroad. Sarah gave him logic puzzles to train his mind. One of them was: "A woman is laying on a bed, and she's dead. There's a puddle of sticky purple liquid and two small sticks next to her.

What happened?" Vincent knew immediately: "Poisoned popsicle."

In middle and high school he flirted dubiously with sports, soccer first, then lacrosse, but Vincent was more interested in video games than field games. His bedroom was cluttered with video game DVD boxes, Agatha Christie and Len Deighton novels, and horror movie memorabilia like plastic figurines from Todd McFarlane's Spawn series. In tenth grade—the year Sarah went to Africa on a PI job and did not return—Vincent liked a girl in his class, Hope, but they had no formal relationship; she seemed to treat him as a Platonic friend. He had more friends who were girls than boys. One of them, Heather, got him a job at a Regal Cinema at a local mall for the summer. He had never really processed his grief about Sarah, and neither had Gwen. It was difficult to do with such little closure, not knowing whether she might still be alive. From the Namibian police to the U.S. State Department, the world seemed indifferent to whatever had happened to Sarah Brinson.

The manager at RiverTown Crossings Regal Cinemas, Duane, a man in his late 20s, sees himself more as a friend to the employees—mostly teenagers—under him than a boss, so he sets an informal tone for the crew. For this reason, Duane's office is often open and accessible even when he's not there, and employees sometimes use it to make private phone calls. On a Thursday afternoon in early August, Vincent closes the door, which is unusual, sits down at his boss's desk, and takes a piece of paper from his pocket. It's wrapped around a credit card, which drops to the desk when he unfolds the paper. After staring at the phone for a while, whispering rehearsed words under his breath—some of them are written on the paper—he picks up the phone and punches in a number.

He does not know this, but Oceans For Christ's offices share a small office space in Woods Hole, where the clients, most very small or absentee businesses, rent the services of a mail drop, an accountant, and a telephone receptionist. The woman who answers the phone—Angela Carranza—fields calls all day for nearly a dozen clients; her contact with anyone who actually works with Evan Tyler's organization is minimal. But when the line lights up with a particular numerical code, she picks up the call with a crisp, pre-scripted greeting: "Hello, and God bless you. This is Oceans For Christ, how can we help you?"

Vincent, sitting in Duane's chair, lowers his voice by an octave or so. "Um, yes, hello. My name is John Carrigan. I'm thinking of sending my son to your school. But I got some questions."

"Of course. How old is your son?"

"He's sixteen."

"And why do you think he'd be a good candidate for our program?"

"He's been screwing up real bad lately. He got arrested a couple weeks ago. I found pot in his backpack. He got fired from his job. He got a girl pregnant. He's about to be expelled from school. I want to send him to some place where he'll, you know, shape up."

"That does sound like he's a lot to handle. Are you here in the area, Mr. Carrigan?"

"No, that was one of my questions. We live in Michigan. If I put my son on a bus, like a Greyhound or something, and sent him there, could somebody pick him up?"

Angela Carranza working from a script of responses, coded with colored tags in a small binder notebook. She scans the index on the first page but there's nothing specifically responsive to this question.

"Well, um, we don't, uh—" One of the notes in the binder, written by Marcus Holcomb, reads, *Accept any student from any area. Work out enrollment details. Be flexible.* "That's not really regular, but we might be able to work something out."

Vincent has his own script, written on the paper; it's only a few words scribbled in ball-point ink. He is nervous, apparently. Beads of sweat are popping out on his forehead. His notes include one entry, *DATES?*

"Well, that's great. Um, when do you, um, the next—well, term or whatever you call it?"

"The *Global Redeemer* will be leaving Woods Hole for the first part of fall semester on August 23rd, sir."

"Well, um, thank you, that's just great. Can I sign my son up over the phone?"

"I can take his information, yes."

Another word is written on his note sheet: *MONEY?* "How much does the program cost?"

"Four thousand for the semester. We can arrange a payment plan, if you like."

Angela Carranza's script reads: *Get payment up front if at all possible. Most important thing is enrollment!*

"That's, uh, fine. Can I pay all at once?"

"Sure! Can I have your credit card number, please?"

With quivering hand he picks up the credit card. It has Gwen's name embossed on it. "This is my wife's card, is that OK?"

"Sure. What's the number?"

He reads it off. The receptionist types it into her computer. The charge goes through.

"Okay, I think we're all set. Can I get your son's details, please?"

Vincent's sigh of relief is audible, even on the other end of the line in Woods Hole. "That's great. My son's name is Vincent Carrigan. He's in the tenth grade."

Chapter 20: Windhoek

Giuseppe Colvino's quest begins in Rome. Within a few days of the meeting with Bishop Vitacchi, he's assembled a dossier on Evan Tyler containing the most basic information that can be gleaned from public records and the Archdiocese of Grand Rapids. Colvino knows Tyler's birthdate, approximate height and weight, his educational history, and the home address of his family in Grand Rapids. He has seen the yearbook of Sacred Heart Academy (1990) and the official announcements of Tyler's graduation from Catholic Theological Union and his ordination as a priest. He's even received a faxed copy of Tyler's driver's license, issued in Michigan in 1997. But he has not spoken to anyone who knew Tyler.

This preliminary research is necessary, but not illuminating.

He does not tell his wife that he's going to Africa until two days before his departure. Colvino and Melina are having breakfast on the terrace of their house in the hills above Civitavecchia. The terrace faces southwest, offering a view of the sparkling Mediterranean beyond the town and its harbor. She is wearing only a baggy white bathrobe. He broaches the subject casually, before digging into his grapefruit: "I have to go away the day after tomorrow on a job. I'm not sure how long I'll be gone."

"Where this time? London again?"

"A bit farther away than that. Namibia."

"Where is that?"

"Southwestern Africa."

"That is quite a way."

She does not inquire beyond this. Colvino travels often in his job, but the trips are usually short, three days at most, and almost always to other European banking centers: London, Zurich, Hamburg. The year before, he made two trips to New York City and one to the Cayman Islands, but that was as much a vacation as a business trip. Colvino rarely volunteers any details about his work. He tells her merely that he'll call her when it becomes clearer when he might be back. When he leaves for the airport, two days later, she doesn't say goodbye. She's in her study, working on fashion drawings. Discarded designs litter the floor beneath her drafting table. Out the broad windows, the Mediterranean glitters on.

The trip does not begin well. He has booked Qatar Airways and flies from Rome to Doha, Qatar, but mechanical failures of his connecting flight to Windhoek strand him in Qatar for a day and a half. When he finally makes it to Windhoek, Colvino is jet-lagged and visibly ill, blowing his reddened nose into a handkerchief. He stays two days at the Weinberg Hotel in Windhoek, popping cold medicine and ordering jugs of tea from room service. The next morning, he's still on the mend when he reserves an SUV from a rental car agency in the capital and starts the long drive northward through the bush toward Rundu, and eventually Tondoro. Unwittingly, his journey is an eerie reenactment of Sarah Brinson's, six months before. When he arrives in Tondoro, he still has never heard her name.

"The Lord has answered our prayers. You're from the Vatican Bank, aren't you? I've been writing letters to Rome for months. No one ever answered. Why didn't you call ahead and let us know you were coming?"

The man who says this to Giuseppe Colvino, in English, is slight and short, with dark eyes. Father Moctesuma Suarez, formerly a parish priest in his hometown of Papantla, Mexico, is in his mid-30s and has a nervous energy, as if he is forever twitching or quivering, though in reality he is not. Colvino meets him within minutes or arriving at St. Ambrose Parish. It is now deep winter in the Okovango region. The river has had its annual swelling, and the greenery around its banks has begun to retreat. The year's eco-tourists have come and gone.

"In my line of work," Colvino tells him, "it's best not to announce one's presence ahead of time." He does not correct Suarez's misconception that he works for the Vatican Bank. "I've read your letters. I've come for more information. You have records, more than the copies you sent to Rome?"

They are walking along the pathway next to the parish church that Evan Tyler helped to rebuild. "I have everything that was left to me. What I sent to Rome were representative examples. There is more, much more, but it's very confusing. Many records are missing or otherwise incomplete."

"Surely you can request duplicate records from the bank."

"Father Tyler closed the bank account the parish was using, just before he departed, and opened a new one. The old bank has been reluctant to share anything with me."

"What do you know about Father Tyler?"

"Just that he's held in regard here second only to a certain carpenter from Nazareth. I don't even believe the Holy Father himself would get such a reception as Father Tyler would if he returned to this town. It's uncanny, how much everybody talks about him. I never met him in person."

Colvino has arrived in the late afternoon, and while Suarez shows him the office and its records, he suggests they leave the deep dive until tomorrow. Just as there was the night Sarah Brinson arrived, the employees of St. Ambrose Parish and several locals who are fixtures at the mission host a dinner for the guest. Father Ubate was not replaced, though his grave on the premises is garlanded with flowers every Sunday. Father Hague moved up into his position as leader of the parish.

During dinner, Hague remarks, "We certainly have had many visitors this year. In Tondoro, for years we see only the same faces, but this year is different. An American visitor and an Italian. Perhaps Tondoro will make it on the map after all."

It is a few moments before Colvino catches the reference. "You had another American visitor, earlier this year?"

"Yes, the woman. And she was also searching for an American, though none of us had seen him."

"Who was this woman, this American?" Colvino looks across the table at Father Suarez, who merely shrugs.

"What was her name, Joe? Do you remember? It began with a B."

Joe Kimbeta remembers: "Brinson. Sarah Brinson."

Colvino regards everyone around the table with a penetrating stare. "Who was she? Tell me everything about her."

So this is how Giuseppe Colvino learns of Sarah Brinson's visit nearly six months ago. Hague never spoke to the Namibian police when they looked for her, but he knows they were here.

"Let me be sure I understand. An American private investigator came here in February, disappeared after leaving this town, and has not been seen since?"

"I heard she disappeared from Rundu," says Joe Kimbeta. "Not from Tondoro."

"How soon did this happen before Father Tyler's departure?"

"Two weeks," says Hague.

Colvino now fixes his stare upon Father Suarez. "That was not in your letters to the Vatican."

"Father Tyler was the best thing that ever happened to Tondoro," says another woman at the table, Mrs. Kaimbi. Several others at the table echo this sentiment almost reflexively, as if repeating a shibboleth that has been deeply imprinted into their psyches.

After the dinner breaks up, Colvino takes Suarez aside. "Father, I'm beginning to see what you meant when you said earlier that the people of the town idolize Father Tyler. It's almost like he brainwashed them."

Suarez sighs. "*Now* you see what I've been dealing with? Yes, it's exactly like that. All they talk about is the wonderful things he did here and how he was the best thing that ever happened to this town. No one trusts me, because I don't do things the way he did, and I don't go singing his praises morning and night."

"Do you get the sense that he was a manipulative man, that he played mind games with the people here?"

"I think that is an understatement, to be honest."

"Is there anyone in Tondoro who *doesn't* think Evan Tyler was a hero?"

Suarez flashes only a glance into Colvino's eyes. "Yes, there is someone. I'll take you to her in the morning."

The Mbwele residence is a modest house of gray cinder blocks, with a metal roof and a large dusty yard surrounded by a stone fence. Anika Mbwele, who meets them outside the house, is shy and retiring. She speaks in short, clipped sentences. She has trouble understanding English in Colvino's Italian accent, so Father Suarez, who went to seminary in Texas, sometimes repeats his questions to her. An invisible veil seems to drop over her face when he asks her about Father Evan Tyler.

"I am a good Christian. I do not harbor hate in my heart. But I have very strong feelings about Father Tyler. He is a thief."

"What did he steal?"

She looks deeply into his eyes. "My son."

"I don't understand. How did he do that?"

Anika brings him inside the house. She takes him to a door that is slightly ajar, but motions to Colvino with a finger across her lips. There is a figure inside the adjoining room. Moses Mbwele sits on the edge of a narrow bed. He's dressed in jeans, a black button-up shirt and patent leather shoes. He is also wearing a secondhand marine life jacket, very old and worn, its bright orange fabric fading and its straps tattered. A closed suitcase sits on the bed and there is a Bible on top of it. Rosary beads hang from between Moses's intertwined fingers. He stares at the window with unseeing eyes, murmuring something inaudible to himself. He rocks softly back and forth.

The mother seems to have to screw up her courage before swinging the door open farther and speaking to him. "Moses. *Moses!* We have a visitor. I'd like you to meet him."

The young man's head turns. He surveys her, Colvino and Suarez standing behind him.

"Have you brought a letter?"

"What?"

"A letter. Have you brought a letter for me?"

"I'm sorry, I don't have any letters."

Moses is silent for a moment. When he next speaks his voice is soft but harsh: "Leave me alone."

The visitors retreat to a patio that is little more than a few metal chairs beneath a nylon awning that flaps gently in the breeze. Anika Mbwele serves them coffee but drinks none herself. She does not speak. Father Suarez, perhaps sensing the awkwardness of the silence, finally offers explanation.

"Moses was Father Tyler's star student at the parish school and something of his assistant. He was also extremely devoted to him. He stopped attending school right when he left."

"I see." Colvino drinks from a coffee mug that is chipped on its rim. "What was he doing in there? I couldn't make out what he was saying."

The mother finally speaks up. "He was praying. He just sits there, praying to himself and to God, all day long. He's waiting for word from Father Tyler. That's why he asked you if you had a letter. He waits for the mail all the time, hoping there will be a letter from him. Every time the mail comes and there's nothing, he becomes even sadder. Sometimes he cries."

Suarez says: "Father Tyler evidently made some kind of promise to him. I don't fully understand what happened."

"Father Tyler promised that he would send for Moses to come join him at his new ministry. He's supposed to take him away with him and they will go around the world together spreading the gospel. Moses says he has to be ready as soon as word comes, and he still thinks it will at any moment. That's why he keeps that suitcase packed. He's been waiting months now. It has affected his mind."

"Why the life jacket?" Suarez must repeat Colvino's question to Anika.

"Tyler's new ministry is supposed to be aboard a ship."

"A *ship?*"

She nods.

"Where is he supposed to meet the ship?"

"Moses doesn't know. Thank the Lord he doesn't know. If he did, he would have run away there long ago."

More to Suarez than to Anika Colvino asks: "Is there anything that can be done for him? A doctor, a psychologist?"

"The nearest one is in Rundu," says the priest.

Annika shakes her head. "He won't go. He barely leaves that room, and then only to eat."

"Maybe something can be done."

They finish their coffee in silence. The air of sadness and resignation that cloaks the Mbwele home is impenetrable.

Once back at the parish, Colvino goes truly to work. He spends the day cloistered with Father Suarez in the business office. Piles of documents and bank records, carefully sorted by Colvino, start on the desk, but soon begin to grow on the floor as well.

Colvino asks a thousand questions. "What is this tax bill for? Did the Tondoro Catholic Community Fund receive a $9,000 donation in March of 2000? Where did it come from? Here's another transfer to that entity,

Oceans For Christ, Ltd.—is that Tyler's new ministry? What is GTSM, Ltd.? Have you ever heard of that entity? Here are more hotel bills. Father Tyler stayed at hotels in Windhoek on six different occasions and charged them back to the parish. What's the official policy on that?"

"I don't know," or "That all happened before I got here," are Suarez' most common responses. Still, Colvino never grows short with him. He continues to make notes in a small notebook and on his laptop computer.

Colvino finds one page in the records which he compares to documents from two separate piles, in front of which he sits on the office floor. He peers over his reading glasses at Suarez.

"TCCF's old bank, the account Tyler closed in March, was at Bank of Namibia, yes? And the new one, the one you use now and that he opened, is at Bank Windhoek, yes?"

"Yes, that's right."

Colvino holds up the statement. "This is from neither of those. This statement is from FNB Bank, September 2001. There's no other statement from this bank in the whole bundle. Has the parish ever done business with FNB Bank, to your knowledge?"

Suarez shrugs. "No. But again, before my time. What does it mean?"

"Well, look at the balance." Colvino hands the page to Suarez.

"Two hundred and eighty thousand dollars. American."

"Did you know the parish ever had that much money?"

"No."

"There was a third account. One whose existence Tyler tried to conceal. Notice all the records of the other accounts have missing pages or missing months. Probably because they showed transfers going into or out of *this* account. Tyler burned or shredded every paper that referred to this account, and he scrambled the rest because he knew Father Ubate was too daft to sort through it and his successor—you—wouldn't have the knowledge to make sense of it. But he missed this page. You see? He missed *this* page. He doesn't make mistakes often, but he made one here."

Suarez looks at it, but hands the page back to Colvino without saying anything.

The Italian takes off his reading glasses, puts them in a small case and hauls himself to his feet.

"Father, I'd like to use your telephone, please. It will be a long distance call."

Two days later, Colvino is ushered into an office in a glass-enclosed low-rise tower in downtown Windhoek. Benjamin Nyambe is in his late thirties, well-dressed, in a gray suit and yellow tie and the desk across which he sits from Colvino is clean and uncluttered. He offers the Italian walnuts from a bowl, but he declines; Nyambe cracks one himself with a silver nutcracker and tears at the meats with his thin fingers as he listens to Colvino.

"Well, Mr. Colvino," says Nyambe in his crisply-accented English, "I would certainly like to help you and the Vatican Bank, but I'm afraid there is not much I can do. We cannot disclose financial information of a customer, or a former customer, to a third party without that party's permission, or a court order."

"Mr. Nyambe, I just showed you the letter, signed by Fathers Suarez and Hague, directing you to release this information to me. You have it in your hand. That's the permission of the customer, isn't it?"

Nyambe sets the letter down on his desktop and pushes it away from him. "The principal on the account was under another name. In any event, the account is no longer active."

"It's an institutional account under the name of Tondoro Catholic Community Fund. Father Suarez speaks for that institution."

"If the names do not match, there is nothing I can do."

"What happens when a corporation changes officers or directors? That must happen all the time. Does that corporation lose access to its accounts for all time when someone changes positions?"

"I'm sorry, I cannot disclose this information to you. It is a rule."

"I've been in the banking business over 25 years and have never encountered a rule like this."

"You've been in the banking business in *Italy*, sir." Nyambe's voice now suddenly has an edge of hostility. "This is Namibia. I'm afraid we don't operate our businesses under European rules here."

"Oh, it's like *that*, is it?"

"Like what? You come here from white Europe and tell Africans what they may do with their money? I understand the Vatican has been operating that way for centuries, but that's not how it works in our country." Nyambe pops a walnut meat into his mouth. It crunches loudly between his teeth. "Now, is there anything else I can do for you?"

Colvino leaves the offices of FNB Bank a few minutes later without further incident, and even without voices raised. A few hours after that, at 6:32 PM, Benjamin Nyambe also leaves the building, walking, briefcase in hand, to his car parked in the lot below. A white SUV, its sides streaked with reddish-tan dust from a recent trip through the bush, is parked on a curb just beyond the FNB Bank lot. There is a dark figure behind the wheel. When Nyambe's car, a 1990 BMW, pulls out of the lot, the dust-streaked SUV comes to life, moves away from the curb and begins to follow.

Exactly two hours later, at 8:32 PM, Benjamin Nyambe is back at the bank building, swiping his electronic access card at the front door. The bank is closed and the lobby empty. Nyambe is still wearing his gray suit and dress shirt, though the tie is gone. The collar of his dress shirt is flecked with blood. His lip is split, still bleeding, and one of his eyes is bruised and swollen nearly shut. He is quivering. Giuseppe Colvino stands behind him. Once the lights on the door mechanism glow green, Colvino opens the door to allow Nyambe to enter. The banker is now walking with a limp, favoring his left leg; his right knee is swelling beneath his suit pants.

They do not go to Nyambe's office, but rather to a computer terminal in one of the work cubicles on the ground floor. Nyambe switches on a banker's lamp at the work station and signs in to the system. He taps on the keyboard and clicks the mouse. He says nothing, just wheels the office chair backwards and aside to allow Colvino access. The Italian snatches a neighboring chair and pulls up to the work station. The glowing screen reflects on his reading glasses.

"What key do I press to print these records?" he asks. Nyambe, still silent, does it for him. A printer in the neighboring cubicle begins spitting out sheets of paper. Colvino, however, is absorbed by something he sees on the screen.

"This is a property transaction. Idowando Ranch Holdings, S.A. That's not a Namibian corporation, is it?"

"S.A. is South Africa." Nyambe's voice is terse and strained.

"They don't happen to have an account with your bank too, do they?"

Nyambe glowers at him through his one un-swollen eye, and then reaches for the computer keyboard.

Chapter 21: Omaruru & Silvermist

Idowando Ranch is located on the outskirts of the town of Omaruru, Namibia, in the scrubby countryside two and a quarter hours' drive northwest of Windhoek. The town lies in the shadow of Mt. Erongo along the banks of a river through which flows nothing but sand. It is a beautiful landscape, but a sad country: Imperial Germany, which used to hold Namibia as a colony, conducted the first genocide of the 20th century here, leaving tens of thousands of Herero, Tama and San people to die of dehydration or to waste away in concentration camps. One such camp was in fact located on the very spot where Idowando Ranch sits. But there is no plaque or marker. The road leading to the property is dusty and unpaved, blocked by a rusty chain drooping between two bollards. A sign hanging from the chain reads, *"PRIVATE PROPERTY—KEEP OUT."*

Giuseppe Colvino, sitting in the driver's seat of the idling dust-flecked SUV, stares at the site first with naked eyes, and then with binoculars. After a while, he parks the car under one of the few trees on the winding road, puts a straw hat on his bald head, and gets out to walk back to the barricaded driveway. He steps across the chain and walks up the driveway. A row of low trees, overgrown and unkempt, shield from the view of the driveway a ranch house that would, if it were properly rehabilitated and maintained, be attractive. It has white stucco walls and a thatch roof, but both are crumbling and badly in need of repair. The yard surrounding the ranch house has shot up in weeds. Some of the windows are covered with plywood. Colvino looks around the house, peering into what windows are un-boarded, but there is not much to see inside except the shadows of big-game trophies collecting dust and cobwebs. This place has been deserted for many years.

There is a back patio. It, too, would be comfortable, if the place were fixed up. There is a large outdoor brick fireplace and a spectacular view of the wild hills beyond, which his map shows are also part of the ranch property. Colvino stands on the deserted patio, listening to the calls of birds and the quiet rustle of the warm

African wind in the trees. At one point, he sees movement on some of the buff-colored hills. Two springboks are barely visible moving off into the bush. Colvino watches them through his binoculars. When they are gone, he walks back round the house, down the driveway to his car, and starts back to the main highway.

Two days later, on Friday, he is in Cape Town. That morning, he walks up to a low-rise office building on a narrow stretch of Jarvis Street, only blocks from the Victoria & Albert waterfront where the *Sea Diamond* once docked. The building is old, but was recently remodeled and covered in white stucco. There are bars on the windows. He waits in a lobby decked out with modern art canvases painted with colorful shapes that vaguely resemble human faces. A receptionist answers a telephone, speaks briefly and then announces: "Mr. Krueger is ready for you, sir. Second floor, first suite on the right."

"Thank you."

Lucien Krueger is a short South African in his fifties with a bushy white beard and a pot belly. He wears an open-necked sport shirt, shorts, and deck shoes. The outer lobby of his office is decorated with photos of sailing vessels and a large map of South Africa dating from the mid-19th century. There are no other people present in the office besides him. "Mr. Colvino? Good to meet you in person. Lucien Kruger, we spoke on the telephone. My! You've come a very long way, haven't you? How was your trip from Italy?"

"I've been in Africa more than a week now, so I'm slowly getting used to it. Beautiful country. I was in Namibia until last night."

"I love Namibia. Truly God's country. I hope someday soon to make it my home. Not only is it much more beautiful than smoggy old Cape Town, but taxes are considerably lower." Krueger punctuates this with an explosive laugh. "Please! Step into my office."

The inner office has the same décor: sailing ships and maps. The view from the barred windows looks up onto Signal Hill. The photos on the wall behind Krueger's desk show him in various adventurous poses: hoisting a swordfish aboard a sailboat, posing with a shouldered shotgun next to an enormous dead wildebeest, sitting in the back of an open Range Rover with a much-younger woman, smiling.

"So!" Krueger, sitting in his office chair, slaps his bare knees. "You are an examiner from the Vatican Bank. To be honest, I expected a call from someone like you. I did *not* expect you to physically come all the way from Rome. What records would you like to see?"

"Why did you expect someone from the Vatican Bank to call you?"

"You're the guarantor of the loan, yes? The transaction *was* extremely irregular—that much is certain. Father Tyler insisted he would handle all the details with the Vatican, but to be honest I didn't entirely trust his reassurances. I figured someone would be following up directly. I'm rather surprised it took this long. In any event, I have nothing to hide, and I'll show you anything you want to see. Financial statements, the books of my businesses, the development plan for the ranch itself, anything. I intend to satisfy the bank completely. Allow me to point out that I've made all my payments in full and on time."

"I'm glad to hear that, but let me be absolutely frank, Mr. Krueger. I'm not interested in you or your businesses. I'm not really that interested in Idowando Ranch except to the extent it fits into the larger picture. I'm investigating the man you made the deal with, Father Evan Tyler. We believe he defrauded the Vatican Bank, and he also defrauded you. We were never involved. We never guaranteed the loan. The assurances he gave you to that effect, and that he gave the bank in Windhoek, were false. The signatures on the guaranty documents were fake. This is why I'm here. Will you help me?"

Krueger's expression changes. Suddenly he looks as though he will be physically ill. His pallor goes green, and his eyes widen slightly. "Fake? It was *fake?*"

"I'm afraid so. The Vatican Bank doesn't get involved in this sort of transaction. Tyler's purpose in involving us seems to have been to facilitate the deal—and obtain an asset you owned that he wanted. If I'm not mistaken, that asset was a sailing ship. Is that right?"

"Yes, the *Sea Diamond.*"

"Would you tell me about the transaction, and about Father Tyler? I want to know everything—how you first met, how the deal came together, everything."

Krueger is quiet for a moment. He looks so despairing that if he broke down in tears it would not be surprising. "Mr. Colvino, I..." He sighs. "I want to help you with that. I really do..."

"If it's any consolation, I'm not after you, and I have no intention of reporting you to authorities. Whatever *you* did in the course of the transaction is immaterial to me. I'm investigating Tyler."

"Yes, but when FNB Namibia finds out the guarantor was fake, they'll declare the loan in default and call it in full. I can't afford that. I'll lose the ranch. This deal was my whole lifeline. It was going to rescue my entire business. Even if you aren't out to get me—and I accept that you aren't—I'm still going to lose everything. Is there *any* possible way you can think of that we can avoid that?"

Both men are silent. Then Colvino says softly: "Do you have a financial statement I could look at?"

Krueger's face brightens. "Right here." He opens a folder on top of the desk—placed as if he was expecting to have to use it—and takes from it a small packet of papers stapled at the corner. Colvino puts on his reading glasses and examines it.

After a few minutes of intensive study he peers over the rims of his glasses. "These numbers for your business, this Gold Horizons Safari—they're accurate?"

"Absolutely. Do you want to talk to my accountant? I can get him on the phone."

Colvino passes the statement back to him. "Not necessary. Why don't you tell me what happened, *all* that happened? If your information is helpful to me, and I have no reason to suspect it won't be, we might be able to work out an arrangement where we may not need to inform FNB Namibia of the full circumstances. I stress, *might*. I need to hear your story first."

"I'll happily tell you everything. Mr. Colvino, I don't know how much of Cape Town you've seen yet, but what would you say if I took you to lunch? I'd be happy to take you to La Colombe. It's literally the finest restaurant in Africa. Overlooking a vineyard. That's a much more civilized place to do business. I can drive you. What do you say?"

Colvino shrugs.

La Colombe is beautiful. Krueger, who knows one of the restaurant's owners, secures a private table on a terrace overlooking a vineyard called Silvermist. With the green rows of grapevines marching across the hills, and misty clouds atop them, it's hard to believe they are so close to the bustling city. Over a dish of fresh tuna steaks in tarragon and wine reduction, freshly-baked bread infused with rosemary, and a wine that seems to glow gold in the glass, Krueger humbly and loquaciously sets out the story. Colvino eats, sips wine, and listens.

"I went into the yacht chartering business in 1985. That's the year I bought the *Sea Diamond*. Oh, she was beautiful then! A real looker, and very fast. There was some money in my wife's family, you see, and she came from a seafaring background. This was, of course, when things were very different here in South Africa. The apartheid era was terrible and unjust—we all knew that —but the rich whites who controlled politics then, descendants of the Boers—I am a descendant of Boers— they threw their money around like there was no tomorrow...and, in fact, there really wasn't...but we did not know that at the time..."

It is nearly 20 minutes before he even gets to the subject of Evan Tyler. By the late 1990s, Krueger's yacht charter business was in severe decline. He had divorced the woman he started it with, and her family's money went away. Krueger had by now a new business, chartering junkets for people on land instead of water, safaris for the burgeoning eco-tourism trade.

"Things were going well, very well. But the yacht business, and particularly the *Sea Diamond*, was a millstone dragging me down. Not only was the maintenance on the ship breaking me, but the negative cash flow on the charter yacht business made me a poor credit risk. Golden Horizons was doing well, but I could only ever operate safaris on rented lands because, without a loan, I could never afford to buy any property of my own. I had my eye on Idowando Ranch for a long time. Years, really. It's a beautiful piece of property—oh, you saw it? So you know. It's in Namibia, which has significantly lower taxes. When it went into foreclosure two years ago, I thought I had an opening. I would sell the *Sea Diamond* and use the proceeds to buy the ranch from the Namibian bank that owned it. Then, recession! My cash flow dwindled, and the banks called my loans. The tax authorities descended on me like a horde of Zulu warriors. The *Sea Diamond* sat on the market for a very long time. Yachts sometimes take years to sell, you know? While she was waiting to sell, I leased her out to a company called V&A Charter Rentals, which used to be a competitor of mine. They used her mostly for training cruises, but there was a little money coming in. Not enough even to cover the docking charges, though.

"Then *he* contacted me—Tyler. It was through the agent who listed the ship. He was searching for a ship, a certain kind of ship, and he wanted to buy it from a South African. I have no idea why. We were in talks for, I don't know, three or four months. Always over the telephone, though. I never met him in person, which I admit does seem strange in retrospect. He wanted a yacht, but *he* had cash-flow problems too. So we worked out this deal..."

Due to Krueger's slow and halting explication, the lunch takes a long time, but it is a pleasant three hours. The sunlight changes and begins slanting over the vineyard, casting long woolly shadows amid the rows of bright green. Krueger orders a second bottle of wine; eventually they crack a third. He grows quite drunk, and ends by groveling.

"So you see, Mr. Colvino, I *need* Idowando Ranch. I'm on my third marriage, and that's not going well. My wife is 20 years younger, and what do I really have to offer her? My son and daughter won't speak to me. After two years of litigation with the South African tax authorities I've fought them to a draw, but they might renew the assault at any time. I knew the deal was shady, the swap of the *Sea Diamond* for Idowando Ranch. To be honest, I suspected Tyler was scamming me, or if not me, someone. But what would you do in my place? You're my age, younger, even. You know that at this age it's too late to start with a new career, especially in this country, where the path out of apartheid has been rocky. If the bank calls the loan—if I lose the ranch—I'm finished. *Finished.* I'm begging you, sir. *Please* don't tell them. Anything you want me to do, I'll do. But let me keep the ranch. You won't regret it. Gold Horizons is profitable—you saw my financial statement. I will make the payments on the mortgage. I guarantee that."

Colvino finishes the wine in his glass. He puts his linen napkin on the wrought-iron table. "Well! This has been quite pleasant. It was nice to be treated to one of South Africa's finest restaurants. I won't trouble you for a ride back to town—can I get a taxi from here? To be honest, you may want to take one yourself."

Krueger, hand around the stem of his wine glass, nods. "Yes. Yes, I suppose so. What are you going to do about...?"

Colvino rises from his chair and takes the leather folio from the other side of the table. He leans down to whisper in Krueger's ear.

"Make the payments. So long as they're made in full and on time, you'll have no difficulty. But if you fail to make them—a dollar short or a day late—you'll receive another visitor from Italy. And that person won't be as charitable as you've convinced *me* to be with your fine wine and hospitality. In fact, he probably won't speak to you at all. You might not even know he's there, because your encounter will end very quickly. Do you understand me?"

"Yes, yes. I understand."

"*In full. On time.* Yes?"

"Yes. Absolutely."

"Very well. Good luck with your business. We're finished here."

That night, Colvino sequesters himself on the terrace of his sea-facing room at the Ellerman House Hotel in Cape Town. Showered and wrapped in a terry-cloth bathrobe, he lies on a deck chair facing out to sea, composing a document on his laptop, which he eventually sends to a secure fax number in Vatican City. It arrives late at night, is printed out and delivered in hard copy to Bishop Leonard Vitacchi at his office in the IOR the following morning. He reads it while sipping coffee.

In part, the memo reads:

My investigation in Africa has, I believe, reached the end of its usefulness. I will be returning to Italy. I have been able to reconstruct a picture of what happened. My preliminary findings indicate that, while no IOR money was directly embezzled in St. Ambrose Parish, fraud was committed that implicates IOR by reputation.

Fr. Evan Tyler ran an extensive, long-term, well-concealed operation to launder money through St. Ambrose Parish. As he had direct and generally sole control of the parish's finances, which he handled in an entity called the Tondoro Catholic Community Fund, he was not subject to oversight from the Missionary Oblates of the Mary Immaculate. From the beginning of Tyler's presence in Tondoro in September, 1998, he began receiving large cash donations for the TCCF. Many of these "donations" came from his (Tyler's) personal bank account in the United States, and from a few other sources that I suspect were merely aliases of Tyler ("Jeffrey Wright" and "Gavin Grove" among them). I will refer to this original source of funds as the "seed money." For reasons I explain later, while I cannot be sure, I suspect the seed money was cash stolen by Tyler from an organized crime entity.

Tyler established several bank accounts in Windhoek to handle TCCM "donations," which ultimately totaled over $280,000 USD and possibly considerably more. Tyler did use TCCF funds to improve St. Ambrose Parish. I saw such improvements firsthand: a renovated church, school building, offices and other infrastructure as well as a medical clinic for the people of Tondoro. Tyler did receive significant legitimate donations mainly by advertising and promoting his prowess as a Catholic fundraiser. However, even the legitimate improvements in the parish were used as vehicles for money laundering. Tyler routinely overpaid contractors and material providers who then refunded excess funds back to TCCF, thus concealing their likely original status as tainted cash.

The most significant transaction in which Tyler engaged was to purchase real property known as Idowando Ranch in Omaruru, Namibia. Using money from the TCCF as a down payment, Tyler (acting in the name of TCCF) obtained a mortgage loan from First National Bank (FNB) of Namibia to purchase the ranch. The property was acquired by a shell company, GTSM, Ltd.

(which stands for Generous Tears of St. Mary's), which FNB was told was owned by the Vatican Bank, and IOR is the guarantor on the mortgage, obviously fraudulent. Immediately after the transfer, GTSM exchanged Idowando Ranch with a private property owner from South Africa, Lucien Krueger, for an oceangoing schooner called the *Sea Diamond*. Krueger, whom I spoke to, seems to have understood that this transaction was fraudulent, but acquiesced due to the desperation of his private financial circumstances.

As part of the deal, Krueger assumed the mortgage on Idowando Ranch. GTSM was liquidated, and the *Sea Diamond*, its only asset, transferred to a non-profit religious organization founded in South Africa by Tyler, Oceans For Christ, Ltd. The Vatican Bank remains (officially) the guarantor on the mortgage now held by Lucien Krueger on Idowando Ranch, which Krueger intends to develop as a safari resort. Krueger is strongly motivated to continue making regular payments on this mortgage. He is desperate to avoid the unwinding of the transaction, which he knows will result in him losing control of Idowando Ranch.

To summarize this transfer succinctly: Evan Tyler laundered at least $280,000 USD through St. Ambrose Parish, then fraudulently obtained a mortgage loan by misrepresenting that he was backed by the Vatican Bank. Using this artifice, Tyler was able to embezzle from St. Ambrose Parish and from Lucien Krueger a sailing ship worth at least $800,000 USD. In essence, Tyler used his laundered funds, and false indicia of involvement by IOR, to steal approximately $520,000 USD, in addition to the $280,000 seed money he already possessed.

There is a slang term used in American video game culture: "level[ing] up," which means a video game player achieving a sufficient number of accomplishments to gain access to the next-highest level of the game where more and bigger prizes are within reach. To employ this analogy, Tyler "leveled up" with his acquisition of the *Sea Diamond*, which boosted his personal net worth by at least $520,000 that he did not earn. He seems to have planned this transaction as sort of an escape hatch. If and when his money laundering scheme was discovered or IOR investigated, he would (and did) simply quit the parish and decamp to the *Sea Diamond* (now rechristened as *Global Redeemer*), which Tyler leased out to a charter tour company until he needed it.

Tyler is also stealing additional monies by defrauding U.S., Namibian and South African tax authorities, as his Oceans For Christ foundation, tax-exempt, has control of this asset, the sailing ship now called the *Global Redeemer*, on which he has paid no taxes.

Tyler is now currently operating the *Global Redeemer* as a floating "reform school for troubled teens." He seems to have a personal interest in psychological manipulation of vulnerable people, particularly boys and young men. As his ship is apparently in international waters much of the time, it is clear that one purpose of stealing this mobile asset was to remain one step ahead of any authorities who may pursue him. Having a group of teenage boys aboard his ship also obviates the need to employ a professional crew.

Given a number of clues I have uncovered, I think there is strong reason to believe that the man who operated this scheme in Tondoro, and who is now operating Oceans For Christ, is using an assumed or appropriated identity. The Evan Rodgers Tyler of Grand Rapids, Michigan, USA who was ordained as a Catholic priest in May 1998 is almost certainly not the same "Evan Tyler" at the center of this case. I am not the first to harbor this suspicion. Last February, an American private investigator, Sarah Brinson, appeared at St. Ambrose parish. She did not disclose her true mission to the people of the parish, but she disappeared shortly after leaving the town, a case Namibian police have not solved, and in fact bungled badly. "Father Tyler" resigned from OMI and fled Tondoro only two weeks later. Sarah Brinson was from Grand Rapids, Michigan. That is not coincidental. She must have been hired by Tyler's real family, who I believe suspect he is not the real Evan Tyler. The perpetrator seems to have realized this; he may have killed her to keep her from reporting back to her clients in Grand Rapids.

This is what I believe happened, most likely in August or September 1998, just before "Father Tyler's" arrival in Namibia: an unknown perpetrator, an American who bears some physical resemblance to Evan Tyler, discovered him, probably during the brief window of time when Tyler was in Rome on his way to his OMI posting in Tondoro. The perpetrator stole his identity and credentials as part of a plan to launder the seed money fund. He also probably murdered the real Tyler. The perpetrator's discovery of Tyler was likely opportunistic. This is why I believe the seed money, however it came into the possession of the perpetrator, belongs to organized crime. Someone was chasing him, and it was not the authorities, or not primarily the authorities. Why would he have gone to such lengths simply to evade police, when he could simply have parked the seed money in Switzerland or the Cayman Islands? The answer can only be that he was more afraid of pursuers who could employ illegal means to track him down, recover the seed money, and kill him.

The perpetrator's discovery of Tyler was, for him, an incredible stroke of luck. Tyler's identity provided him the opportunity both to elude his pursuers and to hide in an obscure location in Africa until well after his pursuers and the authorities gave up trying to find him. Once in Africa, he had literally years to finish laundering the seed money and to organize his eventual escape.

My investigation will now shift to a determination of who the perpetrator is and how he insinuated himself into the orbit of OMI and the Catholic Church. While the decision about what action to take in a strategic sense is yours (or IOR's), I feel it is my job to provide you with all possible information before any action is taken, any authorities are contacted, or before IOR's implication in this matter is made public. I will be returning to Rome shortly, but suggest we have no contact until this phase of my investigation is complete.

Chapter 22: Giuseppe

Giuseppe Marovisio Colvino spoke with authority on matters of banking, financial fraud and organized crime. These three heads of the same hydra had been spitting at him all his life, and to a large extent the animal they were attached to had warmed and comforted him since birth.

Giuseppe's life and family circumstances were deeply shaped by the Second World War, even though he came into the world seven years after it ended. He was born relatively late in the life of his father, Lorenzo, who had been just entering adulthood as Mussolini's *fascisti* caught the country in their iron grip. Lorenzo Colvino joined the Banca Nazionale dell'Agricoltura, headquartered in Milan, the working people's bank that specialized in loans and economic development of Italy's agricultural sector. Lorenzo himself was not a fascist, but he collaborated with the regime, sending to the government information the bank gained on the financial and sometimes personal affairs of Jews, Communists, dissidents, and other undesirables. Insofar as Jews were concerned, it did not matter for a long time, as Italy generally resisted applying antisemitic persecution measures similar to Germany's on its own population. That changed—as much else did—when the Allies and the Nazis invaded Italy in September, 1943. After this time, Germans began sending off Italian Jews in trains, and they found the information Lorenzo Colvino provided quite useful in looting the property they left behind.

More tragedies and sins were to come. In February 1944, Lorenzo's young wife was caught in a crossfire and killed. Giuseppe's older brother Matteo, a year old, starved to death on the terrible blue oily milk that was given to young babies during the German occupation. Lorenzo was also forced by Mussolini's thugs to stash some of Il Duce's blood-soaked assets in hidden accounts when the dictator retreated to the fascist puppet state of Salò late in the war. When Mussolini fell and the war ended, Lorenzo Colvino was a thin spindly scarecrow of a man with sunken eyes and prematurely gray hair who lived in a tiny flat in Milan, alone with his guilt and faded photographs of his dead wife and son.

As there were in most occupied countries, there was a backlash in Italy against collaborators with the regime, and Lorenzo was quickly targeted. Though he abhorred what he'd done during the war, Lorenzo was a coward at heart. He sought protection from the local Mafia, which ran most of the black market operations in Milan in the desperate first months of peace. The Mafia granted its protection in exchange for Lorenzo's occasional help in laundering money through the bank he still worked for. He was quietly removed from the list of collaborators and spared reprisal. In 1947 he married again, a much younger woman called Clara. Their sons, Paolo and Giuseppe, were born in the years that Italy struggled to stitch itself back together after the wreckage of fascism and the war.

Despite the challenges, Giuseppe grew up relatively happy. He was a burly barrel-chested lad who was a fast swimmer and pugnacious wrestler. He was fascinated by movies, especially American ones, and frequented a crumbling old movie theater in Milan where he fell in love (sequentially) with Greta Garbo, Vivien Leigh, Rita Hayworth, Doris Day, and Sophia Loren. He had generally fond memories of his childhood, or at least he said so to his wives and daughter years later. The family grew prosperous, though never rich. At age 16, however, political violence again changed the trajectory of Giuseppe's life.

On December 12, 1969, a bomb exploded at the Milan headquarters of Banca Nazionale dell'Agricoltura, one of three bombs detonated in Milan that day. Seventeen were killed outright and many wounded, including Lorenzo Colvino. Surgeons used forceps to pluck keys from a typewriter out of a gaping hole in his skull. Lorenzo was left unable to walk, his left leg and arm were useless, and he had a severe speech impediment. What became known as the Piazza Fontana bombing was initially suspected to be the work of radical leftists, but as court cases and investigations stretched through the end of the century and beyond, increasing evidence accumulated that the culprits were neo-fascist terrorists.

The pension afforded Lorenzo from the bank for which he'd worked all his adult life covered only a fraction of his ongoing medical expenses. Giuseppe had been attending a private school in Milan, but he had to drop out and go to work to help defray the family's costs. There was, fortunately, another lifeline: the Mafia, for whom Lorenzo had also worked. A local enforcer, Guglielmo Famigi, recognized the plight of the Colvino family. Famigi gave Giuseppe a job unloading trucks of Mafia-purloined merchandise at a local warehouse. Giuseppe was eventually able to return to school, though not the private school he'd once enjoyed. Clara, Lorenzo's wife and now chief caregiver, deeply disapproved of her son's relationship to the Mafia.

Famigi, as it happened, was looking for a surrogate son. His own boy had been murdered years before over a vendetta. He began to take the young Giuseppe under his wing, frequently having him over to the family's house for dinner. Famigi also recognized the financial value in investing in Giuseppe's education. Within a year of the bombing the boy was attending an even better private school, Istituto San Remo, and his tuition and expenses were paid by Famigi. Giuseppe thrived at San Remo, joining the swimming, wrestling and football clubs. He also became friendly and eventually romantic with Famigi's daughter, Katerina. This match may have been part of Famigi's initial motivation to take an interest in Giuseppe Colvino.

Lorenzo Colvino finally died of his injuries in 1972, nearly three years after the bombing. On his deathbed in a Milan hospital, he warned his son: "Do not become entangled with Famigi and his people. When they get you, they'll own you forever."

Not long after his father's death, Giuseppe enrolled at Bocconi University in Milan, again with Famigi's blessing and financial backing. His surrogate father steered him toward accounting and the financial world. Giuseppe did study accounting, apparently to please his benefactor, but there was never any explicit quid pro quo between them. Aside from unloading those trucks at the warehouse when he was 16, Giuseppe Colvino never directly worked for Famigi or any Mafia-connected enterprise, and Famigi was careful to keep him ignorant of all aspects of his illegitimate businesses. Famigi groomed Giuseppe as the ultimate secret weapon of a mafioso: a totally legitimate businessman, with deep knowledge of complex financial matters, who could eventually be placed strategically into some high position in banking, corporate management, or government.

Famigi's investment paid off—or at first he thought it did. Upon his graduation from Bocconi in 1975, Giuseppe went to work for Banco Nazionale dell'Agricoltura, the same bank his father had given his life to. He was a gifted accountant and rose quickly through the ranks of the bank hierarchy. Famigi also had reason to believe he had cemented Colvino's loyalty: Giuseppe and Katerina were married and soon had a daughter, Sofia. Though he had an almost preternatural understanding of illegal and black market finance, which made him quite valuable as a forensic accountant, Colvino still had done no work directly for Famigi or the Mafia. He was apparently being groomed for a specific purpose, one which required that there be no hint of suspicious activity in his work history.

Ultimately, whatever this purpose was, either Famigi was too patient or Colvino was simply too good a forensic accountant—or both. In 1982, another bank, Banca Commerciale Italia in Rome, made Colvino a handsome offer to serve as the deputy head of the forensic accounting department. Giuseppe and his wife discussed and agonized over the decision. Famigi was strongly opposed. Taking the job would mean a split from him, and from Sofia's family. Colvino chose the new job. The rift between him and his adopted father never healed; and a new, smaller, but equally terminal rift opened between him and his wife, Famigi's now-estranged daughter.

While working at BCI, Colvino began to notice a number of financial irregularities within the bank, especially in affairs connected to the IOR, the "Vatican Bank." On his own, he quietly conducted a five-month investigation and collected extensive documentation. The scandal focused on eight men scattered across various departments in BCI, with four opposite numbers in the IOR. Colvino appreciated quickly that BCI was involved in a vast money laundering scheme for the Vatican.

Colvino did not make his conclusions public, and he did not contact authorities or bank regulators. Over lunch one day, he informed a friend in BCI's management, Davide Bucciarelli. Bucciarelli suggested that Colvino continue to monitor the "deficiencies" and feed him periodic reports. Colvino took it upon himself to investigate Bucciarelli, who had been appointed in the wake of the 1982 Vatican Bank scandal, and who was known to be absolutely honest and incorruptible. Colvino found the secret account in Switzerland that collected the kickbacks Bucciarelli received from the IOR. He kept the documents that proved this relationship in a sealed package which he locked in a safety deposit box at another bank. Bucciarelli's corruption was never made public, but Colvino kept this ace in the hole in his safety deposit box until the very end of his tenure at BCI, a decade later.

This was how Giuseppe Colvino operated: he did nothing, and attached himself to no benefactor, without first quietly arranging a stealthy potential retaliation that he could unleash against his target whenever he wished. But he never had to use these time bombs, and the targets themselves, like Bucciarelli, often never knew he possessed such damning information. Colvino continued to funnel reports to Bucciarelli, knowing full well the scale of BCI's money laundering operations. In the meantime, his salary grew. He and Sofia bought a condo in Rome, located on one of the Seven Hills, and they also purchased a vacation time share on the Dalmatian Coast. Giuseppe enjoyed fast cars and his Great Dane dogs. And he never lost his passion for classic movies. He never reconciled with Famigi, who died in 1993.

That same year, Colvino changed jobs again. The next lucrative job offer was from the Banco Catolico di Civitavecchia; the proposal was for him to head their compliance and forensic accounting department. Unlike the last major career move, this one was easy and required no deep reflection. Colvino's salary nearly doubled. The directors of BCC seem to have understood that Colvino knew full well the depth of corruption in his previous bank. The source of that corruption—IOR— owned the controlling share of Banco Catolico di Civitavecchia. Instead of the Mafia possessing a powerful man with a clean background to run interference for them, it was now the Vatican Bank who had Giuseppe Colvino as a quiver in their shadow arsenal.

Although Colvino's job with BCC was ostensibly to oversee legal compliance by the bank—an important task given the emphasis placed on cleaning up official corruption in Italy following the so-called "Years of Lead"—his real value was as a troubleshooter, investigator, and sometimes unorthodox fixer of financial irregularities. One of his major cases in this period was to direct the final disposition of a major fund, held by various banks in Switzerland for shell entities controlled by the Vatican, derived from Jewish properties looted during the Holocaust. The existence of this fund was so secret that almost no one knew of it even 50 years after World War II ended; had knowledge of it reached the world press it would have turned the Vatican upside-down. Colvino ultimately recommended quietly disbursing the fund to banks in various tax havens, including the Cayman Islands, in exchange for shares in various securities and loans packages, all legitimate. These recommendations were followed. By the turn of the century IOR had laundered all of its remaining money that could have been traced back to Holocaust assets. Few people in the Church even knew the fund had existed and fewer still knew what happened to it. Even the Pope never knew about the bullet that Giuseppe Colvino had helped the Church dodge.

By the late 1990s, Colvino was in his mid-40s, balding and vain. His own personal demons—a mid-life crisis —split open the fissure that had existed for years between him and his wife. Colvino had an affair with his much-younger secretary, Melina Callegari. The divorce occasioned by this lapse occurred just as their daughter Sofia entered university, where she became enamored of various far-leftist causes. Colvino's politics had always been conservative, but grew even more so in this period. Eventually, he was estranged from both his ex-wife and his daughter. He married Melina on the understanding that they would never have children. His job, his fast cars, the Great Danes, and the house on the Dalmatian Coast would be enough to satisfy him. Perhaps it would not be enough for Melina, but that reckoning was still many years off.

This is who Giuseppe Colvino was in the late summer of 2002, when he joined the pursuit of the agent of chaos whose name he did not yet know was Marcus Holcomb.

Chapter 23: Nassau

Far out on the Atlantic, about 80 nautical miles from the coast of Delmarva Peninsula, the blue-white speck of the *Global Redeemer* rolls and heaves in choppy seas. The sails are full, but she is not making her top speed, 12 knots. Indeed, she has been struggling since departing Woods Hole yesterday. The wind is brisk, and the seas have been higher than predicted. Nonetheless, she clips along, headed south, far outside the 12-mile limit.

In the main salon, which serves as classroom and communal dining area, eight boys sit around the table.

They range in age from 14 to 18. Several of them have the greenish pallor of seasickness, though they're well enough—barely—to attend class. Two other students, David and Mike O. (there are two Mikes in this semester's class), at this moment lie groaning in their berths in the crew foc'sle. One of the greenish-looking boys at the table is Vincent Carrigan, who sits at the end of the main dining table, farthest away from Father Tyler. Walter Birch, one of the two teachers aboard the *Redeemer*, stands behind the kitchen counter in the galley, mixing up a protein shake. He is young, fresh out of grad school.

The boat is pitching, but Tyler is doing his best to ignore it. Two items sit on the tabletop next to his right hand: a leather-bound Bible and a walkie-talkie radio. Tyler is in mid-soliloquy, as he's been for the past 20 minutes. A few of the boys are pretending interest, but most look bored.

"The Greys are not our friends. You've heard the stories of alien abduction, right? It's a punchline, I know. They make fun of anal probes on *South Park* and in movies. But it's a psy-op. That means psychological operation, psychological warfare. The media wants you to think alien abduction is a joke. The Grey aliens are sent by Satan to exploit mankind. They collect DNA from people. They're breeding part human, part-alien hybrids. When He comes back, Jesus and the Annunaki are going to end all of this. There will be a war, a big war between the followers of Christ and Satan's minions. You all have to be on the right side. What you're learning now is—"

Spontaneously Vincent pitches forward, spewing pinkish vomit across the tabletop. Droplets of it splatter on Tre, who sits across from him. The other boy recoils. "Goddammit!" he shouts. "You fucking puke on me?"

"Tre, stow that talk!" Tyler's voice is loud and sharp. "Vincent, how dare you?"

The boy coughs and wipes his mouth. "I'm sorry. I'm real sick, Father."

"Get some wet towels and clean that shit up. Noah, Tre, help him."

"Can I go to my cabin?"

"Not until you clean the table."

"But, Father—"

"Don't talk back to me! You're close to getting lashed, Vincent. I'm going to fucking lash you, man. Tre, you too. Clean this fucking puke up. I mean *now*."

The boys stir to action. Walter helps the boys wet some towels in the galley sink. Vincent comes out from around the counter to move back to the table but suddenly totters and vomits again in the sink. Tre, exasperated, drops one of the wet, now vomit-covered towels into the sink basin. "This is fucking gross, man."

"Tre, *shut up*. Get another towel from the aft head. Vincent, maybe you better go to bed."

At that moment Tyler's walkie-talkie squelches. "*Skipper, May here. Can you come up to the cockpit please?*"

"Can it wait?"

"*I think you should come up here. Over.*"

He grimaces but rises from the table and reaches for his jacket, which has been draped across the back of his chair. "Walter, why don't you take over? I interrupted your class anyway; you can get back to it." Tyler moves aft, toward the hatch leading up on deck. Two boys are sponging vomit from the tabletop; Vincent, hanging on to the walls and doorknobs, makes his way forward to the foc'sle.

May Pinder, in a red jacket, stocking cap and sunglasses, stands at the helm. She is here in the cockpit many hours of the day. She trades shifts with the assistant mate, Ben Korla, who doubles as the math and science teacher, but he is below trying to fix the diesel engine, which has also been giving them trouble.

Tyler grips the railing at the edge of the cockpit. He is surprisingly unsteady on his feet in heavy weather. Those used to sailing, like May, can immediately recognize a man who has no seafaring background and limited experience on the water.

"What's up, May?"

"Weather is getting worse. A new advisory was posted a few minutes ago. We're going to be facing a 30-knot wind soon. The patch job those kids did on the gaff sail is for shit. It's going to tear to ribbons in a 30-knot wind. I really think we should put in until things calm down and we can do a better job on the gaff."

"I want to be in Nassau on Friday."

"It's not going to happen."

"*Make* it happen."

"Evan, I'm not making this up. The gaff sail won't take a 30-knot wind. Considering all the problems we're having with the diesel, I strongly recommend we put in somewhere and get everything fixed."

Tyler glances at the compass, a glowing dial spinning in a glass tube. "Where do you suggest?"

"Closest port is Ocean City, Maryland. About three hours."

"All right, let's do it. Who do I punish for doing a shit job on the sail patch?"

"It's nobody's fault. These boys don't know sailing. I tried to tell you that. They're good at scrubbing and painting, but don't count on them to make vital repairs that all our lives depend on."

"Don't tell me how to run my school." Tyler's voice is again sharp and barking. "Get us to Ocean City. I still want to try to make Nassau as quick as we can."

Tyler clambers away from the cockpit. May turns the wheel; the compass slides several degrees, the sails flap, and *Global Redeemer* is now headed due southwest.

On paper, Oceans For Christ is a brilliant grift, playing both to Marcus Holcomb's strengths as a con man and to his apparent vanities and proclivities. In reality, it's something else entirely. Holcomb has learned the hard way that anything is more difficult—and more unpredictable—when attempted at sea.

Though of course it's not written down, OFC does have a specific business plan. Various actions Holcomb has taken serve as tantalizing clues to it. In the months since he left Tondoro, he's been spending money like water, much of it to refit and rehabilitate the *Global Redeemer,* and also to launch and promote the teen reform school. For this phase of the business, one might consider Michael O'Cuinneagain an unwitting investor in the venture: all of Marcus's capital, now carefully stashed in various offshore bank accounts, originated in the blue Umbro bag for which Shannon O'Cuinneagain, João Broka and Stephen Trask were killed. Marcus has never been in legitimate business in his life, but he seems to understand that one must spend money to make money.

There are other subtle frauds built into the background fabric of the business too. The *Global Redeemer*, for example, is over-insured; Holcomb altered the appraisal he sent to the insurance company to inflate its book value. Ruinous unenforceable provisions and exclusions lie like ticking time bombs in a codicil to the agreement which desperate parents sign when they turn their kids over to Marcus: that they can never sue, that they absolve OFC of all consequential liability, that the venue for arbitrating disputes is Pretoria, South Africa, and that they waive any rights to refunds or restitution. OFC's "model of instruction" includes an insistence that, in order for Father Tyler's miracle works on the characters of wayward young men to stick, they must continue to listen to his lectures and motivations even after they complete the program, for which their families pay on a subscription model. When he's not barking orders at them or expounding fantasies of UFOs and the Rapture, Holcomb spends much of his time in his cabin at the rear of the ship, talking into a computer to make these follow-up sessions, which he mails out on CDs when the ship reaches a port. These lectures are milquetoast motivational speeches sprinkled with Bible verses, tidbits from Dale Carnegie and bromides lifted wholesale from books like *Chicken Soup For The Soul*. A dedicated CD burner, hooked up to Marcus's computer in his cabin, prints these discs nearly round the clock.

But behind these careful machinations, a lot is going wrong. The monthly expenses of maintaining and supplying the ship are vastly greater than it seems Marcus anticipated. On the transatlantic voyage alone—when Holcomb and May Pinder sailed with no other passengers or crew from Cape Town to Woods Hole in early August—lines snapped, a sail tore, the bilge pump quit, the GPS system died, and they nearly ran out of fresh water. Marcus, down with seasickness, spent hours in his cabin at a time, unable even to come on deck. May has never complained. The brief sexual affair she and Marcus carried on in Cape Town seems to be over by now. He has promised her a significant share of OFC's profits, once there are some. There aren't any yet, though finding ten students for the first semester with parents desperate enough to pay OFC's outrageous tuition does seem to be forward momentum.

As a school, though, the *Global Redeemer* is an unmitigated disaster. In Massachusetts, Holcomb was obliged to hire two teachers, Walter Birch and Ben Korla—the latter as much of a handyman around the boat as a teacher—but the problem is that they are more or less honest, which means the fact that the school is a grift will eventually bother them. Walter is the only person aboard who has any experience with special education or troubled youth. Only a few days into their fall semester voyage he's already had it out with Holcomb twice. "When are you going to let me do my job? You've got these kids swabbing the deck and polishing the brass so often, they're not learning anything other than menial labor skills." To this, Marcus replied that the longer he could keep them at menial tasks, the less chance they had to get into trouble. This is true, but a lot of trouble goes unremarked and certainly unpunished aboard *Global Redeemer.*

These are, after all, troubled kids. Gabe, from Worcester, Massachusetts, has fits of temper and once beat a classmate senseless at his previous school for flipping him off in the hallway. David came aboard the boat with various baggies of pot and pills stashed in his luggage and is doing a fine business selling to the other students. Mark, a preening bully, has already appropriated Walter's aimless "group therapy" sessions into tirades of verbal abuse against the other students. Noah and Mike A., who hated each other on sight, have already had two rounds of fisticuffs below decks. Vincent is the only student who has never been in trouble with the law. He tries to project a tough-guy image by mouthing off to Father Tyler, Walter, or Ben whenever possible. "You're a fucking chickenshit pansy," growled Jim at him, the first day of the voyage. "I'm gonna fucking kick your ass the first chance I get." The boys are starting to develop derisive nicknames for each other: Fatass (Mark O.), Dumb-Shit (Jim), Mr. T (Tre), Squidbrain (David), Fuckhead (Nate). After vomiting on the table in the main salon, Vincent is coming to be known as Little Puke.

Day to day life aboard the *Global Redeemer* is difficult, whether by neglect or design. The ship is naturally what seafarers call tender, meaning she rolls a lot in heavy swells or even not-so-heavy swells, making seasickness endemic among all but the hardiest passengers. Because Holcomb has had to spend so much on maintenance he's skimped on food. Most meals are beans, rice or prepackaged macaroni and cheese. The crew's head that the boys are assigned to use is a stinking mess and one must constantly wait to use it; they typically urinate over the railing rather than go below. The boat is infested with cockroaches. Portholes leak, condensation forms on nearly every surface and dampness is endemic throughout the ship. Though originally built in the 1960s as a luxury yacht, for this ship those days of comfort are long over.

The question may arise whether Marcus Holcomb truly believes the ideology he feeds to the students when they're not scrubbing the deck (and sometimes when they are), or going through the motions of having English or math lessons droned at them by Walter or Ben. As to the question of belief, there is this evidence: several of the books on the shelf in Marcus's cabin are popular UFO and occult books, from which he lifts concepts, details, and phrases liberally and without attribution. One such book is a crude memoir from the early 1950s called *The Flying Saucers Have Landed* by George Adamski, a crank and former burger stand owner whose UFO tales were later appropriated by Theosophist followers of Russian occultist Helena Blavatsky. Marcus also owns and frequently refers to a more recent (1987) book, *Communion*, briefly a best-seller, whose fanciful tales of alien abduction are interwoven with Catholic mysticism. He has several small volumes of *Star Trek* paperbacks. There's also *The Late Great Planet Earth* by Hal Lindsey, which was an evangelical and eschatological fad in the 1970s. Judging by its dog-eared and worn condition, the book on his shelf he refers to most frequently is Dale Carnegie's 1936 manipulative and motivational classic, *How To Win Friends and Influence People.*

Draw from these facts the inferences you will. But if he does not believe the UFO mythology, there is evidence that some of the boys aboard *Global Redeemer* are beginning to. While sequestered in their berths from seasickness, Squidbrain and Fatass, who seem to tolerate each other well enough, whispered for a time about alien abductions. Mike O.—Fatass—even said, "You know, I'm wondering if something like that happened to me. There was this one real weird night a couple summers ago."

After three days of waiting around in Ocean City for repairs and another two at sea, *Global Redeemer* finally puts in to Nassau in the Bahamas, late on a Tuesday afternoon. There are by now several more pressing problems. The water maker is broken and fresh water is again running out, oil is leaking somewhere in the bilge, and Noah, stabbed in the hand with a chisel by his arch-enemy Mike A. (now known as Psycho), needs medical attention. When the injury happened at sea, Ben patched up the wound with an ace bandage from a first aid kit, but no one aboard the ship has any medical training; now the wound is becoming infected. Ben confronts Father Tyler with this fact, below decks, as the ship is half a day from Nassau. "You've got to get him seen by a doctor. He could get sepsis. I'm serious."

Tyler grimaces. "These are juvenile delinquents. Nobody can be ashore without being guarded, and nobody can be left alone on the ship. I've got banking business ashore, you and May will have your hands full with repairs, and Walter will be guarding the ship. Who's left to take him to a doctor?"

"Well, you're going to have to take him on your way to your business. It's got to be looked at."

Tyler grimaces again. He gives a noncommittal answer about Noah and suggests Ben get to work on repairs. "It'll be taken care of."

What he ultimately does is task three students—Mike O., Jim and Vincent—to take Noah to Doctors Hospital, which is only a few blocks from the waterfront where the *Redeemer* is tied up. He chooses these three probably because they seem to be the most responsible of the surly lot, but that judgment is certainly relative. On deck, he threatens and tongue-lashes the three before letting them off. "You miserable fucks better do this right or I'll lash every one of you. Don't think I won't do it. Take Noah directly there. Mike has the map. Don't stop anywhere else. Make sure Noah gets looked at, bandaged up and gets a shot or two. No X-rays. See if you can get some pills or something for him. You'll bring any medication directly to me or Walter. Again, any fuck-ups, it's your asses, all of you. Got it?"

A few minutes later the four boys walk down the gangplank. Tyler himself is not far behind, carrying his laptop case, the tropical sunset reflecting off his sunglasses. The Nassau harbor front bustles with yachts, fishing and pleasure craft, cars, and people. Tugs are pushing a large cruise ship toward the passenger terminal. Fronds of palm trees sway in the tropical breeze. The buildings fronting the harbor road are painted pink and baby blue.

As might have been expected, the shore party falls apart almost as soon as they pass out of sight of the *Redeemer*. "I'm gonna get some booze!" Jim cries cheerfully. Fatass thrusts the map into Vincent's hands. "Catch up with you later." He's off, too. Vincent, hesitating, stares at the map and Noah's bandaged hand. "Come on. I'll take you. Think we can score some drugs at the hospital?"

There's a long wait for a doctor in the main lobby of the emergency room. Noah is as surly as the rest of the group, but his hand hurts badly enough for him to stick with it, and he waits. Vincent goes to a bank of pay phones at the front of the hospital lobby. He picks up one and punches 0. "Hello, um, can you help me? I'd like to make a collect call, please. To the USA. The number is..."

In Grand Rapids, it's only an hour earlier than in Nassau, and Vincent knows when his mother is likely to be off her shift and home. The phone in the kitchen of the Juneberry Avenue house rings and Gwen Carrigan answers. "Yes, yes, I'll accept the charges! Vincent? *Vincent!* Can you hear me?"

This is the first she's heard from him in real time since he left. He recorded several voice mail messages for her the day he left for Woods Hole and when he arrived, but despite her attempts to find him in Massachusetts—futile, since the *Global Redeemer* already sailed—she has not spoken to her son directly.

"Are you all right? Where are you?"

"The Bahamas. Mom, I can't talk for long—"

"Vincent, get out of there. My God. You're in so much danger, honey. Why did you do this crazy thing? Never mind—how do I get you home?"

"I told you I can't talk long. I'm not in danger. Okay? I'm *not* in danger. We're in Nassau, the Bahamas. Somebody has to get him. You know, expose him..."

"But it can't be *you*, Vincent. This is crazy. We're crazy with worry. I can't believe you did this! I'll get you home. I can get you a ticket home—"

"Mom, listen. *Listen* to me. The boat, it's got ten students. Most of them are from Massachusetts someplace. I think we're going to a couple islands down here, but I don't know which ones. This guy, Father Tyler, he's got us scrubbing decks and polishing brass and stuff. And there's this weird shit, he talks about UFOs and the Rapture and wars between armies of angels and aliens and stuff. He's trying to brainwash people. I don't know if he really believes it or if he's just a faker."

"Has he hurt you? Or anyone else?"

"No. He keeps threatening to lash guys if they get out of line. But he hasn't done it yet. A guy got stabbed, though. Not by Father Tyler, another kid did it with a chisel. He's all right, he's going to be all right, but—"

"Vincent, you have to get out of there." Gwen's voice is pregnant with fear. "There's nothing more you can do. And if he finds out who you are..."

Vincent is looking over across the hospital lobby. Noah disappears behind a curtain with a doctor.

"I have to go. I'll be real careful. I'll call the next chance I get."

"Vincent, wait. Vinc—"

The boy hangs up the handset. He turns away from the phones and walks back toward the chairs outside the curtained cubicles. From behind the curtain Noah's voice is audible, explaining to the doctor what happened. He says it was an accident: he stabbed himself with a chisel while scuppering the deck of a sailboat.

Chapter 24: Vatican City

It is a sunny mid-morning on a Wednesday in Rome. Giuseppe Colvino has been touring the campus of the Missionary Oblates of Mary Immaculate on the Via Aurelia. The buildings, many of them fronted in tan-pink stucco, crouch amid trees and brick-lined walkways that wind through the compound. The tour has been a courtesy, but he is not here for that. In the shadow of a large poplar near the main chapel, he walks with a petite lady in nun's habit and thick Coke-bottle glasses. Sister Marabella Gasparri has been at OMI for nearly 40 years. She and Colvino converse in easy Italian.

"He was a very nice young man," she tells him. "Always pleasant and polite. I only met him a few times, but he did impress me with how polite he was."

"Was there anything strange about him, or his visit? Anything connected with him that was at all out of the ordinary?"

She thinks for a moment. "Well, come to think of it, there was one thing. I'd forgotten about it. It was four years ago, after all."

"What do you recall? Anything."

"He was staying at the rectory. Over there. Our visitors from out of town often do. There was some mix-up with accommodations regarding him. He was supposed to leave, if I have it right, but he didn't check out or turn in the key. He just sort of disappeared. Then I got a phone call from him. Something had happened. I don't remember what he said—he was robbed or, I don't know, I don't remember—but he wanted us to pack up the suitcases and belongings held left in his room and send them to a hotel. I do remember that was unusual because that never happened before."

"He wanted his things packed up and sent on, but he didn't come for them himself?"

"Yes, that's the way it happened."

"Where was the hotel that you sent his bags to, can you remember?"

"Turin. I think Turin. No! Bologna. Yes, it was Bologna. He paid for the shipping, of course."

"Thank you, Sister Marabella. You've been very helpful."

Colvino's interview with Father Bertholdi occurs in the latter's office. The banker takes notes on his laptop. There is much to tell: Bertholdi speaks at length about Father Evan Tyler, his exemplary record at seminary, and how excited he was to be going to do the Lord's work in Tondoro.

"Yes, thank you, Father. What can you tell me about the week that Tyler was here? I understand the OMI convention was going on."

"Oh, yes! It was a great pleasure to finally meet Father Tyler in person." After several more minutes of description—in which Bertholdi manages to explicate the story of the founding of OMI by Eugène de Mazenod in 1816—he eventually returns to the subject of Evan Tyler. "He was so polite and knowledgeable. I haven't met a lot of Americans who have served with OMI. Canadians, many, but not Americans. There was another American who happened to be here that week too. Not a priest, but a student. I introduced him to Father Tyler and they seemed to take to each other well and quickly."

Colvino is still typing on his keyboard. "Another American? If he was not with OMI, what was he doing here?"

"Some sort of research, I think. He was a student from Sapienza. Another very nice young man. I gave him a tour of the campus, and also the Vatican itself."

"Do you remember his name, this student?"

"I'm sorry, I don't."

"What did he look like?"

Bertholdi shrugs. "Late 20s. He had long hair. That I do remember."

"Blond?"

"No, black. He looked like one of those American rock and roll stars. Grunge, I think they call it? Which was why I was surprised at how interested he was in Catholic missionary work."

"You gave him a tour of the Vatican?"

"Yes, all the secret spots. The Gardens, the Niccoline Chapel, the Cabinet of the Masks. Oh! I just remembered. The student was from Boston."

"But you don't remember his name?"

Bertholdi shrugs and shakes his head.

The secret grottoes of the Vatican—the Niccoline Chapel, the Gardens and such—are not open to the public. To see them one must be on a private tour, in the company of an authorized person. The Vatican keeps records of who is admitted in, and in whose presence. These records are kept in a computer database. Colvino not only knows this, but he knows the woman in the visitors' office who keeps the records. Half an hour after he has left Father Bertholdi, he's in this office, peering through his reading glasses at the screen of Mrs. Veata's computer, over her shoulder, as she scrolls through the visitor records.

"Wait, was that it? Go back up." The column scrolls upwards. "Bertholdi. That's it." Instantly he spots what he has been looking for. "Wright! Jeffrey Wright. Of course." He has already come across this name in the TCCF bank records.

Mrs. Veata highlights the entry. "You were right about the date. Last week in August, 1998. Would you like a print-out?"

"Yes, thank you. May I use your phone in this office, please?"

Colvino uses the phone to call the registrar of Sapienza University. A mile or so away in another part of Rome, another clerk scans another computer screen. The Sapienza clerk, a man, reports: "Jeffrey Elgin Wright. International students program. American, home address in Boston, Massachusetts. Attended two terms, fall '98, spring '99, as well as summer courses."

"Does your computer system interface with campus security? If there were any security or police incidents involving that student, would they show up on your record there?"

"No, they wouldn't, I'm afraid. You'll have to contact campus police directly."

Colvino thanks the clerk and hangs up the phone. He takes the print-out that Mrs. Veata hands out to him. "Did you find who you were looking for?"

"I think so. Thanks, you've been most helpful."

But he hasn't found who he's looking for, not just yet. In the library of Sapienza University, Colvino finds a directory of international students from the 1998-99 school year, which includes photographs. Jeffrey Wright is a chubby short-haired lad with dark hair and eyes. He could not reasonably be mistaken for a much thinner and decade-older blond man with blue eyes and a differently-shaped face. In any event, it is clear Wright was still on the Sapienza campus in the spring of 1999, when Father Tyler was already in Tondoro.

Colvino's visit to Sapienza campus police is fruitless: "We can't disclose the private records of university students, even past ones, to a member of the general public, Signore Colvino."

This doesn't prove an impediment for long. Back at his office in Civitavecchia, which he reaches late in the afternoon, Colvino makes a phone call to a younger man in Milan with whom he occasionally does business. "I want anything in the database of Sapienza University campus police on a person, an American, named Jeffrey Wright. It would date from 1998 or 1999."

Colvino knows the hacker only as Igor G. "If there's anything to get," he says, "I'll get it. Give me your secure fax number again, please? I know I've got it, but it's not right here on my desk."

An hour later, Sapienza campus police's file on Jeffrey Wright curls page by page out of Colvino's fax machine. He had been investigated by the police following a complaint by UniCredit Bank, who alleged Wright had abused the privileges of banking offered as a perk to Sapienza international students. The campus report does not disclose precisely how, but it does contain a multi-page statement, handwritten by Wright in English, in which he claimed that his identity had been stolen. Ultimately no action was taken against Wright.

Reading glasses perched on his nose, Colvino strains to read Wright's handwriting, rendered more inscrutable by the pixelly distortion of the fax. Its key passage reads:

I never opened an account with this bank! I never even heard of Uni Credit. But what I think happened was ID theft. One night I went to a party. July 98. When I woke up next morning my wallet was gone. My passport too. 2 days later someone I been at party with returns wallet & passport to me – no cash missing & credit cards not used (I called my bank to check) but I was sespicious & this is where it must have happen.

The person who did it was named Kyle Barnes. Tall, long hair, blond dyed black, wore Nirvana & Pearl Jam T-shirts. He told me he was from La-hoya [*La Jolla] Calif. He hung with our group of friends during Open Days, internat'l student orientation. But he just left right after that and never seen again around campus. I did not suspect my ID had been stolen until campus police contact me (Nov. 98).

Jeff E. Wright

Colvino does not need the help of Igor G. to access the computerized banking records of UniCredit Bank, or any other bank in Europe. Within minutes, his office printer is spitting out a complete record of transactions from Jeffrey Wright's account with that bank. Even before the lengthy file has finished printing, he's clutching the initial pages, circling entries in red and punching numbers in a running tally on an adding machine. The names of payees he is circling are ones he has seen before: *Grove, G. Dortgard, G. Blakeney, N. Tyler, E.*

When the pages stop printing, Colvino snatches the last one and stares at it. The final transaction—the one that finally drained Wright's account, almost to the last lira—is dated 14 September 1998.

MT. OLYMPUS CRUISES — VENEZIA, ITALIA.

Chapter 25: British West Indies

After departing Nassau, everything aboard the ship seems to be working for the first time in the career of the *Global Redeemer*. Sails are full and patched. The bilge pump is functional and the water in the bilge is clean. The V-drive is working. So is the water maker; there's enough fresh water for passengers and crew.

There is fresh meat and vegetables in the galley, and meals aren't canned beans and macaroni and cheese. The ship makes eleven knots east-southeast through the Antilles. It's a bit of a digression from the normal course —next destination is George Town in the Cayman Islands —but May Pinder told Father Tyler that the previous course around the west of Cuba was a mistake. "You see this?" she said, tapping a computer screen with a weather map splotched with color. "That's called a tropical depression. The wind is blowing this way, and it'd blow us right up on shore here. This island is a Communist dictatorship. You want to end up in a prison camp? We're going the easterly course. End of story."

All is going well technically, but this afternoon, as the *Redeemer* is passing Inagua Island in the British West Indies, May, who is down in the nav/comm room, intercepts a radio call. She squawks Tyler on the walkie-talkie, who is pacing the foredeck, Bible in hand, as the students scrub the deck, a task they now do almost daily. Noah's hand is bandaged but he still pushes a wire brush mindlessly forward and back. The foredeck is covered with suds. Ben is minding the helm, but the ship is on auto-pilot.

May's South African-accented voice crackles over the intercom: *"I've got a radio call you need to take. Over."*

"Is it urgent?"

"Yes. Law enforcement, over."

Tyler puts Walter in charge of the deck-scrubbers, goes below into the main cabin and walks aft to the nav/comm room, on the port side of the stern right across from his own cabin. He takes the radio handpiece from May. "Hello, this is Father Tyler. Who is this, over?"

"This is Captain Brody Collins of the Bahamian Coast Guard." The voice, slightly choked by static, has a Caribbean accent. *"Do you have a passenger on board named Nathan Hamra, over?"*

"I can't confirm or deny the presence of any specific person in our program without proper authorization. Over."

"We're not going to play games with you, sir. We've received a call from the United States Coast Guard. They have a request for the immediate return of Nathan Hamra to the United States. We understand this person is a minor and his parents have revoked permission for the child's continued presence aboard your vessel. We request your immediate return to Nassau. If you refuse this request, you will be considered to be committing the crime of kidnapping and we'll be forced to classify you as a pirate vessel. Do you understand what I'm telling you? Over."

"Wait a minute—pirates? You think we're pirates?"

"We're responding to an official and legal law enforcement request by your Coast Guard, sir, as required by international treaty. Please return to Nassau immediately. We will be taking the child into our custody so he can be returned to the United States. Copy?"

Tyler pauses for a moment, holding the radio, staring alternately at May and at the computer screen at the nav station, which shows a cataract of red splotches on the weather map. At last, he puts the radio to his lips.

"Copy, Bahamian Coast Guard. We're altering course. Over."

"Please call us in a couple of hours with your ETA. Over and out."

With a disgusted look on his face, Tyler hands the radio back to May. "What course do I tell Ben to steer? Let's get there and back out again quick as we can. I've got business in George Town."

He returns to the deck-swabbers. May comes back up on deck and relieves Ben. She spins the wheel, directs Ben to set the sails to beat into the wind, and *Global Redeemer* begins making a great white foam arc in the blue-green waves.

It's a day and a half back to Nassau. During the voyage the picture of what has happened becomes clearer, but it is not yet complete until the ship docks and the little drama involving the Bahamian Coast Guard plays itself out.

A few days earlier, an article appeared in the Falmouth *Enterprise*, a local paper covering Falmouth and Woods Hole, Massachusetts. Entitled "Floating Teen Boot Camp Is Weird Cult, Sources Say," the item, by one Wade Harris-Carson, appeared in both the print and online versions of the *Enterprise* and described goings-on aboard the *Global Redeemer,* including rap sessions involving UFOs and the Rapture. The article also mentioned reports of violent incidents aboard the ship. One source reported a student was stabbed in the hand with a chisel and required medical attention ashore. Harris-Carson had also apparently corroborated some accounts of the school with another student who sailed aboard the *Redeemer* from Cape Town in July. Though not named in the article, Lucas Weyrenga was the corroborating source.

Most—though not all—of the ten students aboard the *Redeemer* were recruited from the Falmouth area. Thus, several of their families saw the article. It was Nathan Hamra's father who'd paid to send him aboard the *Redeemer*. Though long estranged and divorced from Nathan's mother, she still had say, according to court orders, in the boy's education. When she saw the article and called Oceans For Christ, encountering only stonewalling from Angela Carranza, she ultimately contacted the Falmouth police department. Her request to bring Nate home then went to the FBI, the U.S. Coast Guard, and eventually the Bahamian authorities.

At the time the *Redeemer* docks in Nassau the following afternoon, Tyler has not yet seen the text of the article, but he has heard of its existence during a terse radio call with the Bahamian Coast Guard. He is uncommonly gracious to Nate himself—Fuckhead, the other students call him—as they approach Nassau. He calls the boy to his cabin.

"It's a shame you won't be continuing the semester with us, Nathan. I'm really sorry to see you go."

"It's gotta be my mom. She's kind of a bitch."

"You know her best. I hope you don't forget what you've learned here. And I hope you don't repeat it too often to people on the outside—they may get the wrong idea about what we're trying to do here. Now, there's nothing you'd like to confess to me before you go, is there?"

Nate shrugs.

"You sure?"

He shrugs again.

"Okay. Go get your bags and get ready to disembark."

The transfer of Nathan Hamra goes off without incident. Two uniformed guards are waiting at the quay. Nathan himself is the first to get off. He wears a brand new Oceans For Christ T-shirt and carries a crisp new Bible, just handed him by Father Tyler, along with the small athletic bag of belongings he brought on board. Tyler chats with one of the officers on the dock, Brody Collins. "I hope your report shows that we've cooperated fully with the authorities in this matter. Please make sure the American Coast Guard is informed."

Collins, a dark-skinned man in a crisp white uniform, smiles, and hands Tyler an envelope. "Official order. You and your vessel have six hours to leave port and Bahamian waters. If you return to any port in the Bahamas so long as this order stands, your vessel will be impounded, and its crew and passengers detained by customs."

Tyler accepts the envelope and tucks it under his arm. He smiles. "God bless you and keep you."

During the brief layover—Ben and May seize the chance to top up on food supplies—Tyler obtains a copy of the offending article from the Falmouth *Enterprise*. It comes out of the cellular fax machine in his cabin, faxed to him by Angela Carranza. She also reports there are a number of phone messages, some from reporters, some from parents, two from a U.S. Coast Guard official. He makes no calls before the *Redeemer* is again underway, sails full, headed away from Nassau for the last time.

Just after the shore of New Providence Island vanishes astern across the horizon, Father Tyler orders the nine remaining students to assemble on the forward deck. They have all been instructed to remove their shirts and shoes, stand up as straight as possible, look straight ahead, and not speak or acknowledge one another. May is, as usual, at the helm. Ben and Walter stand by the foremast, watching.

"We have an unfriendly presence among us." Tyler's voice is eerily calm; he is not shouting. "An article in the press, full of lies, was published back in Falmouth. This is why Nathan left us. I've read this article. It contains details that only someone aboard this ship would know. That means someone talked to someone back home about what we do here. I think the person who did this is standing right in front of me. So I would like to know. Who talked? Who told the secrets of our group, in direct violation of my orders? Ben, Walter—I can't imagine it was one of you, was it?"

"No," says Ben. Walter merely shakes his head.

"Well, then." Tyler paces the deck in front of the nine boys. "It was one of *you* shit-bags. You miserable fucks—you fucking ungrateful cocksuckers. I want to know who it was."

His voice is still not raised.

"I think it must have been somebody who went ashore when we were in Nassau the first time. I have my suspicions who it was." He is standing in front of Vincent Carrigan, but not looking at him directly. "Don't you know what the Bible says about betrayal? Judas betrayed Christ for thirty pieces of silver. Satan betrayed all of mankind, and God, for the promise of power and glory. The war going on up there, and down here on Earth—the war of the archangels, the Greys, the Blues, the profaners of the Annunaki—whoever talked has lined up on the side of the betrayers. So who was it? Who among you pieces of shit is the Judas in our midst? Who has the balls to admit to what they've done and suffer the punishment?"

All the boys remain silent.

Still Tyler does not rage. He turns away with a casual gesture. "Very well. All of you will stand at attention, just like you are, indefinitely, until Judas confesses."

The deck is silent. The wind blows: the sails flap. A seagull caws overhead. Tyler remains for a few moments, then moves aft toward the cockpit.

"How quickly can you have us at the Caymans, May?"

"It'll take the same amount of time as it did before. About three days if the wind keeps up. The good news is we can take that westerly route around Cuba now. The tropical depression dissipated."

"'Good news,' the way you said it, implies the existence of bad news."

"There's another storm. This one coming from the east, across the Atlantic. Another tropical depression. They're calling it Lili."

"Can we get to Cayman before it hits us?"

"Probably."

"Just get us there."

On his way forward to the line of his students, Tyler seizes three of the buckets the boys have been using in their scrubbing chores. He hands one to Walter, another to Ben, then goes to the side rail—the *Redeemer* is heeling over, as she does when making high speeds—and drags the bucket in the ocean to fill it.

"Still don't want to come clean, Judas?" Tyler comes up behind the line of students. "You will stand there, not moving—all day, all night if necessary—until I hear from the Judas." He heaves the contents of the bucket at the line. Seawater splashes the boys' shoulders, heads, and backsides. It is not cold—the Caribbean in late September is as warm as it ever gets—but the unexpected nature of the dousing causes several boys to flinch. The water runs off them onto the deck.

Tyler nods at his employees, "Walter? Ben?"

They follow suit, filling their buckets and splashing the boys. Walter seems to go about it with significantly less enthusiasm.

Tyler goes back to the rail for more water. "Still nothing?" *Splash.* "Again." *Splash.*

The water is warm, but after multiple drenchings and the continued cool blast of the wind driving them toward the Caymans, several of the boys are shivering and gooseflesh stands across their bare shoulders.

Walter, finally, puts his bucket down. "I can't do this. You hired me to teach English, Evan, not to do...*this.*"

"Fine. Go below, then!" Tyler hauls another load of water from over the rail. "How long will it take, you piss-ants? Miserable little cocksuckers. You fucking traitorous bastards, who the fuck do you think you are?" *Splash! Splash!* Seawater runs in rivulets down the deck and spills over the side. "The water's going to get colder, you know. We'll be out here all night! No dinner. No sleep. No one goes to the bathroom. You'll just have to piss your pants. Nothing gets done 'til I get an answer!" *Splash! Splash!* Now Ben, too, has given up; he stands, clutching the rail, bucket in his other hand.

After another violent splash of seawater across his shoulders Vincent finally goes down. He drops to hands and knees on the deck, coughing, sputtering, wiping wet hair out of his eyes. "It was me." *Splash!* Another bucketful of seawater rains down on him. "It was me!"

Tyler drops the bucket and kneels down, his face inches from the boy's. "You? *You* did it? I knew it. They call you Little Puke, don't they? Who did you talk to? Who'd you call?"

"My mom. I called her from the hospital where we took Noah." He coughs again.

"All right. All of you, down below, now. Not you, Vincent. Ben, take them below. I want 'em copying Bible verses in longhand. Word for word. Matthew, Chapter 26 —the betrayal of Christ. And you, Puke, you're coming with me."

In Tyler's cabin Vincent sits, his sweat pants soaked, a towel covering his bare shivering shoulders. Father Tyler sits across the desk from him. The *Redeemer* is still heeling, so the room is canted slightly to one side.

"Give it straight, Vincent. You know telling anyone about what goes on aboard this ship is breaking the highest rule. Why'd you do it? Hoping your mom is going to get you out of this, are you?"

Vincent is shivering violently. His teeth are clacking. "She...she sent me."

"She *sent* you? I don't understand."

"She sent me to this school to spy on you. She thinks you're a cult leader. She sent me to get info she can tell, you know, the papers and stuff. I didn't want to do it, but she forced me."

Tyler is silent for some time. He shows no visible reaction. After a while all he says is: "You came by bus, didn't you? Ben went to pick you up at the Greyhound station."

"Yeah."

"Where did you come from? You told me you were from Cleveland."

"I lied, sir." His teeth chatter again. "I came from Grand Rapids, Michigan."

Tyler's stare grows colder. "Who is your mother?"

"I have two moms, sir. Or I had. My other mom was Sarah Brinson."

For several moments, Tyler looks gobsmacked. But soon, stony stoicism covers this. "I see. And you say you didn't want to do it, but she forced you—"

Tears are squeezing from Vincent's eyes. "She told me I had to. She thinks you're bad. I even thought so at first. But I'm starting to think you're right. About the Greys and Satan and the Rapture. I'm sorry about what I did. Real, *real* sorry. I'm scared, I don't know what to think."

"Vincent. Look at me. *Look at me.* I had nothing to do with your mom's disappearance. If that's what your other mom thinks, I'm just gonna tell you—I had nothing to do with it. I was very concerned. I was the one who called the police and gave them the report. You understand that?"

He nods. "Yes, sir."

"I'm sorry about what happened to her. Whatever it was. It was on the road from Rundu. There are bandits in that part of Africa. That kind of thing has happened before, especially to Americans, people they think might have money. It's one of the reasons I wanted to leave. You believe me?"

"Yes, sir."

"Now, do you want to stay aboard, stay in school, or do you want me to send you home? If you don't want to be here, you can go, just like Nate. I won't keep you here against your will."

Vincent pulls on a corner of the blanket. "I want to stay. Please."

"I'm going to have to punish you. The other boys, they have to see what happens when you break the code. If you stay, you have to accept punishment. Are you willing to do that?"

He nods again.

"And we're going to call your mom from the Cayman Islands. This spying bullshit, it ends now. You're going to tell her what I just told you about Sarah Brinson. Right?"

"Yes, sir."

"You mean it? You don't want to take any of it back?"

The boy shivers, "I mean it."

"All right. Go back to the foc'sle, change clothes, get dried off. Go join your friends in the main salon. Your punishment will be tomorrow, on deck."

The boy leaves the cabin, shutting the door quietly on his way out. Marcus Holcomb remains in the chair at his desk, for a few moments staring aimlessly. Then he stands up and goes to the safe whose door is set in the paneled wall. He spins the dial. The combination is 21-11-1978. That date was Rafael Moreira's birthday.

He swings the metal door open. Inside are several bricks of cash, bound together in a thick waterproof bag, a folio of papers also in a waterproof case, and the 9mm Vektor SP1 that killed Vincent's mother. Holcomb takes the gun, pops out the magazine, and checks it. He pulls back the slider and sets the safety. He puts the gun in his desk, in a locked drawer, re-locks the safe and closes the hidden cabinet. The cant of the room shifts slightly; the *Redeemer* has turned a few points to port.

Chapter 26: George Town

In the morning, Vincent Carrigan is brought to the foredeck above the foc'sle. The other eight students are lined up behind him. At the front of the ship, just before the root of the bowsprit, there is a Revere life raft packaged inside a hard white plastic canister that resembles a barrel on its side. Father Tyler instructs Vincent to take off his T-shirt, climb onto the Revere raft canister and reach up with both hands and grasp the taut line connecting the staysail to the bowsprit. The boy complies. He looks like a monkey, caught in the act of vaulting upwards to a higher branch in a tree.

Father Tyler gets up on the foot of the bowsprit and stands behind him, holding another length of rope with a knot tied in its end, like a rope used for carpet beating. He steps forward and whispers something to the boy that is inaudible to the others assembled on deck. Vincent nods. Tyler stuffs a length of surgical tubing in his mouth, which Vincent clutches between his teeth. Tyler stands, brandishing the rope.

"I gave Vincent a chance to leave. I told him I'd put him ashore at George Town with no questions asked. But if he chose to stay with us, he'd have to be lashed. I just asked him again if he still wants to stay. He said yes. I'm sorry this is necessary, but there it is."

"Wait!"

The call comes from Tyler's left. Walter is standing on the deck, an indignant look on his face.

"You can't do this, Evan. This is sick. This is not what I came here to do."

"If you want to go ashore at George Town too, no one's stopping you."

"Yeah, but you can't do this. This is completely immoral."

"Are you in command here, or am I? Consider yourself relieved. Go below."

A pregnant moment seems to stretch into eternity.

"Go below!" Tyler roars.

Walter clambers through the hatch and down the companionway. Tyler rears back with the knotted rope and catches Vincent across the shoulder blades. His scream is pinched and distorted through the surgical tubing. *"HRRRRRRRRRMNNGGGGGHHHHH!"* The rope seems to float through the azure sky before it lands again. *"RRRRRRRRRNNNNNKKK!"* Bright red stripes are already appearing on Vincent's back. He takes three more lashes, his body convulsing each time, but does not let go of the line. Finally, Tyler drops the rope to the deck. Vincent collapses over the Revere raft barrel like a dummy stuffed with straw.

"Now listen up, you bitches," Tyler sneers. "Vincent, from now on, is gonna be the most loyal member of this crew. You know why? He suffered for it. Our savior suffered far worse on the cross. You just remember that."

David and Jim more drag than carry Vincent below. Tyler bellows at the remaining students: "What are you all standing around for? Get your brushes and get to work scrubbing! Anyone gets out of line gets what Vincent just got! Now you finally know I'm fucking serious."

Later that afternoon Walter Birch pays a visit to Tyler's cabin. The pseudo-priest is engaged in his usual task, droning endlessly into a microphone with motivational and Christian inspirational tidbits. A stack of CD-ROM mailer envelopes, ready to be posted from George Town, is already prepared, in one of the drawers of Tyler's tiny desk built into the wall of the cabin. The bundle is inches from the Vektor that was, until yesterday, in the wall safe, but is now in the desk drawer.

Walter minces no words. "I'm getting off at George Town. And I'm taking as many of these kids as will come with me. I had some misgivings about this operation before, but I've got to say, you are a fucking maniac. What you did to that boy is a crime. It's child abuse. You hired me to teach English, not torture children. I can't be a part of it anymore."

Marcus Holcomb shrugs. "Sorry you feel that way."

"Are you even a real priest? I'm starting to have my doubts. I was raised Catholic, you know. Why do I get the feeling you weren't?"

"Your employment contract is very specific. If you go shooting your mouth off and disparaging this operation to the press or anyone else, I'll sue you."

"You go ahead and try." Walter turns toward the cabin door. "You sick bastard." He slams the door behind him.

During the conversation Tyler's hand was within an inch of the drawer containing the gun.

From this moment on, the *Global Redeemer* is a powder keg. Tales of sailing ships with tyrannical captains who drive their crews to the brink of mutiny are mostly fictional, but the charged atmosphere aboard the schooner beginning this night is at least similar in character. The students split into two distinct factions: those eager to disembark and go with Walter, and those willing to stay. May and Ben take shifts at the helm, but say little to each other as they change up. In the rear cabin, Tyler sleeps with the door bolted and the 9mm pistol in his hand.

There is no mutiny, but the exodus from *Global Redeemer* when it reaches George Town is disastrous for Oceans For Christ. When the boat docks at the marina at 2:00 in the afternoon on the second day after Vincent's punishment, Walter and Ben Korla, who have both quit, lead four students ashore: Gabriel, David, Mark and Mike A. Only five remain: Noah, now called "Chiselfist," Tre, Mike O., Jim and Vincent Carrigan. The *Redeemer* has no crew save for May Pinder and Evan himself. There is no semblance of classes anymore. It's not even clear where the ship is headed next, though Tyler has given no outward indication that he's planning to give up the enterprise. Walter and Ben, for their part, have told the defecting students that they'll help them get back to the United States. They don't all stick with him. Gabe deserts the group and vanishes somewhere into George Town on his own. A few months later he'll be arrested by Cayman Islands authorities in a drug raid and deported back to American shores.

Strange as it may seem, the situation aboard the *Redeemer* significantly improves after the exodus. Docked in George Town Harbor with half their complement gone, May speaks to the survivors frankly: "There's a lot going wrong with the boat, and we've got a lot to do. We've got to run down these sails and check every inch of them. The galley and the heads are a filthy mess. And there might be heavy weather coming, so we might have to batten down. I'm not gonna yell at any of you, but there's lots to do and we all got to pitch in. Can I count on you?" For the first time since the ship left Woods Hole, the boys begin going about their tasks not out of compulsion or a plan to prevent idleness, but with genuine effort and cooperation. The rising wind and gentle gray rain that begins later in the afternoon seems to underscore May's prophecy of heavy weather.

Father Tyler and Vincent, however, have business ashore. Before he leaves the boat, with the CD-ROM mailers and a plastic sheaf of business papers in hand, Tyler consults with May in the nav/comm room where she's checking the weather reports. Vincent—who has stuck to Tyler closely since the day of the punishment—stands next to him.

"Where are we on that tropical storm, May?"

"It's going to hit us head-on, but it'll weaken a little before it gets here. We're probably going to have 60-knot winds by this time tomorrow, but at least it's not getting worse."

"If we stay here in port, should we be all right?"

"Yeah, if I can get the boat battened up. Once you're done ashore, I could really use both your help back here."

"Okay. When can we be back underway?"

"If the storm passes us and we don't suffer too much damage, maybe day after tomorrow."

"We'll be back in a couple of hours. I may send Vincent back first without me."

"There'll be plenty for him to do."

They leave her to it. Tyler and Vincent rush down the gangplank in the quickening rain. Tyler has a straw hat; Vincent just bears it as best he can.

In the spacious lobby of the Grand Cayman Marriott Beach Resort—a space filled with white columns, wicker chairs and potted palms—Evan Tyler marches up to the front desk, Vincent in tow, and speaks to the desk clerk: "Would you please tell Mr. Simms that Father Evan Tyler is here and wishes to see him?" The clerk makes a phone call and soon a man in a gray suit and yellow tie emerges from a nearby office.

"Father Tyler? I'm Jason Simms. So good to meet you in person."

"Good to meet you. After all our phone calls, I feel like I know you well."

"Would you like to come into the business center, please?"

Their meeting is brief. Tyler claims from Simms— the hotel's manager— a room that he's apparently reserved on a standing will-call basis, but he speaks cavalierly about it; Tyler will pay for the room but not use it tonight. "I do have some business to take care of while I'm here, however."

"Of course. That little office right through there, you can use that."

Tyler opens one of the plastic waterproof satchels and hands Simms the stack of CD-ROM mailers. "Would you post these for me, please? They're international, but go ahead and put the charges on my room."

"I'll do that. Thank you."

"Thank *you*."

When Simms leaves, Tyler and Vincent go into the small windowless office that the manager indicated. It has a computer terminal, phone, desk and two chairs but nothing else. Tyler closes the door. "It's the same time here as it is in Grand Rapids. What's your mother doing now?"

"Probably working. Her shift won't be up 'til seven."

"Then we'll get voice mail." With a twitch of his head Tyler motions to the telephone on the desk. "Put it on speaker."

With quivering fingers Vincent punches in his home phone number, after Tyler has entered the number to make a credit card call. The line rings twice and picks up. *"Hi, this is the Carrigan residence. I can't come to the phone right now. Please leave me a detailed message and your number and I'll call you back as soon as I can.*" BLEEP.

The boy hesitates at first. Tyler nudges him.

"Mom, it's me. It's Vincent, I'm okay. I'm perfectly fine. I'm in—" Tyler makes a sudden wag of a scolding finger. "I can't tell you where I am. But I'm safe. You don't need to worry. Look, Mom...you were wrong. *I* was wrong. What's going on here isn't a bad thing. Father Tyler isn't responsible for doing something to Sarah. We had a long talk about it. I told him everything. We talked about Sarah. No one knows what happened, but he didn't do it. Something happened after she left that place, I can't pronounce it. Father Tyler feels terrible about it. He was the one who contacted the police about her. So we got it wrong, I know it looks bad, but he didn't do it. I'm sure of that.

"I'm staying with the boat. I'm learning so much. Father Tyler has taught me how sinful I am, how filled with sin I am. I want to follow Christ and be a good person and get my shit together. You remember that time I tried to kill myself back in 9th grade? And you said I was gonna find something in my life to live for, something, you know, to believe in? Well, I found it. It's the Lord. I'm gonna stay. Father Tyler allowed me to leave, he said I can leave any time. I'm staying, though.

"Please don't come after me. I'm gonna be okay. It's not like that time in 9th grade where I was all screwed up. I know what I'm doing. Father Tyler isn't a bad man. I want to be here, and I'm staying. I'll call again when I can. I love you. Give Cracker a kiss for me."

He quietly clicks the speaker button to end the call. There are tears in his eyes; he sniffles and wipes them away.

"That was very good, Vincent. I believe you meant that."

"I did." He sniffles again.

"Now dial the number again. And let me talk this time."

The line rings twice as it did before. Gwen's bright voice dispenses the message, and the cold beep sounds.

"Ms. Carrigan, this is Father Evan Tyler of Oceans For Christ. You just heard from your son. Now you're hearing from me. It's over. He told me all about your little scheme. I'm very sorry for the loss of your partner. But if you continue to insinuate that I had something to do with it, or if you continue to feed negative reports to the press about Oceans For Christ, there *will* be consequences. I'll sue you. This has nothing to do with money. I'll even refund Vincent's tuition so you can't say I've taken a single dime from you. Expect to see a reversal of that charge on your credit card today. He's choosing to stay voluntarily. But if you ever try to have contact with him without going through me first, and if you ever threaten me or this organization again, you'll be sued to the fullest extent of the law. I hope we're clear on this. Goodbye."

He presses the button on the telephone. Tyler looks up at Vincent Carrigan with his cold blue stare.

"That's that. Can you get back to the marina by yourself?" Vincent nods. "Then go right back to the boat and do whatever May tells you."

"Yes, sir."

Vincent does return to the dock and the *Redeemer*. Tyler remains at the Grand Cayman Marriott long enough to have a Martini. While sipping it he watches the television above the bar, which is tuned to news coverage of preparations for the coming storm. On a satellite weather map, a whorl-shaped splotch of digital red is headed directly for the Cayman Islands. Tyler finishes his drink, pays for it with a credit card, puts on his straw hat, tucks the plastic folder of documents under his arm and steps out of the lobby into the parking lot facing West Bay Road. The rain has intensified.

There was a veiled message in Vincent's voice mail, but its meaning is not entirely clear. He referenced twice a suicide attempt in his freshman year. No such attempt occurred. It may have been merely a means to convey to Gwen that what he was saying was an artifice. She did not need him to tell her where he was. On her caller ID, the record clearly showed the call was made from the Marriott Resort on Grand Cayman Island.

There are several large banks located along Market Street in George Town, located in modern, attractive buildings fronted with palm trees and colorful canvas awnings. Few are conspicuously marked. Tyler steps out of the rain into the lobby of one of them, ERG Bank Cayman. The room gleams with brass and polished granite. A receptionist smiles at him. "Mr. Antrim, please. My name is Evan Tyler. He was expecting me some time today."

This meeting is almost a repeat of the rendezvous with Sims at the hotel only a few blocks away. Marius Antrim is in his early thirties and speaks English with a

Dutch accent. He has never met Tyler before, but they've spoken on the phone several times and corresponded by email. Antrim shows him into a quiet office facing Market Street. Just outside the windows the fronds of the palm tree in front of the bank snap and whip in the wind. The glass is covered with sideways slashes of wind-blown raindrops.

"What business can we do for you today, Father Tyler?"

He is opening the document sheaf. "I have some funds I'd like transferred from the business account of OFC to the personal accounts I opened. I'd like this done right away, if possible."

"You have your corporate resolutions for the transfer?"

"Yes, right here. Also, I have some stock certificates here. I purchased some stocks on my personal account and I don't really have any place to keep the certificates. Could you arrange to keep them for me?"

The business they conduct is relatively mundane. Tyler is transferring money between accounts, and he reverses the charges on Gwen Carrigan's credit card. There is not much business here that an ordinary clerk downstairs couldn't do, but Antrim never says anything to this effect. He handles Tyler's papers, makes the appropriate transfers, and obtains signatures on documents—most were already ready for him, awaiting signatures—related to his establishment of the various accounts he's opened with this bank.

Only as their business is completed and Tyler is buttoning up the document pouch does Antrim volunteer something. "Oh, I should inform you. We did receive an inquiry about the OFC business accounts just a few days ago. And our digital security department logged an attempt by an outside server to access our database regarding your account. That attempt was not successful."

"Who made the inquiry?"

"A man named Colvino. He was calling from Italy. I confirmed that he is head of the forensic accounting department for Banco Catolico di Civitavecchia in Italy. That bank is a front for the IOR, which is commonly known as the Vatican Bank."

"What did he want to know?"

"Standard information. Whether OFC was a client of the bank and whether you were personally. Of course, I told him nothing, and that we can't even confirm whether any person or entity is a client. He's a banker, so he would know that. But clearly he did try to access our system. He probably knew he couldn't get in, but he tried nonetheless. The outside server was disguised, but definitely originated from southern Europe."

Tyler smiles. "Thanks for telling me. A report like that is exactly why I wanted to do business here." He extends his hand across the desk. "Thanks, Mr. Antrim. It was good to meet you at last."

Chapter 27: Athens & Boston

Athens steams in 95 degree heat. Its downtown streets are a choking mess of honking cars and buzzing scooters. In the city's business districts, far from the ancient ruins that tourists take pictures of, it seems nearly every other block is under construction with chunks of asphalt torn to pieces and bored men in orange vests directing traffic around them. Much of the construction is related to preparations for the 2004 Olympics. Giuseppe Colvino sits in the back of a taxicab, drumming his fingers on his laptop case. He has not had much rest. He was up until nearly one AM and just an hour ago his flight landed in Athens. The research work on Mt. Olympus Cruises, now bankrupt three years, has been considerable.

The taxi drives him to the curb of a bland-looking office building on the same block as a sandwich shop and a store selling sunglasses. He pays the driver, gets out and hurries into the lobby to get out of the heat. Inside, a receptionist sits at a desk beneath a glass-enclosed model of a cruise ship. Colvino speaks English to her.

"Hello, my name is Giuseppe Colvino. I called late yesterday about the records of Mt. Olympus Cruises."

A short fat Greek man eventually emerges from the inner office to greet him. He also speaks English, in a fashion. He talks while leading Colvino through the office, a maze of cubicles and glass-enclosed smaller offices. "We don't refer much to records of Olympus. Investment no good for us. All their ships, just scrap. Good for none but scrap. You in, ah, shipping business?"

"No, I'm a banker. My bank was a former creditor of the line."

The Greek clerk does not seem to understand this but doesn't ask about it. He shows Colvino into a file room with buzzing fluorescent lights and dozens of steel racks of banker's boxes. Threading through narrow aisles he leads the Italian to a stack of cartons. "Here you are. These here. You may use that table. I cannot allow copy or file to leave the place. You understand, yes?"

"I do. Thank you."

The boxes are marked *Mt. Olympus Cruises* in handwritten marker, but the printed labels stuck to them, identifying their contents, are all in Greek. They are barely organized. Colvino sits, takes off his suit jacket, rolls up his sleeves, and begins rifling through them.

It is a complicated tangle. The cruise line, already beleaguered by falling revenues, tax and regulatory problems and legions of customer complaints, was on its last legs in September 1998, the month for whose voyage records Colvino is searching. The company finally went under in February 1999, and the shipping company in whose offices he is sitting bought the carcass of the line out of receivership. There are binders of court documents, all in Greek. But after an hour of searching, in a box marked 14C, Colvino discovers the booking ledgers for August, September, and October, 1998.

The pages are computer printouts of ticket sales and cabin assignments. His thumb moves down the columns. It stops moving as it touches a line reading *GROVE, GAVIN.*

He continues through the column. These bookings wrap around to the next page. As soon as he turns the page his finger stops at the first line, *TYLER, EVAN.*

The police report, or at least a copy of it, is located in box 14D, in the operations and compliance records. It's a Xerox copy, but the report contains detailed photos of the cabin aboard the *Golden Isle*, the guitar case, the stacks of cash and the envelope in which was found the suicide note. There is also a copy of a passport. This one is genuine, and it includes a picture of a man who resembles Evan Tyler—if he had long blond hair.

"*Ti ho preso,*" Colvino whispers. *I've got you.* And for the first time he pronounces the name he's just now learned: "Marcus Holcomb."

Within 24 hours, Colvino is back in Italy. The desk in his office in Civitavecchia, usually clean and uncluttered, grows stacked with files, papers, faxes and pages of notes. The no-copies restriction by the clerk at Piraeus-LGS Shipping is meaningless. Soon he has the entire report filed by the Greek police, a copy of Interpol's file and parts of the Hertfordshire police's. Finding the name of the man masquerading as Evan Tyler broke open the floodgates. Colvino is very good at obtaining records and files, regardless of their confidential, restricted, or classified status.

The dossier he constructs on Holcomb is thorough. Colvino soon possesses, electronically, copies of his passport, the last driver's license issued to him (in Arizona in 1995), his Canadian immigration file (one of the universities he scammed was in Alberta), credit reports from the three major American credit agencies and the wanted-for-questioning bulletin sent by the Hertfordshire police after the Traffic Circle Murders. He also constructs a timetable of Holcomb's travels and major crimes that proves startlingly accurate; the only one of his victims unknown to Colvino is Stephen Trask. This information and analysis accumulates over the course of a single work day.

There is more. Since the beginning, Colvino has kept tabs on the position of the *Global Redeemer*. Late on this afternoon he receives an electronic update reporting the schooner has again left Nassau after doubling back there, probably as a result of the Falmouth *Enterprise* article, which Colvino has read. On his computer, Colvino plots the ship's last reported position. He understands exactly where it's going—the Cayman Islands—and why.

After less than 20 additional minutes of sleuthing with various pieces of bank software, Colvino calls Igor G. in Milan. "Can you get me an encrypted bank database record? I have the bank and account number. ERG Bank Cayman. The account number is..." He rings off. It is 10:30 in the morning in the Cayman Islands. Colvino calls ERG Bank, and gets a manager's standard reply: "Our policy is not to give out any information on potential clients, even whether they are or are not clients." The nonchalant way Colvino hangs up the phone without saying anything seems to indicate he was expecting this; in any event, he can leave no stone unturned.

Igor G. calls back almost as soon as he's hung up with the bank. "Can't do it," the hacker reports. "Multiple firewalls. I tried a couple of ways in, but it locked me out. Those Cayman banks are good at that sort of thing."

"They are indeed. Thanks." He clicks off and immediately hits the speed dial for his travel agency. "Lucia! It's Giuseppe. Glad I caught you at the end of the day. I need to be in Boston tomorrow."

* * *

Late the next afternoon, a bleary-eyed and jet-lagged Colvino gets out of a South Boston taxi on E Street in front of a small low-rent apartment building painted red. There are bars on the ground floor windows; the street-level retail space is an old dive bar that closed long ago. Colvino, zippered leather folio in hand, checks a slip of paper on which he's written this address. He ducks into a doorway with an intercom buzzer and a directory of names in peeling tape on the red-painted wall. He presses the button next to a label reading *WRIGHT, J.*

"Hm? Yeah? Doug, that you?"

"Er, no. I am looking for Jeffrey Elgin Wright. Is this the right place?"

"Who are you?"

"My name is Giuseppe Colvino. I'm affiliated with a bank in Rome. You attended Sapienza University there a few years ago? May I come up and speak to you a few minutes? I'm following up on a report you made four years ago."

"You gotta be kidding me."

"I'm quite serious, Mr. Wright. I need your help. It's about the man who stole your identity. Please?"

There is a long hesitation. Then the intercom crackles. *"Two-A."* The buzzer sounds.

Wright, who at 24 is four years older, has lost considerable weight and gained considerable muscle. The apartment into which he lets Colvino is dominated by weight lifting and exercise equipment, including a bench press and a rowing machine. Three cats swirl at the Italian's feet the moment he enters. "Don't mind them. My girlfriend's cats." Wright is wearing basketball shorts and a Boston Celtics jersey. The apartment reeks of curry and marijuana smoke. In the main room, hardly visible behind the weight rig, a large-screen television is on, but muted, tuned to *The Simpsons*. "Can I get you something? Glass of water? A beer?"

"No, thank you." Colvino sits on a sagging sofa; Wright takes the equally dilapidated armchair next to it. Colvino begins un-zippering his folio.

"You reported to Sapienza University campus police that your identity had been stolen. It was after a problem involving a bank account in your name, opened in Rome. Yes?"

"I never opened any bank account in Rome. I thought I made that clear. My identity was stolen, and the guy who did it obviously opened the account in my name."

"Yes, yes, I know all that. The man who—"

"You *know?* What the hell, man? I couldn't get anyone at Sapienza to believe me. And no one at the credit agencies either."

"The officers who originally took your report—how do you say in English—screwed it up. We now understand you were telling the truth. This man—"

Wright scoffs. "*Four* years later? It took you four years to believe me?"

"Please. The man who stole your identity. You said his name was Kyle Barnes?"

"If I ever find that fucker, I'm going to beat the shit out of him. My credit is totally fucked because of him."

Colvino hands him a color Xerox of Marcus Holcomb's passport photo, enlarged. "Is this Kyle Barnes?"

Wright studies the paper. His face shows no emotion. He hands it back.

"Abso-fucking-lutely. That's him. Except his hair was dark, black, dyed. And he wore glasses sometimes, but they looked fake."

Colvino hands him another Xerox: several more photos on a single page. One is from Holcomb's driver's license. Another is from the University of Arizona law school. One, black and white, is a promo photo for a heavy metal band called Circumlocution, now more than a decade old.

"Same man?"

"No question."

Colvino begins putting the pages back in his folio. "Thank you, Mr. Wright. You've been very helpful."

"That's it?"

"I needed a positive identification. You provided it."

"This isn't about me at all, is it? You're chasing this guy Barnes. What'd he do?"

"Let's just say that you're fortunate all he did to you was steal your identity."

Colvino rises. Wright gets up to walk him to the door but before he gets a step he says: "Hey, you can't help me clean up my credit, can you? I mean, now that you finally believe me?"

"Write down your social security number and date of birth for me. I'll see to it."

"You mean it?"

"I do these things all the time."

He is as good as his word. Colvino is out of Wright's apartment in less than 20 minutes. From his hotel room in Boston, on his laptop computer, Colvino taps into

Wright's records with the three major credit agencies in the United States. Erasing several entries and retyping a few others is the work of half an hour or so. When he's finished, he closes the laptop and lies back on his bed, massaging the bridge of his nose where his reading glasses rest. He means only to rest for a few minutes, but he is so jet-lagged he slumbers for several hours.

By mid-morning, he is back at Logan Airport. Still sleepy, nodding off in chairs, Colvino shuffles aboard a 737 bound for Houston and a connecting flight to Grand Cayman Island later in the afternoon. The GPS reports on the *Global Redeemer*, which Colvino can access on his laptop through a tracking service designed for the shipping industry, have it still in the harbor at George Town, at least as of the time Colvino boards his flight. When he arrives in Houston for the layover he visits an internet kiosk on the airport concourse and checks the site again. It is slow to load, but it shows the position of the *Redeemer* unchanged.

Unfortunately, it is not easy to get to Grand Cayman Island on this day. As Colvino walks to his connecting gate he passes a digital billboard of flight information. The words *DELAYED* and *CANCELED* are frequently appearing. Indeed, his flight to Grand Cayman Island has been scrubbed. But so are many others to Miami, Key West, Kingston, Cozumel, and similar destinations. Outside the airport windows, a leaden gray drizzle leaks from the clouds.

The digital board is within earshot of a television monitor bolted to the ceiling in a nearby gate area. CNN Airport Network is audible. *"...tropical storm watches and warnings all over the Caribbean as Lili continues to wreak havoc. The island of Jamaica is under a tropical storm warning, with 50-mile-an-hour winds and heavy rain reported…"*

He goes to the ticket counter and stands in a queue that takes 45 minutes to reach an agent. A blond woman with a narrow face and too much lipstick examines his ticket and taps on her computer keyboard.

"Well, I'm afraid there's not really much going in that direction. Nearly everything headed south or southeast is being affected by the weather."

"How long do you think it will be until we know what might become possible?"

"This is a big storm. If I were you, I'd get a hotel here in Houston and check back in the morning. I don't think anything's going out tonight. You are entitled to a hotel voucher."

"Thank you. Can you recommend a hotel?"

The airline will cover only a Quality Inn. Colvino goes there, having retrieved his suitcase. He pays to upgrade the room to a suite. There is no urgency now. After watching television coverage for half an hour—reports on Lili are interspersed between updates and shrill political analyses of the forthcoming Congressional resolution to authorize an American attack on Iraq—it is clear that there's little danger of the *Global Redeemer* going anywhere soon. He eats dinner in a restaurant near the hotel, returns to his room, checks email and messages, then takes a long warm bath and crawls into bed.

In the morning, when he checks the marine positioning site Colvino does a double-take at the computer screen when it loads, displaying the schooner's position. "What the hell is he doing?" Not only has the *Global Re-*

deemer left port, but according to GPS it's headed north-east—chasing the storm that just deluged the Cayman Islands, and which, in the next 24 hours, will become a hurricane.

Chapter 28: Hurricane

The night that Giuseppe Colvino spends in a hotel room in Houston is a harrowing one for the company of the *Global Redeemer*. Though the schooner is tied at a quay in George Town Harbor, the high winds and lashing rain make for a noisy and uncomfortable night. Even in port the waves and swells crashing into the marina are considerable and several of the students are seasick. The five of them—Tre, Noah, Mike, Jim and Vincent—spend most of their time in the main salon, huddled on the floor, as low in the ship as possible. The sound of rain on the teak decks and hatch covers is at best drumming and at worst a roar. May Pinder sits in the nav/comm room, repeatedly checking the weather forecast. The lights are dim; the generator is low on power. No one has eaten in hours. Water from rain leaks into the cabins from multiple tiny cracks around portholes and everywhere else condensation has made damp. The steel of the ship's plates creak and groan.

Evan Tyler—Marcus Holcomb—is in his cabin. He lies in his bunk, an electric torch duct-taped to the bulkhead to augment the dim orange glow of the ship's main lights. He has been sick once today already, but has been popping Dramamine. He calmly reads a *Star Trek* novel. The gun is under the pillow, within easy reach.

At nearly eleven o'clock, there's a knock on his cabin door, barely audible above the lash of the rain on the deck. Tyler sits up, tosses the paperback book onto the bed, and reaches under the pillow. "Who is it? What do you want?"

"It's me, Father." Vincent's voice is well known to everyone left on the ship. He visits Tyler frequently and, while Vincent was never popular, the other boys have begun truly to despise him now that he is seen as Tyler's pet.

Holcomb lets go of the gun, which Vincent never sees. "Come in."

The boy has a damp towel wrapped around his shoulders. The boat is so wet, even below decks, that nearly everyone carries a towel now.

"You asked me to tell you how the other guys are holding up. We're miserable, sir. The other guys, some of 'em talking about jumping ship. The only thing stopping them is nobody knows where to go. In this port, I mean."

"This is going to be the worst night of the storm. If we can get through this, we can survive anything."

"May says we should have gone to a hotel shoreside. We still can."

"May isn't in command. And it's almost midnight. I don't know where to get a hotel at this hour. Besides, all the tourists' flights are canceled. The hotels are full."

"I'm just telling you what they're saying."

"Well, thanks." Tyler leans back in his bunk, hands clasped behind his head. "You boys are going to have to learn about hardship. When the Annunaki come back for us during the Rapture, we may have to spend days or weeks on their ships in conditions worse than this. It's part of why I'm doing all this, to toughen you up. I know the other guys aren't as down with the program as you are. But I know you believe it, Vincent."

The boy nods. "Yeah. I do."

A pause passes between them. Tyler says: "You want me to read to you?"

"Yeah. I'd like that."

Vincent sits on the cabin floor and draws the towel tighter around his shoulders. Tyler reaches for the bookshelf—the cabin is so small it's within arm's reach of the edge of the bed, if he stretches—and takes *Communion* from it. "Where did we leave off? Do you recall?"

"I think the guy was remembering all the times aliens abducted him in his childhood."

"Right." He opens the book. A peal of thunder rumbles through the sky above the harbor; the boat rolls again to starboard.

In the morning Tyler awakens May in her cabin, the owner's stateroom on the port side. Rain is still streaming down the portholes but the rolling and pitching of the boat has greatly reduced. She has gotten as little sleep as anyone, and only returned to her cabin three hours ago. She jerks awake. "What is it?" She snorts. "Oh. It's you."

"The storm is weakening. We have to get underway."

"What?"

"We have to leave. I want to raise sail as quickly as possible. How soon do you think we can make Corpus Christi?"

There is a look of shock and incredulity on May's face. "Corpus *Christi?* What the hell are you talking about? You've never mentioned Corpus Christi before."

"Vincent told me last night the kids are on the verge of mutiny. We need to get to sea to prevent that, and if they still want to jump ship the next place we tie up, we better make sure it's in the States. Corpus Christi is the logical place to go."

May shakes her head. "It's not logical at all. Miami is a couple hundred miles closer. In any event, the hurricane is still out there."

"It's weakening. If we make a dash for Corpus Christi or Galveston, I think we can make it."

"Evan, this doesn't make any sense. We've got to wait at least another day or two for the wind to die down—"

"*No!*" Tyler has rarely shouted at her, but his voice is suddenly a blast of rage. "We're leaving this morning! Make it happen." He does not wait for an answer but turns away and storms out, slamming the cabin door behind him.

Twenty minutes later, May is sitting at her computer in the nav/comm room, listening to weather traffic on the headset. Several of the boys are still in the main salon, sleeping on benches and in chairs, towels wound around them. Tyler comes down the companionway from being on deck. His rain parka is zipped up to his neck, water dripping and running down the edge of the hood. He peeks into the nav/comm cabin. "Well?" he says expectantly.

"It isn't really weakening. Winds are still really high to the northwest. Waves pretty bad too. If you want to get to an American port I suggest Puerto Rico—San Juan, maybe Ponce. It's the other direction. The storm will get farther away from us the farther we go."

He shakes his head. "No. Got to be Corpus Christi, Galveston, New Orleans, something on the mainland."

She looks at her computer screen, then back at him. Her voice is soft: "Can we speak on deck?"

He moves toward the hatchway. May snatches up her own rain jacket.

They go on deck and walk back to the cockpit. The wheel, lashed in place with rope, drips rivulets of rainwater onto the deck.

"You told me never to contradict you in front of students. Evan, what you're proposing is suicide. You want me to sail directly into a hurricane. You realize the hurricane, which just passed over this island, is now to the northwest of us, right? Directly between us and the Gulf Coast?"

"I have my reasons, May. You gonna do this?"

"You want me to kill you, myself and five kids? That's what you're asking me to do."

"If you want to quit and get off here, like Walter and Ben did, I won't stop you. I'll sail the ship myself."

"You don't know a goddamn thing about sailing. You'll capsize the boat five miles out from port."

"Then save me from myself. You want to prove you're a master mariner? Here's your chance."

The South African sailing master stares at him, her lips pursed. "If you want to go, please, let's try for Puerto Rico. Can we compromise on that?"

"This is not a democracy. *I* make the decisions on where this ship goes. Are you gonna help me do this, or not?"

She pauses again. The look she flashes him is sour. "I want the log to show that I do this under protest. The only reason I'm doing it is because if you put me ashore, you'll go off and try it on your own. I *might* get everybody killed. You *certainly* will."

Tyler goes below and begins screaming at the students. The rain is unabated and the wind still coming in occasional sharp gusts, but the *Global Redeemer* begins stirring to life. Boys clamber on deck, begin to zip open sail bags and untie lines. The work is feverish now that they've lost half their complement. But slowly the sails rise, and the schooner makes ready to sail into the roaring gray mass on the horizon.

Once out from George Town Harbor, the little ship is but a dot on the angry ocean. The swells toss and punish her. The wind whips and bites at the sails. May Pinder lashes herself to the wheel. The boys cower below in the main salon, all seasick, soaking wet and shivering. They pass a yellow bucket between them; its sides are streaked with acrid vomit, some of it bloody. The *Redeemer* is barely upright at any time. When she plunges over a wave she heels over, port rail in the water, and becomes closer to vertical only when she crests.

Tyler is on deck, too, sitting in the cockpit with May. Occasionally he staggers to the side to retch. A nylon rope is tied around his waist.

It's eleven o'clock in the morning. They've been out about an hour. They're six nautical miles from the shore of Grand Cayman Island.

When Tyler staggers back to the helm, wiping his mouth, May shouts to be heard over the blast of the wind: "This is madness, Evan! We have to go back!"

"No! Forward! We can't go back!"

"You're going to get us killed!"

"We're going on! We can make it!"

It grinds on. Though the boat takes endless punishment from the waves and rain, it remains afloat. May wrestles the wheel as if it was a live creature. Eventually she too succumbs to seasickness. After puking over the side, she staggers toward the hatch to go below. Tyler takes the wheel, watching the vast canyons of gray-white water mounting and shifting around the ship.

May vomits again—on the floor this time—just as she reaches the main salon. No one notices. The ship's central space is wrecked. Every object in the interior of the ship has fallen loose. Each time the *Redeemer* rolls, a host of debris slides and bounces across the deck: cans of food, plates and cups, cushions now sodden and soaked, a fire extinguisher, Bibles, empty macaroni and cheese boxes, one of the boys' shoes. No one speaks but one of the boys occasionally coughs or sputters. The torment continues, hour after hour, until long after the thin gray daylight vanishes into a wall of inky darkness. The rain and wind is so enveloping that it's difficult to see the light at the top of the mainmast from on deck.

When she has had some rest, May returns to the cockpit. Tyler is just a dark shape now, shivering in his rain parka, one hand on the wheel. She takes over for him. *"Go below!"* She must shout at the top of her lungs to be heard. *"Go rest! Check on the kids!"* Tyler hauls himself up, unties the rope around his waist, and feels his way past the cockpit to the main hatch. He cannot make it to his own cabin. He makes it as far as the head just forward of the nav/comm room. His stomach lurches before he can get the toilet seat up and his vomit splatters across the closed toilet lid. He sinks back into the corner of the tiny bathroom, exhausted.

Seventeen minutes after May returns to the helm, the *Redeemer* begins ascending the tallest wave it has yet encountered. It's so black she can't see any of it. But all aboard feel it, or at least the other side of it: a sudden terrifying free-fall as the ship begins to plunge into the trough of the wave. This time the rail doesn't come out of the water. There's a loud crack and the sound of splintering audible above the roar of the wind. The gaff sail begins to tear loose. May screams as ropes and spars fly directly at her. The schooner lurches again. A moment later the top half of the broken mainmast sails away into the gale, seeming to pull the very innards out of the ship as it goes.

The result is catastrophic. The boom at the bottom of the mainmast smashes into the row of cabin windows on the port side. The mast and gaff sail go into the water, but they remain attached to the remnant of the mainmast with the traveler—the line securing the sail to the mast. Thus, the broken mast and its sail act as a sort of anchor, dragging the port side of the *Redeemer* further into the waves.

Instantly, torrents of roaring white water blast through the broken windows into the main salon and the port side staterooms. Tyler, thrown against the side of the head by the ship's lurch, spills out the bathroom door into ankle-deep water. The boys are shouting. He does not have to order them on deck. They're already clambering up the companionway. One of them is shouting, *"We're sinking! We're sinking!"* Tyler sloshes through the water after them. "Life jackets!" he cries. "Everyone, grab a life jacket!"

On deck, May cannot untangle the traveler and release the broken mast. *Global Redeemer*, listing heavily to port and on the verge of capsizing, is already starting down by the head. The bowsprit is underwater. The wheel is useless. Abandoning it, May clutches desperately at the radio handset. *"Mayday. Mayday! This is the* Global Redeemer! *Repeat,* Global Redeemer, *calling mayday! Need immediate assistance. We're about to capsize and going down. Help us, over!"*

Chapter 29: Gulf of Mexico

The activity aboard the sinking *Global Redeemer* is concentrated at the stern. Vincent and Mike are still shrugging on life jackets. May shouts at Evan over the wind: *"The mast is gone! We're dragging the gaff sail, and it's going to swamp us! We've got to abandon ship!"*

"Can you cut the rope?"

"What?"

"Cut the rope! Noah! Tre! C'mon, give me a hand! Vincent, Mike, get the Zodiac ready! I think we're going to abandon ship!"

The battle with the dragging mast lasts several minutes. May eventually ducks below and comes back with a hatchet. The clanging of its metal blade against the steel remnants of the mainmast throws up sparks in the darkness. With a tearing sound and the final snap of the traveler, the dragging obstruction is free. The *Redeemer* rights herself, but only slightly. As she starts down into the trough of another monster wave, everyone grasps for the lifeline. Rain and water blast in their faces. Coming up out of the wave, the ship's return to buoyancy is sluggish.

"We've got too much water in us!" May shouts at Tyler. "We're going to capsize any minute." At that moment she sees something flash on the radio. The squawk of it is almost inaudible over the wind. "Hello! *Hello!* Can you hear me, over? Do you speak English, over?"

Tyler doesn't wait. "Noah, Tre, Mike, get the survival packs. Get on the Zodiac, quickly. Keep the raft tied to the ship 'til we're ready to cut loose."

The boys begin moving. They are shadows now, driven by terror and instinct. Waterproof backpacks of survival gear, packed hours ago, are quickly thrown into the Zodiac, which bucks in the ferocious water at the stern. Mike jumps into the rubber raft, but loses his footing and falls to its floor. Tre follows. Vincent is still leaning over the stern railing.

"Mexican Navy has us on their screens," May says, climbing out of the cockpit. "But they can't come get us. The weather is too heavy for them to put out to sea."

Tyler's electric torch illuminates a cone of light, alive with falling rain and blowing spray. "We'll have to take our chances. Abandon ship. Get in the Zodiac."

She makes the terrifying leap over the rail into the rubber boat, which bobs and thrashes in the white surf. All the boys are aboard now but Vincent, who still remains at the rail. Tyler flashes his electric torch beam at May. "Vincent, get in! May! When you've got Vincent, cast off! I've got to go back for something."

Vincent crawls over the railing. The Zodiac is lifted by a swell, and he leaps in easily.

May's face, illuminated by the beam of his light, is incredulous. "Evan, forget it! We're liable to sink any moment!"

"Don't wait for me! It's okay! I'm going to pop the Revere raft." He waves his arms. "Go! Get away."

"No! Evan, get in the boat!"

"Everything's in my cabin—the log, the papers."

"Screw them! Get in this boat!"

Vincent Carrigan sits just inside the Zodiac, looking between Tyler and May. Tyler's torch goes out, but his voice is still audible: "It's okay! I'll be okay, there's the Revere raft! Less crowded anyway."

"Evan!"

As May reaches to unhook the rope connecting the Zodiac to the ship, Vincent leaps back aboard the *Redeemer*. "Vincent!" she cries. "What are you doing?"

The boy doesn't answer. A moment later he's on the rear deck, trying to clamber to his feet.

May's voice calls through the darkness: *"Vincent! Vincent!"*

Tyler grabs the boy by his life jacket. "I've got him!" he shouts in the direction of the Zodiac. "I'll get him out on the Revere. Cut loose." A moment later: "Cut loose, damn it!" The roar of the Zodiac's engine growls over the whine of the wind.

Tyler shines his light in Vincent's face. "Why did you do that? Why?"

"I want to stay with you!"

The *Redeemer*, now down at the port side, slumps into a wave trough. Both Tyler and Vincent are dashed to their feet. The sickening pitch of the massive wave leaves the ship even lower in the water. Tyler grabs Vincent and loops a rope around his wrist. "Hang on to this! You fucking stupid kid." He recovers his torch and shines it in the boy's face again. "You know where the Revere raft is, right? That plastic barrel in the forepeak." It is not likely Vincent would forget it, as it was the platform of his punishment. "Go up there, get ready to go over the side once it inflates. It'll pop by itself if the ship sinks. Got it?"

He nods. "Where are you going?"

"I'll be right back." He shakes Vincent by the shoulders. "You really want to stay with me? I mean, like, forever? Not go back with the others, or your family? That's what it means to stay."

"I'm with you, Father!"

"Go, then! I'm going below, I'll be right back up—I mean, *right* back!"

They part. Tyler bolts for the hatch to the main cabin. The *Redeemer* is now listing heavily. When he gets into the cabin, he finds the water up to his knees. The sound of the water burbling in through the port-side windows mixes with the roar of the hurricane wind.

He works fast. Holcomb sloshes through the filling cabin to reach his stateroom. The door is hanging open. He goes to the wall safe; its door is above the level of the rising water. His numbing fingers fly as he spins in the combination. Eleven—twenty-one—one, nine, seven, eight. A dead man's birthday.

He is after the waterproof document folder containing the insurance papers. For this, he has risked going down in a sinking ship.

He snatches the folio, stuffs it in the back of his pants, and begins climbing up the steepening slope of the cabin floor—the water is now thigh-deep—back toward the main salon.

As he exits his stateroom, a dark shape, flashing in the light of an electric torch, flies directly at him. The clang of metal against his skull is audible even over the storm. Tyler falls back, splashing into the water. Vincent Carrigan stands before him, wielding a fire extinguisher. The boy's wet face is a mask of rage.

"This is for my mother, you son of a bitch!"

He rears back to strike another blow with the fire extinguisher.

At that moment, a wave catches the *Global Redeemer* from below, raising it up almost out of the water, and when it sinks down again, this time it capsizes. Vincent is thrown off his feet and the fire extinguisher pops out of his hands.

Holcomb did not lie about the Revere raft. Its mechanism is designed to trigger automatically when it encounters a certain gauge of water pressure equivalent to being submerged. It starts inflating on its way back to the surface, a bright red nylon tent riding atop a yellow raft, like a child's bounce house at a backyard birthday party.

As it capsizes, the *Global Redeemer* rolls left, its port side submerging first. The pressure of the air being blown out of the main salon ejects Holcomb through one of the broken side windows. He pops to the surface, gasping, only meters from the Revere raft whose line trails in the furious ocean. He grabs it and begins inching up. His forehead streams blood from the blow of the fire extinguisher.

At last, he slithers into the door of the floating raft. For a few moments, the bottom hull of the *Global Redeemer* glints in the flash of a lightning bolt. Soon it sinks beneath the waves, leaving a welter of flotsam in the boiling water.

Among the flotsam is a human figure. Vincent was drawn to the surface by his life preserver. He flails, shouting inaudibly into the wind. Whether he's screaming for help—or cursing Evan Tyler with his last breath, from Hell's heart—is unknown. The roar of the wind is too loud. The next time the lightning flashes, he is gone. Holcomb does not call out to him.

Marcus sits in the tent of the Revere raft, clutching the plastic folio he took from the safe. Soon there is nothing out on the stormy ocean to see or hear, except blackness and the banshee of the hurricane.

Chapter 30: New Orleans

Two weeks later, on a cloudy day in mid-October, a group of people, most unknown to one another, gather in a conference room on the seventh floor of the Hale Boggs Federal Building in New Orleans, Louisiana. The room is not a formal courtroom, but it's arranged as such. A table at the front, laid with green felt and pitchers of water, resembles a judicial bench. Three people in military uniforms, two men and a woman, take their seats behind it. There's another table off to the side, and, curiously, an Aeron office chair off by itself to the right. The audience chairs, all facing front, are dotted with spectators. Among them are three of the four boys rescued from the *Global Redeemer* wreck. May Pinder is here too. A few reporters are in attendance; one is Wade Harris-Carson, representing the Falmouth *Enterprise*.

Three men sit in the last row of audience chairs. They are not together and do not appear to know each other. One, in the far corner, is Evan Tyler. He wears a plain black button-up shirt and khaki slacks. A yellow legal pad is perched on his thigh. He clutches a ballpoint pen. Another man, middle-aged, Asian, wears a suit and tie and carries a leather folio. The third, on the far side of the room, exactly opposite Tyler, is Giuseppe Colvino. He speaks to no one.

At 10:02 AM one of the military officers, a man named Wechtler, brings the proceedings to order. His epaulets have four stripes; he is a full captain.

"I hereby begin this proceeding. This is the U.S. Coast Guard marine casualty investigation hearing into the loss of the sailing vessel *Global Redeemer*, a U.S.-flagged vessel, in international waters in the Gulf of Mexico on 2 October, 2002, and the loss of one passenger, Vincent Carrigan, age 16. I remind everyone present this is an administrative inquiry, not a trial. There has been media interest in this case. At the present time we will not be barring media from the room, but if media attention comes to interfere with procedures, we may consider it.

"We have taken into evidence the official preliminary report of the U.S. Coast Guard Station at South Padre Island, which itself incorporated documents and evidence from the Mexican Navy, who responded to the *Redeemer's* distress call and rescued six of her passengers and crew on the morning of 3 October. We've also certified the list of witnesses. The tribunal calls as its first witness—" He stares at the sheet on the table in front of him— "May Pinder, sailing master of the *Global Redeemer.*"

May rises from her chair in the audience and walks to the Aeron. The woman behind the desk, also in Coast Guard uniform, rises too.

Wechtler says to her: "Lieutenant Commander McLaren, you may begin."

Q: "Please state your full name and place of residence for the record."

A: "May Gertrude Pinder. I'm from Port Elizabeth, South Africa."

Q: "You're a South African citizen?"

A: "Yes."

Several particulars are established: that May was in the employ of Oceans For Christ, Ltd., that she holds (or at least held) a ship's master's certificate, valid in both South Africa and the United States, and how she was employed by Father Evan Tyler.

A: "He called me. I think he was referred by the charter outfit that used to run the *Redeemer*, when it was still called the *Sea Diamond*."

Q: "You had served that company and sailed the *Sea Diamond* before?"

A: "Yes."

Q: "In what capacity? What was the purpose of the *Sea Diamond* before then?"

A: "During the time I was with her she was used as a training vessel. People paid for classes to learn how to sail an old-time sailing ship."

Q: "So you were an instructor?"

A: "I was, yes. But that was before Evan took over."

Q: "During the time you worked for Evan Tyler, you did not consider yourself to be in overall command of the *Global Redeemer*, did you?"

A: "I didn't."

Q: "Who made command decisions aboard the vessel —where to go, what course to set, that sort of thing?"

A: "Evan made those decisions."

Q: "He was effectively the captain, even though he didn't have a master's license?"

A: "I guess you could say he acted that way."

Evan Tyler sits in the back row, impassive, watching.

More particulars: how and why the *Redeemer* wound up in George Town Harbor, what sort of navigation and communication equipment she had, and May's advice as Hurricane Lili mounted.

Q: "On the morning of 2 October, Father Tyler ordered you to make sail and leave George Town Harbor, right?"

A: "Yes, that's right."

Q: "You disagreed with this order?"

A: "Yes, I did. The hurricane wasn't over yet. The worst of it had passed by us, but he wanted to go to Galveston or Corpus Christi—the direction the storm was headed. I didn't want to leave port at all. But if we were going to go, I tried to talk him into sailing east, toward Puerto Rico. At least that would take us away from the storm."

Q: "Why Puerto Rico, specifically?"

A: "Father Tyler said he was afraid the remaining students were going to desert. He wanted to get underway, take us to sea, possibly so they couldn't do that. And he said he wanted the next port we touched to be on U.S. soil, so if they did desert, at least they wouldn't be in a foreign country."

Q: "Ultimately, though, you gave in and complied with his request, and steered northwest, not east or southeast, even though you knew the *Redeemer* would face high winds, heavy seas, and hazardous conditions. Why did you do that?"

A: "He said he was going to do it his way no matter what. He'd leave me at Grand Cayman and try to sail the *Redeemer* by himself. The chances of him screwing it up and drowning those five boys, and himself, were close to 100%, I thought. At least if I was piloting there was more of a chance of survival than that. And I also thought, once we got out in it, I mean, once he saw how ferocious the conditions were, he'd realize I was right, and we'd go back to port."

Q: "But that didn't happen, did it?"

A: "No."

Q: "Did you have a romantic or sexual relationship with Father Tyler?"

The Coast Guard officer in the middle of the table— Commander Farrell— suddenly speaks up. "I don't think that's relevant, Commander McLaren."

Wechtler pauses a moment, and then says: "I agree. The witness need not answer. Move on, Commander."

Half an hour later May is still in the Aeron chair.

Q. "Why did Vincent Carrigan climb out of the Zodiac and back aboard the *Redeemer* just as you were about to cut it loose from the ship?"

A: "I have no idea. I was completely shocked. He said he wanted to stay with Father Tyler."

Q: "Why didn't you try to convince him to come back?"

A: "There was no time. Tyler said he was going back for the log and the papers. He planned to get off on the Revere raft. He said he would bring Vincent off that way. I had the other four boys in the Zodiac to look after, and I thought the *Redeemer* was going to capsize on the next big wave. Again, it was math. I had the power to save four lives and my own. If I dithered over Vincent, it could have risked us all if the ship capsized while we were still tied on. I just had to trust that Evan would get him off on the Revere. So I cut loose. I never saw Vincent again, and I never saw Tyler until the Mexicans brought him back on the Revere, back to the naval station at Cozumel."

Q: "Did you ask him, when you saw him again, what happened to Vincent Carrigan?"

A: "Of course I did. He said he didn't make it, that he was washed over when the *Redeemer* capsized, and that once he, Tyler, swam to the Revere, he did his best to search for him, but it was too dark and probably already too late."

Q: "What was the nature of the relationship between Father Tyler and Vincent Carrigan?"

Wechtler interrupts; "I don't think that's relevant, Commander."

Q: "One of the students aboard the *Redeemer* made a statement that Vincent Carrigan was physically punished aboard the *Redeemer* on Father Tyler's orders, that he was whipped with a rope. Did that happen?"

"Not relevant," Farrell speaks up.

McLaren flashes him a glance. Her look is sour. She sighs. "No further questions."

Tre now sits in the Aeron chair. He wears a sport shirt and a knit tie, the kind of ersatz formal outfit thrown together by a high school student unused to wearing business clothes.

Commander McLaren asks: "Please state your name and residence."

A: "My name is Tre Crowson, Wareham, Massachusetts."

A "How did you come to be aboard the *Global Redeemer?*"

A: "My mom sent me there as a student."

There are the preliminaries: how long he was aboard, the stops in Nassau and the Cayman Islands, and conditions aboard during the hurricane.

Q: "How well did you know Vincent Carrigan?"

A: "Not well. I don't think he liked me much."

Q: "Was it your impression that Vincent was especially devoted to Father Tyler and his teachings?"

Farrell interrupts: "Not relevant."

This time McLaren argues. "Sir, I believe it *is* relevant. The question of why Vincent Carrigan got off the Zodiac and back aboard the *Global Redeemer* while it was sinking is a major factor in understanding how he came to be lost in the disaster."

"Let's let her continue," says Wechtler.

Q: "Do you need to hear the question again, Mr. Crowson?"

A: "After he got whipped, Little Puke—I mean Vincent—he starts sucking up to the Father something fierce. I don't know whether it was an act or whether he really believes it, but he starts sticking to the Father like glue and everything is 'Yes, Father.'"

Q: "*After* he got whipped? So the punishment incident did happen?"

A: "Oh, it happened."

Q: "Was it your impression that Vincent was slavishly devoted to Father Tyler, that he would have stuck with him regardless of the circumstances?"

A: "Yeah, it was like that."

Q: "Even though Father Tyler punished this boy by whipping him with a rope in front of the entire crew?"

Wechtler: "There's no real question there, Commander McLaren."

But Tre speaks up anyway. "That was part of it, though. Father Tyler says, when he's done whipping Little Puke, he says he's gonna be the most loyal of anyone on board because he suffered for it. Those were his exact words, as much as I can remember."

Q: "Mr. Crowson, do you feel like you learned anything useful during your schooling aboard the *Global Redeemer?*"

A: "Not unless you count swabbing decks as useful."

"No further questions."

The next witnesses are mostly technical ones: the Coast Guardsmen who took custody of the survivors, the Mexican Navy officer who rescued first the Zodiac with May and the boys and then the Revere raft containing Tyler that was found two hours later, and a general expert on sailing the class of schooner that the *Redeemer* was. Most of this testimony parrots evidence already in the written report. The only thing new is a statement written by a psychologist, opining that Vincent Carrigan was suffering from Stockholm Syndrome as a result of indoctrination by Father Tyler and this was what caused him to climb back aboard the *Global Redeemer.* Farrell objects to this report when Lt. Cmdr. McLaren moves to introduce it, but Wechtler overrules him and allows it.

The final witness of the day is Evan Tyler. He sits down in the Aeron chair at 3:30 in the afternoon. He has spent the day writing on the yellow legal pad, scribbling many words, scratching some out, rearranging others. He brings the pad with him to the Aeron chair.

McLaren: "State your full name and residence, please."

A: "My name is Evan Rodgers Tyler. I'm originally from Grand Rapids, Michigan."

Q: "You are an ordained priest in the Catholic Church?"

A: "I was. I resigned. Ms. McLaren—sorry, *Commander* McLaren—if you don't mind, before we get started, I'd like to read a statement. May I do that?"

The Coast Guard officers confer briefly, Captain Wechtler holding a hand over his microphone. He says: "Proceed with your statement, Father Tyler."

Tyler looks down at the pad, clears his throat and begins to read. His voice is a monotone, completely devoid of emotion.

"I wish to apologize to this tribunal, to the former students and parents of the Oceans For Christ educational program, and most deeply to the family of Vincent Carrigan. Oceans For Christ was an experiment, a brainchild I had years ago when I served with the Missionary Oblates of the Mary Immaculate in Namibia. I envisioned an oceangoing Christian high school, taking troubled youth without direction, instilling them with the word of our Lord Jesus Christ, teaching them leadership lessons, and giving them a powerful bonding experience through educational adventures at sea. I raised and spent vast amounts of money to make this dream a reality. I'll be the first to admit, my experiment failed, drastically and tragically, and Vincent Carrigan paid for this failure with his life.

"I made a number of mistakes. Some of them have already been identified by this tribunal. My familiarity with the sea and sailing is limited. I severely underestimated how much that would affect the operations of the school. I hired May Pinder to sail the vessel, but then I ignored or overruled her advice. I acted as the captain of the *Global Redeemer.* I shouldn't have done that. May was the captain. I was merely the headmaster of the school.

"Even before Lili became a hurricane, I knew OFC was finished. When we put in to George Town, four of my students and two of my remaining employees deserted the ship. On the morning we departed George Town, I had looked at a weather report and erroneously believed the hurricane was weakening. I was concerned the remaining students would desert. If and when they did, I wanted them to be on American soil so at least they wouldn't have to figure out how to get home from a foreign country. I resisted May's suggestion to sail to Puerto Rico because I knew the prevailing winds were blowing to the northwest—they had blown the storm in that direction. If we sailed east and got blown off course, I was deathly afraid the ship would wind up on the shores of Cuba. I didn't want to risk putting the young people in that sort of danger. So, I insisted we sail to the U.S. mainland. It was clearly a mistake. May was right and I should have listened to her.

"Another, even bigger mistake I made was underestimating the impressionability of these kids and my ability to influence them. The testimony that Vincent was quote-unquote 'slavishly' devoted to me—or that he was suffering from Stockholm Syndrome—is absolutely accurate. The second day he was aboard the ship Vincent confessed to me he'd been sexually abused by a clergy member when he was 12. This tragic abuse overshadowed his entire young life. I was horrified, and determined to make up for it. I took it upon myself to rebuild

Vincent's trust in figures of religious authority, and in Christ. I was so devoted to this cause that I refunded Vincent's tuition. I didn't appreciate that I was instilling loyalty in him that overrode common sense—even what common sense a 16-year-old boy possesses under extreme life-and-death circumstances they're not used to dealing with. This was a terrible, terrible mistake on my part.

"I had decided I wanted to try to save the ship's log and papers, but I wouldn't risk May or any of the students' lives to do so. This was why I told her to cut loose in the Zodiac and that I would get away in the Revere raft. When Vincent decided to join me, and was very stubborn about staying with me, I knew it was the wrong choice, but with the ship going down there was no time to convince him of that.

"I made a calculation similar to May's: at least let her get away now, and be reasonably certain of saving five lives, rather than risk them all to try to convince Vincent to go with them. I sent Vincent forward with instructions to get ready to get on the Revere raft. I knew he would obey me, and the Revere raft would deploy automatically, so I thought it was pretty sure that he would make it. I thought I'd be below decks thirty seconds, if that. I went below, went to my cabin and retrieved the papers. As soon as I got back up on deck the wind turned, and I was struck in the head by the broken remnants of the gaff sail boom that swung around. I don't know what happened to Vincent at that point, but the ship was capsizing so he must have gone in the water. The next thing I knew, I was in the water and the *Redeemer* was foundering. I saw the Revere raft in a flash of lightning and caught a line trailing from it. I never saw Vincent. I was desperate to save him. I called out for him repeatedly, but he never answered. It was too dark to see anything. I had no choice but to huddle in the Revere and hope to be picked up, which I was by the same Mexican ship that, thank the Lord, rescued May and the others. That night on the raft in the hurricane was the longest night of my life.

"Oceans For Christ is dead. I've already begun the process of liquidating it. A substantial amount of its assets will be paid directly to the family of Vincent Carrigan. I failed them, and him, and you. I will never again attempt to start a school at sea. I will never again try to teach students or rehabilitate young people. I no longer consider myself a Catholic priest and I will, after this incident, hang up my religious vocation for all time. So no one need be concerned with me repeating any of the mistakes I've made. For all my errors and shortcomings, I express my profound sorrow, to all of you, and to God."

Wechtler: "Commander McLaren, your questions?"

There seems hardly a point, but McLaren persists. She questions him for ten minutes but elicits nothing that was not either in his statement or covered in prior testimony. Finally, the lieutenant commander sits down. "No further questions, sir."

Just before the close of evidence Wechtler addresses the room and asks if anyone else has evidence they wish to present. The Asian man in the suit and tie, sitting in the middle of the back row between Evan Tyler and Giuseppe Colvino, rises.

"I would like to submit a statement on behalf of my client, sir." The man takes from his leather folio a document and begins taking it toward the front of the conference room.

"Who are you, please?"

"My name is James Rhee. I'm an attorney representing Gwendolyn Carrigan, the mother of Vincent." The bailiff—Coast Guard military police—takes the document and hands it to Captain Wechtler.

"Could you tell us the essence of your client's proposed evidence, please?"

"Ms. Carrigan wishes to inform the tribunal of the very serious doubts as to the identity of the man purporting to be Evan Tyler."

Farrell and Wechtler exchange puzzled glances. Says the former: "Excuse me, the *identity?*"

"Yes. Ms. Carrigan sets out in her statement the substantial evidence that this person is not actually Evan Tyler, but someone who appropriated Father Tyler's identity years ago and has been using it to commit numerous frauds on a worldwide scale—including Oceans For Christ and the *Global Redeemer.* The person claiming to be Father Tyler is also connected to the disappearance of an American citizen in Africa, an unsolved missing persons case. The missing person is Sarah Brinson, Ms. Carrigan's partner and the adopted mother of Vincent Carrigan."

"What? I don't understand." Wechtler takes the document from Farrell and eventually passes it to Lt. Cmdr. McLaren. She seems equally puzzled.

It is she who speaks up, leaning closer to the microphone on the green-draped table. "Does your client claim to have direct evidence concerning the loss of the *Redeemer* or the death of Vincent Carrigan?"

"My client, ma'am, simply wishes you to have full knowledge of the circumstances of this case. You'll see her affidavit is sworn. I think it should be entered into evidence."

"And your client's evidence is that Father Tyler is some sort of impostor, who replaced the *real* Evan Tyler for reasons unknown?"

Rhee gives the tribunal a sour look. "It could be characterized as that, ma'am, but, if you'll read the affidavit, you'll see the very solid basis of evidence for concluding there is a serious question in this case."

There is brief discussion among the officers—all with hands over their microphones. Wechtler says: "Thank you, Mr. Rhee. We'll take it under advisement. This proceeding will stand in recess until one PM tomorrow afternoon."

Evan Tyler—who, as you recall, is sitting at the back of the room—is the first one out the doors. Neither James Rhee nor Giuseppe Colvino attempt to go after him.

Chapter 31: Estanica San Isidro

Colvino is missing the next afternoon when the Coast Guard inquiry board reassembles in the same location. This time there are more reporters than participants. May is there, as is Tyler; they sit far apart. Rhee sits close to Tyler. There is an envelope in his hands.

The officers enter at 1:02. They take their seats behind the table. Today is a sunny day. Out the windows, barges are visible plying the green-brown ribbon of the Mississippi River. A large cruise ship is chugging toward the passenger terminal. It is the *M/V Norse Star,* the ship on which Marcus Holcomb murdered Rafael Moreira more than five years ago.

Captain Wechtler clears his throat and reads from a printed sheet.

"This board of investigation finds that the sailing vessel *Global Redeemer,* an American-flagged passenger yacht, capsized and sunk in the Gulf of Mexico at approximately 1930 hours on 2 October 2002, was lost as a result of crew and commander error. The decision to sail the vessel out of George Town Harbor and pursue a northwesterly course, despite obviously and demonstrably hazardous weather conditions, was the ultimate cause of the vessel's loss. We find that, given the conditions at the time, no specific measure or feat of seamanship could have prevented the ship's loss. It was the decision to set sail which led to the loss of the vessel. Once that decision was made, nothing could have prevented its loss.

"As to culpability, we find the master of the *Global Redeemer,* May Pinder, a South African national, wholly responsible for the decision that caused the loss of the vessel. Despite evidence given as to who was purporting to give orders aboard the *Global Redeemer,* the responsibility is with Pinder, and Pinder alone. She, and no one else aboard the vessel, held a master's certificate. She, and no one else, was ultimately responsible for the command decisions made. If she allowed her commander's judgment to be influenced by other factors—personal or financial—she bears the responsibility for not ensuring that her command was enforced and her authority final. Consequently, we find Pinder responsible for the loss of the vessel.

"As to the death of Vincent Carrigan, age 16, of Grand Rapids, Michigan, a passenger aboard *Global Redeemer*, we also find May Pinder, the sole holder of a master's license aboard the vessel, responsible for his death. As master, it was her responsibility to ensure the safety of all passengers and crew aboard her vessel. However, we wish to emphasize that the loss of Carrigan's life was a direct result of Pinder's decision to sail into the hurricane. Once Carrigan climbed out of the Zodiac and back aboard the vessel, Pinder was obligated to maximize the chances of survival for the maximum number of the ship's complement. In this matter we tend to agree with her that trying to convince Carrigan to return to the Zodiac may well have endangered the rest of the passengers. However, as a minor, Carrigan cannot be legally responsible for the consequences of his own decision to leave the Zodiac, especially if his judgment was impaired by Stockholm Syndrome or something else. In simpler terms, he never should have been placed in this situation in the first place. That he was is the responsibility of Pinder.

"As to the behavior of Evan Tyler, CEO and headmaster—his word—of Oceans For Christ, we note that his judgment was extremely poor and his attempts, tragically successful, to convince Pinder to abrogate her command responsibilities to him, were reprehensible. However, it has long been true in navies and merchant fleets all over the world that if a captain delegates command to someone unqualified to command a vessel in their own right, the captain is responsible for the mistakes of the delegatee. Therefore, Tyler does not bear the responsibility for the sinking of the *Global Redeemer* or the death of Vincent Carrigan.

"As to the lawyer Rhee's request to have certain statements placed into the record by his client, Gwendolyn Carrigan, mother of Vincent, we have decided against entering them into the official record of this proceeding. Ms. Carrigan was not present at the loss of the *Redeemer*, nor was she present when any of the operative decisions leading to the loss of the vessel and Vincent Carrigan's death made. I remind all parties that this proceeding is an inquest, not a civil trial. Consequently, as much sympathy as the board has for Ms. Carrigan and her tragic loss, her proposed evidence is regarded as irrelevant to the proceeding before this board.

"This board lacks the authority to cancel or suspend Pinder's master's license as issued in South Africa. However, it will recommend revocation of equivalency status for an American master's license and she will be unauthorized to command any vessel under United States registry. Furthermore, a copy of this decision is being sent to the South African Maritime Safety Authority, which issues what are commonly called there skipper's tickets, for appropriate review, and Customs and Border Patrol has been notified as to Pinder's status—it is noted that, counting the days she was aboard the *Global Redeemer*, a U.S.-flagged vessel, she has extended beyond the limit of her ordinary tourist visa to remain in the United States or any place subject to its jurisdiction. It will be recommended to Customs and Border Patrol that she be immediately deported to South Africa, her country of origin, and denied permission for return to the United States.

"This proceeding is adjourned."

The Coast Guard officers rise from their chairs. So does everyone else. There are brief titters of conversation among the reporters. James Rhee nearly lunges at Tyler, who has just stood up. Rhee thrusts the envelope he's been carrying into Tyler's hands.

"Father Evan Tyler—whatever your real name is— you've been served."

Tyler smiles. "Thank you. God bless you." He allows the lawyer to leave first, then walks out of the conference room. He does not speak to May Pinder or even acknowledge her existence. She's the only one still sitting, weeping into her hands.

Only a few blocks away, down Poydras Street, looms the Hyatt Regency Hotel. On the ninth floor of this building Tyler slides an electronic card into the lock mechanism of room 948. The hallway is dead silent. The room is a suite with a small sitting area. The curtains are drawn across the slider door leading to the balcony. Tyler switches on the lights and immediately freezes. On the settee in the sitting area, sitting casually with legs crossed, is a thick-necked bald man in a business suit and dress shirt—European tailoring—but no tie. He points a semiautomatic pistol at Tyler. It has a long silencer. The man grips the pistol with leather-gloved hands.

"A very nice resolution for you, Signore Marcus Holcomb." The man speaks English with an Italian accent. "You must be very pleased with yourself."

"How do you know what the resolution was? You weren't there to hear them read the decision."

Giuseppe Colvino's smile has an icy quality. "The Coast Guard posted it on their web site this morning. You know who I am?"

"Not precisely, and I don't remember what Antrim said your name was, but from your accent I'd guess you're the guy from the Vatican Bank. When I saw you at the hearing yesterday, I pegged you as European from the suit. Guess I was right."

"Not that it matters, my bank is not the IOR precisely, but close enough. You had to know someone from Rome would pay you a visit eventually."

"What do you want? Money? If you were here to hit me, you'd have shot me as soon as I opened the door. You're Mafia, but you're not a hit man."

"I don't work for the Mafia. I'm just a banker."

"So you *do* want money."

"I also wanted to thank you for one of the more interesting errands I've done for the Vatican in a number of years. You surprised me, which is hard to do after all the years I've been in this business. I was tracking your ship. When I saw you start to move out of Grand Cayman, I admit I was baffled. Your decision to steer into the hurricane was inexplicable at first. Then I realized what was happening. You *wanted* to destroy the ship. You'd given up on Oceans For Christ, and there was nothing left to do but cash out. If the ship went down, you'd collect an insurance payment. That would be your seed money for your next scam. That, and the funds you stashed away in the Caymans. How convenient that you would never try to run a school again, so the authorities can't shut you down. Even if the Holy See made a pretense of defrocking Evan Tyler it wouldn't matter much to your future plans, whatever they are. You're bound to be sued by just about everybody who ever looked at Evan Tyler, but that doesn't matter either. The courts can't reach your money in the Caymans. It can't be that much, though, or you wouldn't have risked your own life for the insurance payout. And then there's Vincent. The Coast Guard board never connected the dots. They were duped by that nonsense about Stockholm Syndrome, but I suspect even you believed he was loyal to you, at least up until the very end. He infiltrated your organization so he could kill you. That's why he jumped back aboard the *Global Redeemer* at the last second, wasn't it? It was his last chance, and his best chance, being alone with you on an already-sinking ship. Your survival was purely a matter of luck, and that's not like you. I've studied your pattern, Signore Holcomb. You only ever really throw the dice when you've exhausted all other options. The whole Oceans For Christ project was a rare thing for you: a strategic mistake."

"Well, thanks for the criticism, I guess. And you're wrong about Vincent. In any event it's immaterial. When will you get around to telling me what you actually want? In case you didn't notice in your investigation, the Vatican Bank isn't out anything. I didn't take a dime of the Pope's money."

"Is that supposed to make me go away and forget you defrauded us?"

"Since you came all the way from Rome to point a gun at me to get me to listen to you, I'm sure the answer is no. I'm just stating a fact."

For the first time Colvino's expression is anything other than affable. His mouth becomes an emotionless line.

"Here's another fact that I happen to know. You altered the appraisal on the *Global Redeemer* for your insurance company. It's over-insured. You told them $1.6 million; it was actually worth less than $800,000, but now that it's at the bottom of the Gulf of Mexico, no one will ever know. The Vatican Bank would regard the insurance payout as adequate compensation for the risk and loss of reputation for you having dragged us into your schemes. You'll turn the insurance payment over to me."

Holcomb is silent for a moment. Then he shrugs. "Okay. I'll see what I can do."

"No, Signore, you won't 'see what you can do.' You will call your insurer right now, on that telephone there." Colvino, still holding the gun steady, reaches into his jacket pocket and takes out a small card which he holds out to Marcus. "I happen to know the company is ready to disburse funds at this very moment, waiting for a phone call from you. You waited until the inquest decision and you had it queued up and ready. They're waiting for your wire instructions. You were going to do it right now, here in your hotel room, right after the inquest. That's why I thought I should be here when you returned. On that card is the Swift code and account number at my bank. Call and give them these wire instructions."

Holcomb looks at the card. "And you'll shoot me if I don't?"

"This is not a negotiation. You asked me what I want —I've told you. You'll notice I haven't asked about how Sarah Brinson, Vincent and the real Evan Tyler really died. All I want is money. You're very lucky, Signore Holcomb, that my employers don't regard revenge as a Catholic virtue. My instructions on that point were clear."

Holcomb sits in the chair next to the end table with the telephone. He makes a call. The business takes a few minutes to arrange, but he reads the numbers off Colvino's card. "When's your wiring deadline for today? Okay, should be no problem, then. Thanks."

He hangs up the phone and passes the card back to Colvino. The gun has never wavered from being in line with his head since the encounter began. But now Colvino rises, begins to unscrew the silencer and puts it and the pistol in opposite suit jacket pockets. "Our business is done, then. Forgive me if I don't wish you luck on your next endeavor. But just keep the Vatican Bank, and the whole Catholic Church, out of it." He steps toward the hotel room door.

"You aren't going to keep me here until the wire goes through? I could call the insurance back and have them change the wire destination as soon as you leave the room."

"Yes, you could. Just as easily as I could call Michael O'Cuinneagain and tell him exactly where you are and how to find you." Colvino chuckles. "I just realized — he's Catholic too. All your enemies seem to be Catholic."

"I was raised Lutheran."

"Why does that not surprise me? *Ciao.*"

These are the last words that pass between them. Colvino opens the door, steps out into the silent hallway, and the hotel room door clicks quietly shut after him.

Fifty-four minutes later the wire transfer goes through.

Three weeks later a hissing old bus, painted light blue, groans and shudders to a stop in front of a low stucco-faced building in Artigas, Uruguay. The doors open and several people, mostly women, plus a stoop-shouldered old man in a straw hat, get out; one man, who has been waiting at the bus stop since dawn, collects his things to get on. He is a good-looking man of about 30 with blond hair, formerly shaved very short but just now beginning to grow out. He's heavily burdened by a large mountaineering backpack with an aluminum frame. A folding camp shovel is strapped to the pack and a large canteen dangles, hooked to the frame with a D-clip. The young man wears a colorful woven baja, mud-splattered jeans and hiking boots that look new but are also caked with mud and he carries a smaller nylon knapsack. He manages awkwardly to navigate his large pack through the narrow bus doors, walks down the aisle and finds a stretch of the overhead luggage rack barely big enough to stow the pack. Another young man, about the same age, sits by the window. The blond man sits down next to him, knapsack in his lap. As the bus begins to move the blond man unzips the knapsack and takes out a silver hip flask. He notices his seatmate noticing him and offers him the flask.

"Would you like some?"

The seatmate stares at him, agog. "You're American? No thanks on the drink. It's eight AM."

"I've been traveling all night. Might as well be eight PM." Marcus drinks. "Yeah. What are the chances, meeting another Yankee here? Where you from?"

"Brooklyn. You?"

"La Jolla, California."

"What are you doing here in Uruguay?"

Marcus looks almost pleased with himself. "I'm looking for a good place to go live off the grid. I read about some place, Estancia San Isidro, in a tour book. The pictures were pretty and it's as far off the beaten path as you can get."

"Estancia San Isidro? I've never even heard of it."

The blond man laughs. "Either had I, until a couple of days ago. What's your story?"

"I'm just traveling around. Trying to find some interesting places to write about."

"A writer, eh? That's a noble profession. You finding Uruguay interesting?"

"*Very* interesting."

Marcus unscrews the flask again. "Here's to Uruguay. The only country in South America that doesn't have an extradition treaty with the United States." He drinks again.

"You don't say."

"I *do* say, actually." He screws the cap back on the flask. "What's your name?"

"Chris Mills."

Marcus extends his hand. "Vincent Moreira."

"Nice to meet you."

"Want to stick with me a while? Check out Estancia San Isidro? You could write about it."

Chris Mills shrugs. "Sure."

The bus hits a bump. Above them, the folding camp shovel clinks against the steel of the overhead rack.

THE END.

About the Author

Sean Munger is a historian, author, podcaster and teacher. He is the author of several novels in various genres, including the international crime thriller *In Deadly Mirrors*, the science fiction/magical realism fantasy *The Valley of Forever*, coming-of-age story *Jake's 88*, the horror novels *Zombies of Byzantium* and *Doppelgänger*, and the short fiction collection *Hotel Himalaya: Three Travel Romances*. He is also the author of the nonfiction book *The Warmest Tide: How Climate Change is Changing History*, based on his expertise as an environmental historian with emphasis on the history of climate change.

As a podcaster, he is best known for the historical show *Second Decade*, which examines the 1810s (the second decade of the 19th century). He is also the producer and co-host of *Green Screen*, the environmental movie podcast.

Sean teaches history classes online at his website www.seanmunger.com. He lives in Oregon.